The Coyote's Tale

Michael J. Vecore

The Coyote's Tale is a work of fiction. Names, characters, places, and incidents are either products of the author's imagination or are used fictitiously. Any resemblance to actual events or locales or persons, living or dead, is entirely coincidental.

First Printing: 2016

ISBN 978-0-692-75181-7

Cover design and editing by S.P.

THE COYOTE'S TALE

www.facebook.com/thecoyotestale

To my wife. Without you,
none of this would have seen daylight.

To Linda. I finally have something new to show you.

Humans

Originating from the planet Earth, humans have proven themselves to be the most nomadic and exploratory species in the Milky Way. Humans were the first species to make contact with another intelligent race, the morkallians. They are the only race that do not primarily live on their home planet. Most humans are spread out among the galaxy, making up the majority population of space stations.

Morkallians

Morkallians are the tall, thin people of the planet Morkal. They vary in shades of green skin, and have silver eyes. Morkallian facial features are minimal; they have nostrils without a nose and small earholes on the sides of their head. Males and females are the same height and weight on average. Most of the morkallian people are peaceful and quiet, focused on careers involving science and art, though a good number of them are shrewd business people.

Deeshie

The deeshie are a race of rough and tough people. Standing average human height, they are nearly twice as wide and extremely strong. Their skin is hairless, though quite callous and bumpy, and they vary in color from pale yellow to dark red. The deeshie evolved as a warlike species, and their history does not contain many artists or great philosophical thinkers. As a result, the deeshie tend to do everything in the most simple and straightforward way, but they are effective in what they do. Their ships fly, their weapons are destructive, and their architecture withstands nature's forces. But creativity is not a strong suit.

Yookallans

The yookallans were the last race discovered by the other three races of the Milky Way. Their home planet of Yookalla is located on the far side of the galaxy, quite a distance from Earth, Morkal, and Deeshie. The yookallan people look remarkably similar to humans. Although yookallans are generally taller and thinner, the biggest differences are the small features. Yookallans' ears are much smaller and shaped in a simpler manner. Their irises, almost always black, blot out any white of the eyes, and their skin color is a ghostly gray. Yookallans are an emotionally repressed people. Most prefer to never leave their home planet, and tend to be employed in the field of the sciences.

1

WHEN a melon-sized fist repeatedly collides with one's face at high velocity, cognitive function slows to a crawl. The mind retreats into survival mode, and the only thought that pops up is, '*How do I not let that happen again?*' The trouble was, I had a plan I was trying to implement, but by the time my brain would recover, another melon would hit me in the face, starting the process all over again.

Under normal circumstances, my thoughts would be more focused on how to defend myself. However, I was bound to a chair, hands tied behind my back with what felt like cordage of some sort.

They didn't use cuffs? Amateurs.

That was the voice in my head. Although he was usually helpful, I didn't need to hear him at this moment. I was unconscious previous to the fist-to-face event and was unaware of my surroundings or situation. I needed my bearings.

The being knocking me around with his melon-like hands was a deeshie. Skin color ranging from light yellow to deep red, this one was as orange as a pumpkin, and the two others standing behind him were more of a yellow hue. Strong muscle mixed with hearty amounts of fat, they were soft but terribly strong. It made for an experience if you were punched by one, as I was about to again be.

Melon was applied to face, and my lip split from the impact. His voice wheezed out between gasps of breath; he was getting winded from dishing out the physical abuse.

"Your name . . . is Cayden."

I spit blood, not quite ready to respond to his useless statement. The floor was made of large metallic tiles, probably leptanium as it was the most common construction metal on the planet. They mined it in droves. It appeared clean, notwithstanding some of my blood, sweat, and saliva shining on its pale green surface.

Though no other walls or ceiling were visible to me, I hypothesized they were identical to the floor. His deep, echoing voice let me know the space was empty for the most part. And it was massive. The lack of light hinted that it was more than likely underground.

Warehouse?

Highly probable.

"Say something!" the deeshie wheezed.

Melon to face. I was sure my left eye would be swollen shut before much longer. The blows didn't hurt as much as previous experiences of mine that involved getting punched in the face. His fat, four-fingered hands felt squishy. Like pillows. Mind you, pillows that impacted my head at a high velocity and with a great deal of weight behind them.

"I have only one question," the deeshie went on. "Why do you associate yourself with this creature called the coyote? I have been reading—"

"You read!" I said, my eyes widening. Well, my right eye widened.

It was a tired trick, but once again, his melon-fist tried to teach my face a lesson. The familiar pull of unconsciousness tugged at me, but I was able to shake it off. No more naps.

Yes, please cease the napping. I find myself so bored when you sleep.

The reason I was here, I remembered as the cobwebs of my mind cleared, was twelve thousand pounds. Money. The motivating factor behind any mercenary. Mercenary was a very crude description of my current occupation, and one that did not at all describe the depth of my life. But today, I was a mercenary. One with a job.

The deeshie leaned down, his bulbous green eyes speckled with black staring into mine. "Coyotes, according to the histories of your home planet, were clever creatures. Crafty. You couldn't have been more obvious."

What he was addressing was what I referred to as the bait. Like an overgrown, ugly fish, he snatched it with greed. The deeshie before me was a gangster. The boss of his little criminal syndicate. He was big time in a small place. The local government of the remote island I was located on, recently established itself. The deeshie pelting me with melons, was giving the new democratic establishment hell, and things were reaching a breaking point.

Taking a leaf from the criminals, a rogue senator with a "do it" attitude hired me to put a significant dent in their operations. Being an all or nothing kind of guy, I decided to just eliminate the whole bunch. People that hindered the growth of society irked me.

I planned the mission for a week, fronting as a young hotshot reporter trying to take down a small-town mob on the vast deeshie home world, aptly named, Deeshie 1. Not too far from the truth. Really, I was a young hotshot jack-of-all-trades trying to take down a small-town mob on the vast deeshie home world. Except, I   wasn't trying.

I was successfully accomplishing.

They thought they caught me spying on their grounds, collecting information. But in fact, I was planting a plethora of explosives. Caution was key with explosives, because I needed to take out a large number of personnel and leave certain merchandise untouched as a bonus to myself. The drugs they stashed didn't interest me, as moving them unnoticed was daunting and required an incredible amount of effort. Not to mention the laws against drug trafficking on Deeshie carried a heavy penalty.

Therefore, in a short time, their drugs were going to go up in flames, along with the bar they always populated, and the apartment building most of them lived in. After careful research, I knew the chance of collateral damage was nonexistent. The deeshie mob lived on their own compound, making it comically obvious that they had no fear of government reprisals. Only their gang was allowed in, which paved the way for me to bring them a surprising amount of destruction.

"You are no coyote," the deeshie said, baring his large square-shaped teeth at me. "You're a dead man."

A thread-edge knife was suddenly under my chin, the tip painfully pushed against my throat. I felt a trickle of blood roll down my collar bone, humbly reminding me the game I played required careful balance.

"What were you doing?" the deeshie asked, not moving the knife. "We know you aren't a reporter, so who are you?"

"According to you, I'm a dead man," I said.

"You will be if you don't talk," he said through a clenched jaw.

"And if I do?"

He smiled and moved the blade to my shoulder. "Perhaps I'll only take a trophy. To teach you a lesson."

I released the breath I was holding. "That's a terrible bargain. You really should work on better business dealings."

My sudden confidence confused him. He was, no doubt, thinking he missed something. Unfortunately for him, he missed a lot of things, including the small chip inserted underneath the skin of my wrist.

He withdrew the blade, placing it back in the sheath at his waist. I tensed as he reached into his jacket, expecting a gun to be revealed, but instead he held a semi-transparent data pad.

"You have an impressive record," he said, his fat index finger scrolling through the information on the data pad. "Most of it seems to be speculative and generic, but that speaks volumes. All of the good mercenaries keep their accomplishments quiet. Don't want others to know their tricks and secrets. I'm almost sorry to mar your career with this failure. But business is business. Did you think we wouldn't notice you? Your actions were hardly professional."

I laughed. Not one of those long evil laughs of doom, just a chuckle of amusement at the lack of intelligence shown by people who claimed to be criminal masterminds. They were an embarrassment. In a larger civilian establishment, their gang would have been a joke, swallowed by more advanced, battle-tested criminal organizations.

"What are you laughing at? You've been had by the Grun'darr, just like everyone else," he said.

A proud deeshie, indeed.

"The Grun'darr?" I asked. "That's the best name you could come up with? That's just sad. Sounds like a noise I make in the morning when I scratch myself, you pathetic stain of wasted life."

The small amount of his composure that remained, evaporated. "We've been running this government since it saw fit to give birth!"

"Spare me," I said, coaxing him into divulging more information on his soon to be extinct syndicate. Digital information was nice, but sometimes people kept secrets away from the storage devices. Memory was the greatest safe, and I was about to crack his. "This government owns you. They only keep you around to do their dirty work, and you know it."

The deeshie waved his hand in anger. "We own the entire district. The police chief and mayor are a part of us, and we have enough dirt on the prime minister to keep him paralyzed in fear. They do what we want, when we want, how we want."

I loved this part. "I almost feel sorry for you. You really didn't think they would just lie down and take your abuse forever, did you? One day, and that's today in fact, they were going to hire someone with the ability to take you out of the picture entirely. Being untouched has made you weak."

The deeshie squinted. "What are you saying?"

"I'm saying goodbye," I said.

My left hand clenched into a fist, and the insert beneath the skin activated. A large transparent bubble surrounded me. It was a shield, able to withstand incredible amounts of damage, including the gunfire the three deeshie rained on me.

It was a clever set of devices, these inserts beneath my skin. The power source was a combination of the electrical impulses that ran through my body, along with micro-generators woven into the linings of my shirt and pants. The soles of my boots contained signal-boosting devices. The tech cost me a great deal of money, but I made good use of them during my time doing such naughty work. They were virtually undetectable, fooling the best scanners.

After a short succession of gunfire, the deeshie in command realized it was useless and began pounding on the shield in frustration, but his melon-fists were no use to him anymore. I took my time wiggling the small lock pick out of the cuff of my jacket. It was loosely sewn onto the material, disguised as a common cuff-clip. Luckily, it doubled as a blade and I cut myself loose.

"What is this?" the deeshie asked, continuing on with his use-less pounding of the shield. "What are you doing?"

I dabbed at my split lip tenderly. "Just doing what I do."

I reached to my other sleeve, pulling off three thin squares of cardium from the outside of my coat sleeve. Cardium was the perfect alloy to use for disguised weapons as it was unusually flexible, making it easy to hide from searches. In fact, the three pieces were so thin, they simply looked like decorative patches. After assembly, the three squares turned into a short-range gun capable of firing five small bullets before the material was compromised.

"What is that? I thought you searched him!" the deeshie roared at his two comrades. His voice sounded muffled from inside the shield.

"They did. You're just vastly incompetent," I said.

You could explain, you know. They're dead anyway.

Your point?

It's not often that you get to talk about it.

I shrugged. He was right. Maybe it would be therapeutic. "You were asking me about why I call myself Cayden the Coyote."

The deeshie stared at me, dumbfounded.

"Interestingly enough it's because I am not alone in my head. In fact, I have some sort of multiple personality disorder. It's fascinating, especially since I don't fit the psychiatric bill. I'm really the better for it. It's like having twice the thinking power wrapped up in one exceptional brain. He's helped me survive my whole life, and he's quite crafty and clever, therefore deserving of the name Coyote."

Nicely put.

"What?" the deeshie said dumbly.

I shrugged. "Or maybe he's an implant."

Not even I'm sure of that.

The deeshie repeated himself. "What?"

Doesn't catch on too quick, does he?

Thanks to a great deal of previous practice, I put the three pieces of cardium together swiftly, and with a final clockwise twist, held a crude looking gun. The shield did not allow things to pass from the outside in, but it had no problem allowing objects from the inside to pass outward. Without hesitation, I aimed and fired at the deeshie's head, following that shot with two more that took out his comrades. Guns were messy, and I averted my gaze from the dark green blood beginning to pool around the bodies.

I squeezed my other hand into a fist, activating another chip underneath the skin. Two seconds later, I felt the familiar vibrations of explosives going off. As I suspected, I must have still been on their compound, but far enough below to be out of the way of damage. It took a couple of minutes, but things finally silenced.

With another squeeze of my fist, the shield dissipated, and I was on my way. It wasn't a long walk to find a lift. The light above the door indicated that I was six floors below the surface.

About as smooth as expected, Cayden.

Could have done without the facial reconstruction.

Sacrifices must be made to achieve our goals.

Perhaps it's an odd idea that there was a voice in my head. To be more specific, the Coyote was a separate being with his own unique personality divided from my own in the most complete way imagin-able. From what I understood, this was supposed to be a defect. For me, it was the secret to my survival. Since I first heard his dry, hyper-rational voice, he always aided me. Without him, I would not have survived my childhood. Before him, the other candidates were better than me. More talented.

I am a part of you. That makes you just as talented, only in a different way.

Maybe.

It was impossible to tell with the organization that raised me. Made me. Games were always played. Was the Coyote some sort of advanced psychological tool naturally developed by my mind that the organization was completely unaware of? Or did the unstable, self-absorbed agents of darkness plant an artificial intelligence in my brain when I was an infant?

I'd tell you if I knew. But I know as little about myself as you do.

Climbing into the lift, I began my ascent to the surface. The bright lights stung my eyes but were a welcome sight. After all the dark and the killing, light felt refreshing.

///

Deeshie 1 was a hot, humid planet. Without a tilted axis, the weather stayed constant year-round. Islands too small to be considered continental, speckled an otherwise water-covered world. An emerald sky was almost always filled with clouds, and rain was often a daily occurrence. Today seemed almost special as there wasn't a cloud in sight.

"What happened to you?" Neg'stella was watching me carry a heavy load of merchandise towards her transport.

She was a morkallian female, about my age, and an associate of mine on Deeshie 1. Just like all morkallians, she could be compared to grass; green, slim, and tall. Her long, oval-shaped head housed shimmering silver eyes. No nose or ears protruded from her face, only a pair of holes above her mouth and on the sides of her head. Her mouth was human shaped, but short, pointy, perfectly symmetrical teeth lined her gums. All in all, she looked like an average morkallian.

Stella, as I liked to call her despite her hatred of the nick-name, stood about ten inches taller than me, which was normal for her people. She was a weapons dealer, and we shared a mutually ben-eficial relationship. Whatever merchandise I acquired on my jobs, I sold to Stella. In turn, I received a discount on the supplies I needed, and we both shared information freely with one another. In our field of not quite lawful activity, information could be expensive.

"Don't worry about it. Just help me get your end of the bar-gain." Only able to see her dark green figure with one eye since the other had swollen shut, I half dragged, half carried my bag of goodies. She didn't argue and helped me load the supplies into her transport. "That small one goes up front with me. It's the information I need."

Our personal relationship was odd. Though time spent together wasn't uncommon, and our conversation was usually cordial or humorous, we shared no real friendship. I couldn't afford to get close to people, especially those that were regulars in my life. Plans could be compromised that way.

And we have many plans.

She climbed into the cockpit. "You got a pretty big bag of merchandise here."

"You're welcome," I said in her native tongue. Languages fas-cinated me, and I frequently exercised my ability to speak many. "Take me back to your shop. I'll get cleaned up and we can divide up our profits."

"So, what happened? Did they get the upper hand on you?" She reverted the conversation back to human.

Like many of her people, she found the accent of humans when speaking her language humorous. The morkallians were well known for their downright creepy ability to learn any language and speak it fluently without any accent. Their vocal chords had a fluid-like attribute, which allowed them to change into any shape they needed to imitate the proper sound.

I climbed into the passenger seat, sealing the door beside me. "When someone gets the upper hand on me, you will know."

"How?" she asked, bringing the small ship's systems online.

"I will more than likely suffer a gruesome and violent death," I said.

She guided the ship upward, laughing. "So, no one can outsmart the legendary Coyote?"

I shook my head. "That's not the secret to my success. It has nothing to do with outsmarting your opponent. I don't outsmart anyone."

"From where I sit, it sure looks that way," she said.

"We are all as smart as we are," I said, dabbing my swollen eye gingerly. "Our intelligence is a preset condition. I have merely exploited my intellect to its fullest degree. Explored its depth and learned its extent. Most other beings don't bother doing that."

Stella banked the transport to the left, taking us west. "And that is the secret then?"

"Of course not," I said. "I just use that hyper self-awareness and think a great deal about everything that I do. Everything. I plan it all over and over. Each moment's possibilities are carefully thought out, carefully considered. I then proceed to the best options available at the time as they fit my plans."

"Sounds like an awful lot of thinking for one person to do," she
said. "How do you keep yourself organized?"

I smiled. "I have a way of multitasking."

2

GUNS, guns, guns, grenades, mines, laser knives, plasma bands, thread-edged swords, and more guns. I was familiar with them all, though I had no real love for weapons. It was my estimation that an individual was more dangerous than any blade or firearm. Weapons were tools, thought up by the mind to serve a purpose. A means to an end.

Stella differed with me on this. Her passion was weapons. Thus the reason to open her shop. I trusted her experience to guide me on what best fit my needs, and so far, she hadn't steered me wrong. And when I needed it, she gave me access to her medical kit.

I emerged from her refresher unit. "All right, how do I look?"

"You're not dripping blood, but you still look awful," she said, pausing in her effort to clean what looked to be an exotic shotgun. "Can you even see out of that eye?"

"Not quite, but the swelling will go down in a day or two," I said, dabbing it gently.

She shook her hairless, green head. "Why don't you just see a medic and get fixed up now?"

"I have my reasons," I said. "Have you gotten a count on the profits?"

She placed the gun back in its case and handed me a data sheet. "Not a bad haul. You want your share in unmarked cards?"

I pocketed the sheet and put on my coat. "Absolutely. If you will excuse me, I have to visit my employer for the rest of my pay."

She squinted her eyes, which I recognized to be a morkallian expression of surprise. "You're going looking like that?"

"Of course," I said, once again dabbing my swollen eye. The bugger hurt. "Nothing like commitment to bring in an extra reward."

///

After an hour-long meeting, in which I exchanged my client's information for the price we agreed to, I walked out of the state building and back to the borrowed transport with a bonus in my hand. The Senator was kind enough to give me a trelai as thanks for my extra effort in completing the job.

The trelai was an ancient form of deeshie currency made from a precious crystal, native only to their world. It flashed light blue in the sunlight. It was good for a couple thousand pounds at least. It was also a valid form of currency on Deeshie 1, which meant I didn't have to worry about any sort of exchange tax.

The Coyote taught me that putting on a performance could add to the weight of one's wallet. From performance was born reputation, which preceded itself, which led back to performance.

A vicious Shakespearean circle.

My success as a mercenary was proof of his theory. With his help, my performances were not only convincing, but also terribly complicated. While tactical strategy was a strength of mine, the Coyote was downright devious. He tended to see what most would dismiss as useless. A scavenger of plans.

Why do you persist in referring to me as a "he", when you know I prefer "it", as "it" is a more fitting description?

It was true. The Coyote did not like to be associated with a sex. He viewed himself as neither male nor female. I said "he" because it would have been even stranger if he were female and not male, as I was male and not female. It was a small comfort to know that even though I carried an unknown entity in my head, at least I would still fall on one side of the sexual identity fence.

Insecure much?

Ours was an interesting relationship. It was difficult to identify just what he was. He was fully self-aware and with a consciousness of his own. He could have made my life a living hell by assaulting my mind or trying to take over my body. But he didn't, nor did he ever try. That alone led me to trust him to some degree.

Trust is earned, after all.

He continued to earn it, in my estimation. There were times . . . dark times in which the Coyote shone as the only light in my life. Without him, my existence would have been shorter.

Considering that I live in your head, your survival is key to my survival. I'm extremely selfish, Cayden. It just so happens that you are me, therefore I care.

And he does believe he is the most selfish creature in the known universe. We talk about it, sometimes. His emotions, his desires, his goals.

I have none of those things. I just am. I exist, which compels me to continue existing. Through your genitalia, our genetic code will be passed on to our half-clone, and we will live on through him, her, or it.

Do you have to be so damned factual about sex?

Is there another way to be?

My walk out the back of the capitol building took me directly into the transport lot, away from the crowds of people. Ghettos, ganglands, and drug alleys I didn't mind. I could handle the people there. But a bustling city full of law-abiding citizens going about their usual schedule gave me the creeps.

Though I had a knack for blending in, I hated doing so among higher society. The kind of deception required to be one of them, left a bad taste in my mouth. To hide such a ruthless, self-serving nature behind a facade of utmost civility made me squirm. At least thieves, pirates, and mercenaries were honest about the lives they led.

After a quick run up the steps to the third level, I reached the transport ship. I wasted no time in walking up the loading ramp and plopping into the cockpit. Time was not my friend. My plans were quickly going into effect. With the ease that came from far too many hours piloting, I took the ship off the ground and made my way back to Stella's, and away from the fabrication of civilized society.

///

"He gave you a trelai?" The crystal coin glinted blue in Stella's slender hand. "Do you know how much these things are worth?"

"About two thousand pounds, right?" I said around a mouthful of rations she gave me.

"Three thousand," she corrected. "You didn't steal it from him, did you?"

I took a seat behind a transparent counter containing a plethora of knives and swallowed a tasteless spoonful. "Of course not. I told you, I had my reasons for not seeing a medic."

She shook her head and murmured an old morkallian curse. "Sometimes, I wonder if you have planned your entire life."

"Illusions, Stella. It's all illusions," I said.

"Enlightening as always, Cayden."

I scraped the last spoonful of gray rations from the can. "The less you know, the less you have to worry about. The less you have to watch out for."

She chuckled nervously. "Okay, fine. Keep your secrets."

I winked. "I will, thank you very much."

"Here, take this," she said, handing me a white pill. "It'll bring down the swelling."

I pocketed the pill and tossed the empty ration container into the trash. "Thanks. I'm headed off to Port Seven for a drink, which will hopefully be followed by a well-deserved sleep."

"Are you going to meet Bronx there?" she asked.

I nodded. "Got a message from him the other day. Want to come?"

"I have too much work to do, but you guys know where to find me if you need any supplies," she said, sitting down at her desk and straightening some data sheets. "Of course, I wouldn't mind if you brought me back a keg of that magnificent ale."

The dank inner store faded away as I pushed the door open and stepped into the slums. A blast of hot, humid air greeted me with the pent up excitement of a neglected puppy. Outside, a floating neon sign told me I was indeed at Neg'stella's Weaponry. Trash littered the metallic streets, along with vendors of exotic food, "misplaced" merchandise, and whatever else you could imagine. The smell was a mixture of rust, body odor, and rotting food.

Raggedy buildings lined the alley, all made of cheaply bought light metals and shaped in squares. That way, it was easy to stack new establishments on top of existing ones. Some of the buildings were homes for what they said they were, and some were abandoned and used for something else. Others were fronts for illegal activities.

The inner cities of Deeshie were melting pots for people, and there wasn't a better place for low-class criminals to make a home. It was rough, but I was perfectly adapted to it. The capital cities, like the one I visited for my reward, were the only bright spots on the planet. Conveniently, they were called "Deeshie Capital" followed by a sequential number. My visit was to Deeshie Capital 27. The deeshie were not known for their creativity.

Reaching into my pocket, I withdrew the pill Stella offered me and tossed it into the streets. I'd see a medic along the way. Stella was a trustworthy person, and that pill was probably what she said it was, but certain rules made life easier. Like rule number one.

Don't trust anyone you don't have to.

Taking a left, I paid a toll for the public transport to Port Seven, a local satellite space dock where pirates, mercenaries, bounty hunters, and all things unholy hung out.

Also known as "home."

3

IT didn't take long after I entered the bar to spot Bronx. He was one of its loudest occupants, which was saying something. The man always had a crowd around him. Most of the time, that crowd consisted of young bucks, listening to his more adventurous, and often exaggerated, stories.

A grin tugged at my lips as I saw him holding a mug of ale and making funny motions with his empty hand. Even though I couldn't hear the exact words he was saying, I could tell by reading his expressions, he was recalling the story about being hunted by the Yookallan Knights in their own asteroid field.

Bronx was there for me since the beginning, before things went dark. He was complicated, just like me. Perhaps that's why he helped me. I liked to think we were kindred spirits.

I still don't like him.

One tangible friend and partner is not too much to ask, I think.

I know he's necessary, Cayden. But be careful.

Since day one, the Coyote was mistrusting of Bronx. I mistrusted them both at first, but over time they became the two people I depended on. I felt like I was the glue of the trio. Bronx didn't know about my personality quirk/possible implant. The Coyote insisted on it, and I complied, though there were times I wanted to spill the proverbial beans. It would have been nice to confide in someone outside of my head.

Not something I have control over, you know.

Bronx was approximately twenty years older than me, which pegged him somewhere between forty or forty-five. He was a big human, standing nearly two meters tall, and made of nothing but old grizzly muscle. Eyes of onyx, skin as dark as coffee, and a presence that would impress the hardest criminal. Despite his cheery personality, I wouldn't want to cross him. It was easy to tell his stories were half fake, but it was easier to forget they were half true as well.

"There he is!" Bronx shouted from across the bar, pointing a thick finger at me. "There's the man."

He walked towards me through the smoke-infested bar, pushing past all sentients in his way, his muscled arms spreading wide. I tended to lie low, but he never let me, especially when we were meeting for drinks. Before I could say anything, he wrapped me in a bear hug, lifting me off my feet.

I do believe he is thoroughly drunk.

"How are you, ya dirty merc!" he asked, putting me down and taking a look at me.

"Hanging in there, I guess," I said.

"Damn, kid," he said, noticing my swollen eye. "It looks like a ship landed right on your face. What happened?"

"Got into a fight with a deeshie," I said.

My reply was an old mercenary trick. When asked a question, tell the truth in a lie. Bronx knew it and knew why I did it. In a bar full of other mercenaries and bounty hunters, it was not wise to acknowledge a job.

"Did you win?" Bronx asked.

"I always do," I said.

He laughed. "Come on, I'll buy you a drink."

///

It felt like two hours passed, but I was sure it was at least double that. A few cups of the ale could interfere with one's time-keeping abilities. I could never keep up with Bronx, who drank like he was dying of thirst every time he was at the bar.

"You know, you're going places, kid." There was a slight slur to his words. "I've seen em' come, and I've seen em' go. It's not just talent that keeps you breathing. There have been people with talent that do what we do, but a simple bullet can kill em'. Not us, boy. We're different. We were born for this."

I nodded, taking another sip of the green-hued ale, grimacing as the alcohol stung the cut on my lip. "You're my only friend, Bronx. We have to stick this out together."

His open hand slammed onto my shoulder with a loud *thud*. No doubt, his version of a pat of comfort. "The feeling's mutual, Cayden. We're the only two of our kind."

I recovered, took another drink and stared into the mirror at the bar. On a normal day, I wasn't able to do something like that, but the alcohol in my system was helping keep my mind from inner thoughts and memories I would rather not have pondered. Those memories and inner thoughts led to incredible confusion, dark poetic musings, and far too many questions. All of that hindered my effectiveness on the job. The job was the plan, and the plan couldn't be compromised. It was too important. But, thanks to the ale, I could view my reflection without much to worry about.

Today, I could stand to look at myself.

Gray eyes stared back at me. I knew I possessed a semi-handsome face. Handsome enough to have received my fair share of offers. Short brown hair, a brow that could hide my eyes when I wanted, an average nose, and a square jaw. One girl told me she liked the single dimple that showed on my right side when I smiled. Olive skin with a natural dark hue. I didn't have to tan to achieve my look, like some other humans. I was of normal height and normal build, though, that build could be deceiving. I liked to take care of my body.

But most of all, take care of the mind.

Of course.

No, really. Stop drinking. I'm counting the dead brain cells.

"I'm going to do it, you know," I said, contemplating the image before me.

Bronx put down his empty mug. "Do what?"

My stare did not leave the mirror. "Do what they think is impossible. Do what they think can't be done."

"You better. Been talking about it for awhile now."

"I'm just waiting for the puzzle pieces to fall into place," I said.

Bronx signaled the bartender for another round. "I believe you, kid."

///

The dock where I kept my ship, and where I lived, was one of the roughest that orbited the planet. Dank, dark, dingy, dilapidated, and drug-infested. That was all the adjectives starting with the letter "d" I could think of with the alcohol running through my blood. It was a huge place, housing a host of people from all different races. I was in dock 13, neighbored by a deeshie drug dealer, and a semi-famous morkallian bounty hunter.

"I almost forgot how rough this spot was," Bronx said from behind me, as I punched in the code to get through the doors.

"You've been retired too long," I said around a burp. Stupid ale.

"It's the reason I retired," Bronx said. "Hell, you've got to have eyes in the back of your head to survive out here anymore. This ship of yours had better be something special. The last time I saw it, it was just a heap of parts on a rusted-out frame."

"And since you laughed at my efforts," I turned around with the door still closed, "I promised that I wouldn't show you my ship until even you would be impressed."

"Ten pounds says I'm not impressed," he said, holding out the light ceramic coin-shaped form of money.

I took the coin and opened the door. "Thanks for the cash."

Bronx's eyes widened, and his jaw went slack. For the first time since I'd known him, he said absolutely nothing. I knew my ship was impressive, and I knew I would win the bet, but I didn't know I'd render him speechless.

"Kid, how did you do this?"

Before us stretched the open dock, and in the middle was the spacecraft I worked on for over a year. My living quarters were small, tucked into an upstairs apartment on the right side of the dock. Most of what I paid rent for was vast open space, twice as large as the gleaming new space vehicle resting on its floor. The far wall was actually the dock door, ready to slide up and reveal the unending openness of space.

"I've been working upwards of a job a week for the past two years, Bronx. My average earning is about ten grand a job, now. I've been pouring all that money into this."

His lips parted into a smile. "This is amazing. She's beautiful.

Tell me about her."

I looked at my labor of love, its familiar midnight blue shell gleaming in the interior lighting of the dock. Her shape resembled that of a stingray. She was my baby. I hadn't christened her yet, but that would come soon enough.

I walked and pointed to the different parts of the ship I wanted him to see. "She's got a Third-class Eagle Plasma Engine that pumps out over twenty thousand shocks of propulsion. That's just the main engine. A Silver Stream SD jump drive gives her wormhole access in as little as ten seconds. I've even added some custom modifications to the boosters that give her a signature and extra kick."

Bronx nodded, patting the outer shell, behind which the engine was housed. "She's got legs, that's for sure."

"I haven't proven it yet, but by my estimation, this thing can only be outrun by single-cockpit fighters," I said.

"I wouldn't doubt it," Bronx said, continuing his walk around the ship.

I followed him. "I built her to run with only one, but it's possible to have a five-person crew. Enough bunks, enough supply space, and more than enough weaponry. You're looking at two automatic Banshee turrets that can hit every conceivable angle. Two high-powered rail guns that swivel just as well as the turrets. I can control them from the cockpit, or just let them automatically target enemies. The automated option is slower, but quite effective. To top it off, I've got a Scatter missile launcher in the middle. That's up to twenty field-seeking missiles shot at one time. They might not be the most accurate or explosive, but they'll do the job just fine. For a last bonus, I built in a mine dropper in the back."

"And you've still got enough power for this thing?" he asked. "How do you figure?"

I pointed to the the tail with a smile. "I figure that with twin neoconductors, I'll be just fine."

"You're kidding!"

"Nope."

"Boy, you are a genius," he said, thumping me on the back.

"Don't you ever forget it, Bronx. That's hyper-polymer ceramics for the exterior, coated with chameleon skin. Just to protect its beauty, I've got a Fendolla Shield Generator."

"What are her dimensions?" he asked.

I waved my hands at the ship, as if the demonstration would help him understand the units of measure. "Eight meters tall, twenty meters wide, and forty-five meters long."

"She's a mean looking predator."

I smiled. "I brought you down here so we could take her out for the first time."

He nodded. Then, flipping his half-full bottle of ale, he threw it at the tail of my ship. The glass shattered. "There, it can fly now. Let's see what she's got."

4

BUTTER. The take off was like butter. White knuckling the control sticks, I guided her out of my humble dock and into infinity. She purred like a giant kitten. The new engine responded with a smoothness that even I wasn't expecting. I only ran it a few times to perform diagnostic tests, so it was the first time I ever let the engine do what it was meant to do. It did not disappoint.

She certainly is a well-crafted machine.

"Listen to her, Cayden," Bronx whispered from the co-pilot's chair. "Bang up job, kid. Bang up job."

I couldn't say anything. I only wanted to live the moment; to appreciate the completion of such a crucial and monumental task. For two years I meticulously planned it out and scrounged for parts. For two years, I sunk every last bit of money I could spare into it. It was finally done, finally ready. Just in time.

Stick to the plan, Cayden, and you'll soon be free.

The black, cold of space surrounded us like an icy ocean. My moment of peace was short-lived, but it would be the first of many such moments to come. I let the excitement take over. A smile overtook my features, and I pushed the accelerator to the max.

Bronx let out an unintelligible cry of surprise as the Third-Class Eagle engine proved true to its reputation. She went from purr to roar in an instant, the powerful plasma surging through the engine, providing a boost that stretched our faces taut. The sleek craft shot like a bullet into the unknown without so much as a shudder.

I adored the power at my fingertips. "She's beautiful."

"Kid, this is a dream ship for anyone who knows how to fly," Bronx said.

"All right, Bronx." I loosened the straps that restrained me to the pilot's seat. "Take over, will you?"

He looked at me in surprise. "Cayden, you just got a hold of her. C'mon, you need to get more time in before you hand over the controls."

I was already making my way out of the cockpit. "Not that big of a deal for me. I want to check on everything while she's flying. So, just take it relatively easy and enjoy yourself."

He shook his head in resignation. "Aye, aye, captain."

///

Bronx's snoring echoed off the small apartment walls. After a long test flight, a few minor adjustments to the engine cooling system, and a loop around the planet, Bronx guided her back into the dock. She did just fine. That was my consensus, anyway. Bronx couldn't stop informing me of the ship's greatness. She still needed work, but it was minor. Overall, her performance exceeded my expectations.

The living quarters were a part of the dock I paid rent for. It wasn't much, but it was enough for a single mercenary keeping a low profile. The dock took up most of the space, but the options of a spiral staircase and small lift led up to the apartment. Only two rooms. The main area, which combined the living, kitchen, and dining space into one. The other was just big enough to fit a bed, a dresser, and a small door that led to the facilities.

Below the apartment, at the bottom of the staircase, was an area where most of my tools were kept. I was provided with crude shelves and a beaten-up workbench. Beyond that, stretched the dock.

What space I had in the apartment was cluttered with clothes, shoes, and ration packs. One might enter my quarters and believe me to be lazy, but there was a definite method to my madness. The clothes, shoes, and ration packs that lay scattered were carefully planted for ease of access should I need them in an escape. And my natural mechanical skills afforded me the ability to plant all sorts of goodies in more places. Weapons, emergency meds, spare money, fake IDs, and whatever else might come in handy were stored under-neath chairs, behind wall decorations, and in hidden compartments in the kitchen.

Bronx was crashed on the couch, still cradling a bottle in his hand. I sat in a chair, shirtless, not too far from him, downing another mouthful of ale. I intended to change my shirt, but I forgot my two spares were in the cleaners. It was hot in the apartment anyway, thanks to a malfunctioning heating system my super kept insisting was going to be fixed for the past three months.

I felt my eyes flutter and realized sleep was calling my name with the longing desire of a forlorn lover. The half-empty beverage dropped from my hand, clinking to the floor, and my consciousness slipped upon the slopes of dreamland.

The slumber I fell into was a strange one. I dreamed of a small hand in mine, holding on tight. But the grip went slack, and the limp fingers slipped through mine. Try as I might, I couldn't hold on as it fell away from me into darkness. An incredible emptiness gripped me, but the world of the living came screaming back to the forefront of my mind as outside stimuli shattered the dreamscape.

A deep voice said my name with great urgency. My eyes were

open, but the imagery around them hadn't sunk in yet. The panicked cry came again, this time much louder. Sense of sight exploded back into my brain. There were people in my apartment. Men restraining someone else. It was Bronx.

"Cayden!" He shook off one of the intruders but fell to the floor under the power of two more.

I was urgent in my assessment of the situation. All men, dressed in black. No, there was one woman in the back, dressed formally in a sharp-looking green suit. Two intruders were directly in front of me, but the sound of a soft footstep told me there was another behind me.

A hundred possibilities formed in a second, and I knew each reaction to the finest detail. What felt like an eternity passed as I waited for the next turn in the game to take place. Finally, the man behind me stepped forward and illuminated my proper course of action.

His hand grabbed my bare shoulder from behind, and I twisted around with practiced agility. His grip loosened, causing him to lose his balance in the process. My elbow intercepted his nose with a nasty crunch. He was a big guy, and the high-pitched shriek that emitted from his mouth didn't fit his physique. He tumbled to the floor, blood gushing between the fingers that now clutched his face.

I dove behind him, reaching under the nearest kitchen chair. Two goons fell on top of me, trying to pin my arms to the floor, but I already grasped the thread-edged knife held to the bottom of the cushion by a small magnet. With a quick flip of my wrist, I cut deep into the arm of the man to my left. He jumped back with a gasp and a curse, but his buddy threw a strong punch to my jaw. It connected, but not too solidly. As he threw another, I shoved the knife into his oncoming fist. He screamed and rolled off me, unfortunately with the knife still embedded between his knuckles.

Between me and the other night-time raiders was my escape plan. They had the lift and stairs cut off, like any sensible assailants would, but they couldn't see the trap door I installed, hidden under the rug between us.

I jumped to my feet and bolted for it. Since I was running directly for them, they tensed, ready for a charge. But I fell to my knees, sliding on the floor and throwing the carpet toward them. With a kick, the door fell out, and I dropped down the unforgiving slope.

"Stop him!" the woman shouted.

"Go, Cayden!" Bronx shouted.

My body rolled uncomfortably down the little tunnel, falling much faster than I would have liked. I tumbled out of the emergency hatch, free falling a solid three meters before making impact.

Thankfully, the end of my little escape tunnel was at an angle, allowing me to make a semi-decent roll upon impact. Getting to my feet, I started running for the ship, but a man blocked my path. A quick look at the exit showed a battalion of the invaders standing guard. The lone ranger in front of the ship was a better bet.

I'm not so sure about that.

I recognized him at once. A face I saw nearly every day before three years ago. But unlike Bronx, his was a face from my past that I would've been happy to never see again.

Jerry.

"Cayden," he said, flashing brilliant white teeth. "It's been a while."

It was important that I let him continue to believe that I did not know who he was. For Jerry and his band of misfits believed me to be suffering from a severe case of amnesia.

Additional perfect teeth were exposed as his smile widened.

"Don't you remember me?"

What's that word you always used to call him?

Prick.

Yes, that's it. Prick.

I heard footsteps behind me and chanced a look. The woman in the nice suit and her battalion of night raiders were out of my apartment now. Bronx floated on a med-sled between two of the bodyguards, unconscious.

The yet-to-be identified woman carried herself like someone with authority. Not especially tall for a human female, but her gate and stature gave her a tall appearance. Reddish-brown hair cropped close, and dark eyes that observed me with distaste.

I have no idea who she is.

That's comforting.

"Enough," she snapped. "Restrain him."

"Gladly," Jerry said, pushing his long blond hair out of his face.

I was a little outmatched, but if Mr. Good-Looking wanted to take me out himself, I might have a chance to get past him and onto my ship. Of course, I would have trouble after that. Shirtless and shoeless wasn't my preferred method of travel. I never had time to move any spare clothes and rations to the ship yet, and therefore I would be in a bit of a predicament, especially if they decided to give chase.

Well, it's a good thing that escape isn't in our plans.

Good thing.

"Jerry, this is not the time," the woman said, her voice more angry than authoritative. "I don't want any screwups."

Jerry, for his part, did not appear to give much thought to her orders. He stepped forward, removing his coat and rolling up his sleeves. "This will only take a minute. He never was as good in this area as me. His talents lie elsewhere."

I remained firmly in my place. "Better than you think, perhaps."

He responded by rushing me. I dodged a right hook, blocked a left, but was caught by a quick knee to the midsection that took my breath away. As I backpedaled, he advanced with a kind of mechanical precision.

I tried to ignore my burning lungs and unleashed a couple of punches. He bobbed his head out of the way, countered with a jab to my nose, and twisted my arm behind my back. I spun out of it, only to receive a harsh kick to my sternum that again made breathing feel like sucking glass shards through a paper tube.

He circled me. "Really, Cayden, you must do a little better than that."

I wiped blood from under my nose. He fought the way I remembered. Skill and precision. Jerry tried to keep his emotions out of the battle because he made mistakes when he was angry. I knew this.

He did not know that I knew this.

"I've been hit harder by the drunks at the bar," I said, but he only smiled.

You're going to need more than that. You aren't children anymore.

I stepped forward. "What do you want anyway?"

He shrugged his shoulder nonchalantly. "I'd like nothing more than to kill you, Cayden, but I'm persuaded to wait for the moment. You're talents are needed."

"Oh, I see. You're just a pawn. No wonder you hate me. You're good at what you do, you're quick, you're good-looking. Killer smile,

39

by the way. Yet, you couldn't do what they wanted you to, and now they need me. You know, someone *better* than you."

Jerry attempted to hold his cool, but the spark of entertainment that was in his eyes disappeared. I was successful in shattering his cool, which gave me some sense of satisfaction. He possessed that look like he wanted to say so much, yet the words eluded him, which of course only enraged him further.

It's a perfectly reasonable thing to be mad about. I'd be mad if I were stupid.

"Enough games," the woman said. "Take him."

He charged me, angry and ready to do some damage. I wanted to be the aggressor and uncorked a strong right hook. My enemy walked through the attack as if it were not there. He blocked the hook and threw a quick jab to my throat. The strike caused me to choke, and I tried to recover by unleashing another punch, but a vicious knee connected with my midsection and bent me over. Thinking I could take him to the ground, I went for his legs, but his same knee came back hard under my chin, bringing me to a standing position.

The smirk returned to his face. He tossed out a quick punch, but I was able to dodge to the left. Grabbing his extended arm, I spun and drove a hard elbow right into his jaw. The strike connected beautifully, and he stumbled back, surprise written all over his face. I'd split his lip.

Again he charged, the anger back in his eyes. Jerry might have been more talented, but he wasn't very good at taking punishment. He brought down a series of punches, which I was able to block for the most part. The fourth punch caught me on my cheek, but I rolled with the strike and let loose one of my own. He caught my arm and cranked it behind my back, but I was ready and threw my head back as hard as I could. The nasty crunch of a nose cracking put a smile on my face.

He pushed me off of him, but I turned and tackled him to the ground, raining down as many punches as I could. I wanted to hurt him. I wanted to hurt him like he always managed to hurt me. However, before I could get started, strong hands grabbed me from behind. Then, something sharp struck my thigh, and the world faded away.

Prick.

5

THE Coyote hated blindfolds.

I hate blindfolds.

It was a cliché, and it bothered him.

It's not just the blindfold. It's the entire charade. So lacking in creativity. A mysterious attack during your sleep. The blond, blue-eyed assassin who enjoys making snide comments about our past, which I admit, is not entirely intact.

It would be a complete loss if it hadn't been for you, Coyote.

I do what I can, Cayden.

With a none-too-gentle tug, the blindfold was removed, and I needed to squint my eyes to the blinding light. With that one quick glance, I was able to see six men, and one woman. The woman was the one that allowed me to see again. The same woman who commanded Jerry.

"Sorry about the rude measures we were forced to take, Cayden," she said.

"Don't apologize for things you're not sorry about." My voice was hoarse and my mouth dry.

She handed me a cup of water. To my surprise, they didn't restrain me to the chair I was seated in. Apparently, they believed a room full of armed men would stop me if I tried to escape. I accepted the cup and drank greedily.

"We had to take you by force. There was no other way," she said.

"You don't say," I mocked.

My vision was beginning to clear, and I was able to discern faces among the plain gray surroundings of the room. The woman talking was seated across from me. The five men standing around her looked like the biggest and toughest of the bunch that were with her during the successful kidnapping. Jerry stood towards the back of the room, a large bandage on his nose.

"How ya doing? Hope I didn't do any permanent damage." He smirked at my quip, but said nothing.

"Jerry will remain silent from now on, I assure you," the woman said.

"Jerry?" I could've stopped the chuckle that escaped my lips, but didn't want to. Perhaps it was immature, but I liked bothering him. "You're an assassin, and you're name is Jerry?"

Both Jerry and the woman stiffened at my response. "How did you know he was an assassin?"

You want to take this one, Coyote?

Are you sure?

Absolutely. You're the more snide one of us two.

Whatever you say, Cayden.

The Coyote and I could switch control of my body at will. A long, confusing time ago, we discovered this. Usually, I remained in control, but I liked to take advantage of his talents every once in awhile. And with a feeling that could only be described as letting my brain go, I switched to the one observing, and the Coyote to the one with the body.

He did not waste any time.

"Please, if you all supposedly know me, then you should know

I have a mind that puts all of yours to shame. Believe it or not, I've had a life outside of the years that are missing from my memory. I've seen more assassins, mercenaries, drug dealers, slave traders, murderers, convicts, thieves, and just plain old bad guys than most see in their lifetimes. I can read blondie over there like a book."

There was a moment of pause, but her frown turned into a smile. "I must admit, you are one special individual, Cayden. I never was much of a fan, but you are indeed special."

"Would you please desist in making confusing remarks about my past. I get it. You knew me, and whatever psycho group you work for is responsible for the loss of my memory. Why don't we get to what it is you want from me? Your superior act is boring."

And cliché.

Yes, thank you, Cayden.

Her composure was not affected, but she did chance a glance at Jerry. The assassin gave her an "I told you so" kind of look. She turned back to me, her expression one of mild amusement.

"Business, please," I said. "What is it you want? Should I say it in another language? I know several. It's no trouble, if that is what you require."

Sometimes, you're brilliant, Coyote.

I'm always brilliant, Cayden. It is my state of being.

She waved her hand to cut me off. "Show him the image."

One of the men turned on a small device. A crystal clear image of a young human woman appeared via hologram by the wall across from me. Her skin was darker than mine, almost golden. Exotic, dark brown hair with streaks of blond fell by the sides of her face, and brilliant eyes drew attention away from everything else.

A beauty in the dark absence of this existence. A reason. A goal.

Don't do the poet thing, please. Not now.

"Her name is Kalista. All you need to know is that you must kill her. She is not alone, however." The woman signaled to the henchman, and another holographic face appeared beside Kalista's. "She has a brother. Dorian. He is not considered a priority, but you may kill him if you must. Still, we prefer him alive. We'd consider paying you more if you do deliver him unharmed. But kill the female. This is not an option."

I snorted. "That little girl's got your panties so twisted that you need her dead?"

The ice queen grimaced. "Let's just say, she's a threat. Kill her. No excuses."

I shrugged. "Fine. What's the pay?"

"Ten thousand if you kill her and deliver her brother unharmed."

I couldn't help laughing, completely taken off guard by their meager proposal. "Ten thousand? Are you kidding me? This is obviously of some importance to you, and I'm sure she will not be an easy kill. I'm guessing her brother presents problems. And there must be something special about her that will make my job even more difficult. Otherwise, why would you want her dead?"

"How much do you want?" she asked, cutting to the chase.

"Fifty." I said with a shrug.

"Excuse me?"

"No less," I said. "I want fifty thousand in unmarked universal cards, and I want half of it immediately. I'll kill your annoyance and
deliver Dorian alive and well."

"This deal isn't done, Cayden. I—"

"This deal *is* done, lady. You want this girl dead, and her brother alive. However, if it were that simple, you would've sent Jerry there to do your dirty work for free. But he's the kind of brainless bastard that will rely on nothing but his physical talents. I haven't quite figured out why that won't work, but there's a strong reason. Maybe Dorian is better than Jerry. So, you want me to go in with a plan, a backup plan, and no room for mistakes. You don't want there to be any doubt. So the price is fifty thousand. It's not like you can't afford it."

There was a moment of pause, and then the slightest of smiles crept onto her face. "Okay, Cayden. You've got your deal."

"Great. Now what?"

She grabbed a needle from the small table behind her.

"Again? Really?"

Soon, the world faded away.

///

Bronx looked behind him as the door opened to the observation room. Margaret walked through, a hard-to-read expression on her face. Frustration, perhaps. It was her first actual interaction with Cayden, and Bronx knew it could be off-putting. None of Cayden's peers were anything like him.

She took a seat opposite him. "I don't see why you are fascinated by him."

Bronx watched her micro-expressions carefully as she spoke. She was trained to hide such giveaways but no one was perfect, and the slight crinkle in her nose showed her aggravation. She was new to the programs she was now in charge of and therefore unfamiliar with the experiments that were Cayden and Jerry. Jerry, she knew and didn't understand. Cayden, she did not know and understood even less.

"Margaret, after that conversation, you still don't understand why he's always been my favorite?" Bronx asked, threading his fingers together.

The crinkle in her nose increased. "I can see his talents. But he is more a threat than anything. He has always been and forever will be a threat as long as we let him live. He is weaker than all the others, yet he found a way to survive."

"There is no such thing as a paradox, Margaret," Bronx said. "Only the illusion of one. Cayden was never the weakest. He was always the strongest. I would not suggest attempting an assassination."

She took a bottle of water from the table between them and drank before speaking. "You don't think our resources could finish him off?"

Bronx shrugged. "Maybe, but what would the price be? Cayden is different than the rest of his peers. He's unique. I've tried to communicate that to our superiors over and over, but they are only concerned about results. Cayden's potential is greater than the rest because what he does is his identity. He can do anything, and anything stretches a long way."

Margaret shook her head. "I have to agree with our superiors, Bronx. Your faith in him is too great. He is a human. Just like any other."

Bronx smiled. "Yes, he is. But he is a fully self-aware human. Not many are like him. He sees past the games everyone plays, and plays his own. I've never encountered someone that could so easily make anyone his pawn. Even our organization."

Her eyebrows raised. "And that's what makes him dangerous? Being self-aware?"

"It make him extremely dangerous," Bronx said. "Extremely uncontrollable. If there ever was someone who could bite the hand that feeds him, it's Cayden."

"Then please explain to me why you like him so much?"

He met her gaze with an unreadable expression. "I enjoy the challenge."

It was that challenge that got him demoted, of course. Margaret was, to a degree, his new boss. The organization he worked for was unsatisfied with Bronx's batch of candidates, which included Jerry and Cayden, and therefore he was demoted. If they were to be honest, though, his superiors simply could not understand the value of Bronx's experiments. His creations were unique, and Cayden stood as his crowning achievement.

However, people with limited vision failed to see the greatness he brought into the universe. Bronx considered leaving, but the twist in Cayden's fate, and the role he played in it compelled him to stay. It was worth it. If Cayden could pull off his plan, Bronx would get everything he wanted.

He stood from the chair and stretched his legs. "I should get down to the shuttle. Good luck, Margaret."

6

DRY mouth. It was one of the many side effects to tranquilizers. Then, of course, there was the dizziness. That feeling of waking up and not remembering anything for the first few minutes. I despised not being in control of my unconsciousness. I also despised not knowing where I was going to be conscious once I exited my unconscious state.

Yes, how annoying.

That was the Coyote, and I was back to being myself within . . . myself. One of the more interesting skills the Coyote was seemingly stuck with was an inability to lose consciousness. Ever. He did not sleep, he did not get drugged, he did not get knocked out. He was always present.

This is true, but that "skill" has only been helpful one time. At all other times it is burdensome and annoying.

He says this because of a tough history. While I sleep, he is awake. And able to keep me awake. This naturally led to a great deal of arguing between us, and arguing with oneself only fuels stress. Eventually, he learned of my need to sleep and allowed me to rest. The biggest problem for him was once I lost consciousness, he was powerless. He couldn't take over my body, and obviously had no one to talk to and nothing to do. For him, my sleep time was like a six-hour silent imprisonment.

"Are you okay?" a deep voice asked.

"I need guns," I said, the sound coming out in a dry croak.

"You need water and food. Then you need guns."

I was able to open my eyes and sift through the darkness. A very large blur was squatting down next to me. It was Bronx, of course. He was holding out a bottle of water. I ripped the cap off and gulped down a few mouthfuls. My throat cleared around the same time that my vision did. Bronx's face had a few bruises, but otherwise he seemed fine.

His dark eyes scanned around the room, giving me the signal we were probably being watched. In other words, we should keep up the act.

"Did they kidnap you, too?" I asked.

"Yeah, but it was you they must have wanted," he said. "Nobody so much as talked to me. Just knocked me out. I woke up in a little gray room, and then, they knocked me out again. My eyes opened about fifteen minutes before yours."

"Why would they bring you along?" I asked.

He shrugged and helped me stand up. "Beats me, kid. Perhaps just to account for any loose ends. Here, I cooked up some bacon and eggs. Lots of protein and salt. It'll get you up and running again."

I slumped into a chair, ate, and explained to him what happened. Bronx already knew, of course. I knew that he knew. He knew that I knew that he knew. However, I had to act like I didn't know, and he had to act like he knew that I didn't know.

So much knowing.

"So, you have to kill some girl?" Bronx asked.

"And bring her brother back alive."

"Cruel," he remarked.

"It is," I said. "I'm extremely low on supplies. I need to pay a long, expensive visit to Stella."

"You're all out of weapons?"

I swallowed some eggs. "I've got a few guns here and there, but nothing good enough for this job. I need to stock up, and I've got the money to do so."

Bronx looked up from his cup of coffee. "How could you possibly have saved money when building that ship?"

"I didn't," I said. "But, they left me twenty-five grand in advance for the job. It's probably in my bedroom, along with information on where I can find my targets."

My friend shook his head with a smile. "All right, kid. I'm going back to my place to catch some sleep. You need anything else?"

"I'm good. Thanks for cooking this up."

He walked to the door. "Of course. You know how to contact me if you need anything. I have no doubt that I'll be seeing you later."

"No doubt," I said.

Left alone to a plate of half-finished food and a trashed room, I pondered my plans thus far. Things were moving fast. Very fast. I knew they would once the organization made its first move, but after waiting for three years, the sudden pace was intimidating.

Kalista was what it was all about, of course. My plan revolved around her. It always had. It was her brother that worried me. Try as we might, the Coyote and I could never come up with a concrete solution for him. I knew that Kalista loved him dearly, but he presented a complex problem for me, and the future I envisioned. There was no surety with him in the picture, which I hated.

Because plans are based on surety, or contingencies that offer an alternate surety.

The problem with Dorian was that the alternate plans offered as little insurance as the original plans. He had the unique power to change everything, mostly for the worse. I was left with no option but to improvise and hope.

I made my way into the bedroom. Just as I predicted, there was a suitcase and a folder neatly placed on the bed. That would be the twenty-five thousand, and I wasn't quite sure what was in the folder. I picked it up, and a small video recorder fell out. A miniature hologram of the psycho lady who gave me the mission popped up when it hit the floor.

"Hello again, Cayden," she said. "I trust your drug-induced sleep gave you pleasant dreams."

Was that an attempt at humor?

I think so.

She should not do that again. Ever.

Agreed.

"This message is simply a warning. Although you are our chief hunter and our chief employee, we want this job completed quickly. Therefore, we have placed a freelance bounty on both of the siblings for twenty thousand. That kind of price will attract a fair share of the market. So, I do hope that you get to them before some lucky bounty hunter claims the prize. Happy hunting."

"Oh, thanks," I said, tossing the recorder into a trash bin.

I opened the folder the rest of the way to find a few digital printouts. There were clear images of Dorian and Kalista with several different angles of their faces playing by slowly. The similarities between them were clear, but the differences were stark. Dorian was a hard-looking young man, with pale skin. His eyes and close-cropped hair reminded me of the color of long-dried blood; deep brown with a red hue. Despite what were probably handsome features, his expression emanated intimidation.

Kalista couldn't have been more different. There were striking similarities in the shapes of their faces, such as their high cheekbones, and almond eyes. However, it was the differences that mattered. Kalista's skin was warm and bronze. Her eyes were hazel, with highlights of green and blue dancing on a background of light brown. Her hair was voluminous, mostly dark brown, but accented with magnificent streaks of blonde. Looking at her always made me wonder what creature would not possibly find her beautiful.

If I currently possessed hands, I would be snapping my fingers several times and redundantly telling you to "snap" out of it.

I ignored his barb, as a reply would only fuel a preachy monologue. The Coyote was constantly reminding me not to get drawn in and to stay focused. But he did not feel what I felt. I don't think he could.

Of course I can't. Love is selfless, and I am the epitome of selfishness.

The report said that they were last seen on the planet Morkal. My best guess was that they were hiding in the city of Je'zulna. It was a lawless section of the planet, and a great place to hide if you were on the run.

Finding them wouldn't be easy, but for me, not at all impossible. I put the folder down and packed all of my belongings. Everything I owned needed to be transferred to my ship. Once I finished purchasing new supplies from Stella, I would not be coming back.

Not ever.

/ / /

"Let's start from the top. What's your list?" Stella asked.

I took a public transport to Stella's shop. My ship was packed and ready, but I didn't want to use it until I had to. Using public transports allowed me to blend in seamlessly, while at the same time

53

study the sentients around me. If someone was tailing me, I would know.

Sleep begged me to surrender to its dark clutches, but time was not on my side. Though very important, REM had to wait. The Coyote was overjoyed that he received more active time, and I leaned on his energy to see me through. A pounding headache, no doubt a lingering effect from the tranquilizer, had taken over my brain. So far, the medication did nothing for it.

Your head hurts because your skull cannot take the enormity of your brain.

Right, and my pants are tight because they can't take the enormity of my—

You're always so sarcastic when you're in pain. Why is that?

"Let's just cover the guns first, Stella." I ignored the Coyote's curiosity. "I'm going to need a pair of Custom Viper pistols."

She winced. "You have good taste, but they aren't cheap. With your discount, you're looking at twenty-eight hundred right there."

I waved her concern off. "That's fine. How many shots does the clip hold?"

"Twenty. The package I'm giving you throws in two spare clips, so you've got eighty shots total."

"Give me a couple of rechargers, too."

"That's another hundred," she said, glancing at me with a worried expression. "You look kind of nervous, Cayden. Everything all right?"

I rubbed my temples with the tips of my fingers. "Just another job. An important one."

"Do you need any help on this one?"

"This is way out of your range, Stella. I just need the supplies."

"Whatever you say." She dropped her wary tone and shifted our discussion back to business mode. It was better that way. We were unlikely to see one another again.

I sighed, taking a moment to mentally organize my supply list. "I'm going to need a sniper rifle. Any recommendations?"

"Well," she said, walking over to the far wall, "in my opinion, the best bang for your buck is this one."

She pulled down a gun that was nearly as long as I was tall, and by the way she carried it, it looked to have significant weight. A rectangular scope was seated on top.

"Is that a Titan?" I asked.

"Close. It's actually the Titan's younger brother, the Achilles. It's a human-made sniper, so you're looking at laser bullet technology. Automatic infrared is available in dark situations. It comes with its own automated tripod, long-distance remote control, and it has a clip of ten shots. More than you need, I guarantee it."

"Why's that?" I asked.

She tossed me a thin, palm-sized transparent control screen from the side of the gun. It lit up immediately, multiple commands displayed across its face. I assumed it was the remote.

Stella leaned forward across the counter and pointed at the lower right-hand corner of the screen. "You see the auto-target icon? If you press that and you spot the person you want to shoot, it will automatically lock in until it senses elimination. So, if you do happen to miss, the rifle will track your target for you without flaw. You can also preset targets you want eliminated. The gun comes equipped with facial recognition software."

I nodded in appreciation. "Nice. I'll take it. Give me three extra clips, and I'll need a standard re-charging unit."

She blinked a few times. "What kind of mission is this?"

I shrugged. "Actually, I'm just stocking up on some of this. I have the money, and I do need the supplies."

"Let me get a packing kit from the back," she said. "That brings your total to six thousand, Cayden."

She walked through the doorway to her left, at the back of the shop, hauling the sniper rifle over her shoulder. I turned around and leaned against the display case, allowing it to take some of my weight. The headache was worsening, stabbing its claws into the backs of my eyes. It was not an unfamiliar feeling.

From before my birth, I was an experiment. Experiments had side effects, and one of mine was headaches that no medicine on the market could help. I tried to distract myself with my surroundings, which I might very well never see again. I spent a lot of time in this shop. Good times, mostly. Remembering it wasn't a bad idea.

Yes, memories are important.

The initial entrance of Stella's shop looked quite similar to most weapons shops. A mix of cheap, basic weapons and their more sophisticated counterparts displayed in three transparent cases that made an upside-down "U" shape upon entrance. On the gray walls behind the cases were larger weapons, such as the sniper rifle I purchased.

Quite out of place, however, were what appeared to be simple, framed digital pictures of various peaceful images. A sunset from planet Earth over an ocean that lit the sky a deep red. A yookallan child playing a game with his friends. A deep-space nebula, shining strikingly blue upon a backdrop of black.

It was all code, known only to mercenaries and bounty hunters. Stella sold highly illegal explosive kits. The sunset picture, or any other image with a red-hued sky, indicated the dealer had a Red Sky explosives kit, which was my particular favorite. Images of children playing were code for Young Gun explosives. Any images of nebulae meant Oblivion explosives.

I used the Red Sky explosives kit on my last mission and came away quite satisfied. The Young Gun kit, from what I heard, was more powerful but less controlled. The Oblivion kit apparently consisted of only one bomb and remote and was the cheapest. I needed complexity and control.

Why would anyone want anything else?

Stella wheeled a large case through the doorway on a handcart. "That's better. Now, what else can I do you for?"

"Shotguns," I said.

She walked to the display case to my left. "How many and which ones?"

I shrugged my shoulders, and the movement intensified the pain behind my eyes. "What do you recommend?"

"Well, my personal favorite is the Mark II. It takes hyperplasma ammo, which gives it some crazy kick. I mean, this stuff will cut people in two within ten meters."

"Sounds good," I said. "I'll need two of them."

She took a moment to run the numbers on her data pad. "Your total is a little over nine thousand."

"Still doing okay. Now I need your recommendation on submachine guns. What do you think?"

She walked me over to another display case. "It's a toss-up between the Gavel 91 and the Leopard Special. Both of them are works of art. The Gavel fires red plasma bullets, which will penetrate any body armor I know about. Its magazine holds fifty shots, but the package you'll get comes with ten full magazines. The Leopard is laser bullet technology, and its magazine holds five more rounds than the Gavel, but it's not quite as powerful. It's faster, though. The Leopard

Special comes with five magazines."

"I'll take two of each."

Stella ran the numbers again. "That brings your bill up to fifteen thousand."

I nodded, but the pounding in my head stilled the movement. "We are quickly approaching my limit. Enough weapons, I think. On to the explosives and miscellaneous items. I'm going to need ten frag, ten smoke, and ten flash grenades. I'll need the holsters for those pistols, and a quality gun-cleaning kit. After that, a new Red Sky explosives kit, and I believe that will be all."

She ran the math again. "Twenty-two thousand even."

"Deal."

"That explosives kit must have worked well if you're wanting another," she said.

I did my best to smile, though the pain splitting my skull made it quite the effort. "I was pleased."

She peered at me for a moment, no doubt trying to discern my intentions. "Planning on blowing something else up?"

"Don't ask a question you don't want to hear the answer to," I said.

I paid her in my newly acquired stash of unmarked currency, and she helped wheel all the supplies out to the transport. A few people gave me strange looks but most just minded their business. No need to start trouble with a guy that was carrying enough firepower to lay waste to a city.

We need to get you back to the apartment. This migraine is progressing at a quick rate.

The Coyote could not feel my pain, but he could detect it. As far as I knew, he could not feel any pain whatsoever. When he controlled my body and was hurt, it was I who felt it. At first, I thought this to be a detriment, but discovered it to be an advantage. In the most intense of times, he would stay calm and keep me focused. It came in handy in the past, and I counted on it coming in handy in the near future.

You may begin to vomit soon.

I know.

You need sleep.

I know, Coyote.

No need to get snippy.

Stella stared at all the weapons. "You starting a war, Cayden?"

I strapped myself in, and did the same to the case of my new goodies. "Something like that."

"Well, you've got a fighting chance at winning."

"I always win," I said.

She shook her head and sighed. "Of course you do."

Stella waved as I departed. I allowed myself to wave back, knowing that it could be the last time I would see her. It surprised me that I was going to miss her.

Don't go soft, now Cayden. War and soft mix about as well as razor blades and jellyfish. And it is to war that we must go.

I took a deep breath and let it out as slow as my lungs would allow as the transport climbed through the upper atmosphere. This planet was one I wished to see again someday. But, for now, I was to leave it behind.

To war.

7

THE bar was a refuge. Dorian found it within the first day of relocating to Je'zulna on the planet Morkal. It was perfectly hidden; deep down an alley between two other bars. The front door was inconspicuous, a small sign at the top right listing its identity. *The Gutter*. Dim lights and staff that only asked what they could get you, complemented the criminal atmosphere.

Despite its small size, six tele-comms operated at all times, the lights of the screens casting long shadows across the bar floor. Each tele-comm broadcast a different news channel. Dorian would often see a denizen of the bar get up and quietly leave as the wanted ads would play.

Today, it was his turn.

In the three months he was on the run, no wanted ads listed him on an open bounty. Instead of bounty hunters, he faced assassins and soldiers sent on specific missions to kill or capture him. He was hunted in silence. But on the second tele-comm to the left, both his and his sister's faces were displayed in full view. The reward was for twenty thousand in unmarked cards.

He commanded his body to relax. His natural instinct wound him like a spring. Twenty thousand was a lot of money. Enough to attract a good deal of bounty hunters, both seasoned and fresh. Since unmarked cards were worth up to ten percent more than traditional pounds, the attraction increased.

After an eternity, his face was replaced by another. Dorian stayed in his seat for three more minutes, sipped his drink with forced patience, and left the money on the table. He took his time walking out of the bar, making eye contact with none of the patrons.

He was not a hider by nature. More a confrontational warrior, willing to engage a fully aware enemy. That was what he liked. That's what he was meant to do.

However, instinct couldn't be followed all of the time. Dorian carried baggage; baggage he willingly accepted. When it was himself in the crosshairs, he felt comfortable. Confidant. He was very capable, that much he knew. That much he *felt*. It was inside of him. The skill to kill swiftly, efficiently. The ability to manage any combat situation, no matter the odds. But when his sister, Kalista, was the target, the equation changed.

His confidence ebbed away, and his capability waned. His instinct demanded risk, but he couldn't risk her. She was important. She was close to him. A part of him.

Dorian attributed it to their genetic connection. It was the physical link. The same blood. The emotional love he felt for his sister was wavering at best. He cared for her, but such emotion felt foreign to him. Still, she was the only one who could stir any emotional feeling from him, even if it was faint.

Perhaps that said something.

Perhaps that was *why* he risked his well being to secure hers. Despite little memory, Dorian was sure of one thing. His instincts were true. He felt to his core that trusting them was his key to survival. With Kalista, his instincts went haywire. He felt protective and at the same time, indifferent. Part of him demanded that he go so far as to sacrifice his life for her, and another part of him screamed for him to abandon her.

His choice was made, and he would not change his mind. Shelter her. Hide her. Run. His instincts continued to send mixed signals, but he did his best to ignore the ones that cried for him to leave her.

It was night on Je'zulna, their temporary home on Morkal. During their brief stint on the planet, Dorian diligently studied the city maps over and over until he was comfortable with knowing multiple ways to each destination. Not only did it make him look more like a local, but it allowed him to take a different path to his apartment each day. He usually took longer routes with unnecessary twists and turns to make sure he wasn't being tailed. Tonight was no different. After twenty minutes, he was home.

The door slid open after receiving the combination, and he walked through the entrance with caution, his eyes scanning everything. He did this automatically, sensitive to any unexpected change. The lights were dim, but that was not surprising. The scent of vanilla hung in the air. A candle Kalista bought two days ago. The atmosphere was warm, almost uncomfortable. She liked the heat.

"Kalista?"

There was no response, but he knew not to panic. She had a tendency to be unpredictable. He made his way past the kitchen and into the living area, still on high alert. She was sitting at the corner of the couch, shaking as if she were caught in a blizzard, despite the room's warm temperature.

The muscles in his shoulders relaxed. "Another attack?"

She nodded. "I-it's okay. I just need some time."

"They're more frequent, now," he said.

Again, she nodded. "It's okay."

After wrapping her in their one spare blanket, he sat down,

his arms wrapped around her frail body. His instincts growled in frustration at the back of his mind. He quieted them and instead focused on his reason for staying.

For him, Kalista represented his humanity. From his observations of all other beings, it was evident that families cared for one another. Half of his instincts supported the observation, and Dorian felt if the other half won that battle of his mind, he would lose more than just a sister. He would lose what made him worth being.

He felt her body cease its shaking. "Are you hungry? I have some food."

She sat up, her eyes growing wide. "Something's wrong. What is it?"

Kalista owned the uncanny ability to detect what the people around her were feeling. She could sense their happiness, their sadness, and beyond. It was no use lying to her, because she knew. Dorian's worry over the new bounty on their heads must have captured her attention. It was not the first time she sensed what he was feeling. If she knew about his conflicted nature involving her, she did not let on.

"Dorian, what is it?"

"We're going to have to run again," he said. "There's an open bounty on both of our heads. The pictures were crystal clear, so it's obvious it's the GS. Apparently, they are trying a different tactic."

A tear crept down her cheek. "I won't go back there, Dorian. I don't know what they did to me, but I'll never go back there to find out. I don't care if I ever know."

Dorian didn't know much about the GS, despite it being the organization that raised him from infancy. He didn't even know what the initials stood for. His memory was thoroughly erased. What he could recall was generic. His personality still felt rooted, his instincts sharp, and his training ingrained, but he did not know why. Beyond the past three months, everything was blank.

Kalista was not like Dorian. She maintained something of a memory, though not much of one. What she could remember was limited, and she described everything as shattered. Like someone had taken a puzzle and scattered its pieces across the room. Still, what she did remember was useful.

Dorian rose from the couch. "We need rest. We will leave tomorrow."

"I can't go back, Dorian."

He did not turn back as he entered the darkness of the single bedroom. Kalista preferred the couch. "I know."

///

Travel in my beautiful new ship was heavenly. The morkallian system was one that inspired awe, with many ringed planets and colorful moons. The actual planet of Morkal was also a sight that pleased the eyes, though it did have its darker sides. Beyond the ornate fountains and primped gardens blooming with rainbow flowers were dark alleys and scummy dens of thieves.

Dorian and Kalista were hiding there.

Getting to the planet only took me half a day, thanks to the wonders of wormhole travel. The longest part of traveling through the holes was the pit stops in between. The holes in the realm could be long or short depending on where one goes and when. For me, it required three stops.

Tracking my targets turned out to be fairly simple. Thanks to my excursions, I made a lot of friends in a lot of places. Visit a few lowlifes, ask the right questions, pay with the right kind of money, and one could find out just about anything. And so, I located Dorian by the end of that very same day.

Amazing what money and wit can accomplish.

Now, I was watching my all too familiar adversary walk out of the bar, the concern of seeing his face on the tele-comm evident in the tension of his steps. Still, to the casual observer, his performance of nonchalance would have been effective.

Bravo.

I didn't want to alert him to my presence, and so I only glanced at him a few times. From the small observations I was able to make, he was everything I remembered him to be. He chose his seat carefully, positioning himself against a wall so no one could surprise him from behind. From his chair, he had the option of three exits, and his peripheral vision caught everything that moved near him. He glanced from patron to patron every forty-five seconds to verify their activities. Before eating or drinking, he swallowed a large white pill, dry. I recognized the pill, as I also kept a stash in my ship. An easily accommodated medicine developed by the yookallans that rendered most poisons harmless.

Smart.

He was justifiably paranoid. Many a bounty hunter paid bar-keeps to slip a target a tainted drink. It was better than risking injury or death in a confrontation. It was such a good method that I adapted it to my own strategy.

Tracking him the old fashioned way was out of the question. He would catch anyone that followed him and no doubt eliminate them. I knew I wasn't a match for him face-to-face, but I was definitely sneakier.

Sneakiness is far superior to violence in my opinion.

My method was not one of poison. I discovered an interesting tracking tool on one of my many adventures as a mercenary. A scent-less, tasteless liquid that contained microscopic chips. The chips were bio-mechanical in nature, so they attached to red blood cells harm-lessly. After thirty six hours, they shut down and were naturally flushed through the waste system of whoever housed them. While active, they gave off a unique electronic signal, which would appear on the device in my pocket.

Considering Dorian left the bar, perhaps you should check to see if it's working.

Right. I finished my cheap, not-so-tasty meal, and then departed the run-down bar. With the coordinates, I would be able to implement the next part of my plan.

That's a good word. Implement. Sinister, yet coy.

As I have previously stated, the Coyote could sometimes be annoying.

Annoyance is in the eye of the beholder.

I made my way back to the ship, which still held that beautiful new ship smell, and crashed into the pilot's chair. It had been approx-imately ten minutes since Dorian finished his drink, infecting himself with my tracers. If they weren't sending a signal by now, then some-thing was failing. I pulled the palm-sized, transparent screen from my pocket. Sure enough, a little white blip showed up less than five kilo-meters away. I keyed the coordinates into the nav-layout on the ship and found the exact address to where my prey was staying.

Perfect.

Indeed. The next step in my plan would be more difficult. So far, I was capable of operating in the shadows, but the moment of rev-elation approached with quickened steps. I would have to face Dorian. More terrifying than that, I would have to face Kalista. I would see her in person again, after more than three years of biding my time.

It's going to work.

I hope so.

Stay calm.

Easier said than done.

8

KALISTA was perched on the edge of the sofa, staring into the dark of the room. Most of her nights were spent much the same way. Sleep evaded her, scared away by the images and words cycling through her troubled mind.

Through this storm, she sails on. Undeterred, she rows on. High or low, she moves on.

It was poetry. Random and confusing. The words would pop into her mind as if the author resided in her head. Dozens of lines, strung together out of order. She couldn't complete a single poem, but it didn't matter. Kalista treasured them above all other memories.

She clicked on the small light she kept by the couch and took pen to paper, jotting down the verse. She did not dare record the verses digitally. Kalista felt they were at risk of being erased purposefully or accidentally. Nor was it as intimate as the handwritten note. Holding the pen between her thumb and forefinger felt right, somehow.

Above the newest line were several others she discovered over the past three months. They were all beautiful, and not a single one belonged to a published work. It was the key reason she treasured them so much. All of her other fragmented memories would be fulfilled when she smelled, heard, saw, or tasted something connected to her past. Always, it was a fuzzy recollection completed by outside stimuli. The poems were completely random and original. It meant that someone had given them to her.

For her.

Kalista was sure of it, because she could see the poet in her mind's eye, shrouded in darkness next to her. His features couldn't be identified, but his voice was clear and comforting. Sometimes he would hug her, kiss her forehead, and speak unknown reassurances. Other times it was he who was upset, and it was she who hugged him. He would leave papers behind, lines of poetry he wrote for her.

Her only concern was the intense sadness she felt when picturing his silhouette. For as good as she felt when remembering him and his poetry, she also experienced pain. Was he dead? Had he left her? What was it?

After storing the notebook back in her travel bag, she turned the light off. Kalista closed her eyes and could almost feel his presence next to her. They spent a great deal of time sitting with one another. Talking. Crying. Laughing.

Kalista fell back on the bed with an exhausted sigh and stared at the ceiling. She didn't slept last night either. If she could only shut her mind off. That was all she wanted. To be still. To be at peace.

She concentrated on the poetry, hoping it would settle the emotional storm.

///

His name was Kintro. He was considered one of the top bounty hunters in the morkallian system. He was ruthless, rich, and readied for his upcoming hunt. What made him so unique, and effective, was his blood contradiction.

He was a yookallan. His people were calm and rational, never partaking in any kind of extreme behavior. They made successful politicians, lawyers, historians, scientists, mathematicians, and the like. And they traveled only when necessary. Many yookallans lived their whole lives without leaving the city in which they were born.

Somehow, his personality rebelled against the norm. He craved the hunt. And it was his genetically inherited patience which proved deadly in his craft. As far as he knew, he was the only yookallan bounty hunter in the galaxy. It was a shame because his people possessed the necessary mix of skills and smarts to be effective in the field.

At the moment, it was that yookallan patience which was saving him from committing murder. A punk human off the streets was begging him to listen to a tip. Kintro was debating on whether to listen and nod or shoot him between the eyes. Humans had a way of irking him like no other race. They were the polar opposite of yookallans. All emotion, all impulse, and the reasoning skills of young yookallan children.

"Look," the young human said, his dirty face uplifted in an honest expression, "I know who you are. You're the famous Kintro. I'm just trying to make my way into your world. Please, let me help you so you can help me."

"What do you possibly have that will help us?" asked Dunch, his partner.

Dunch was a deeshie hunter that Kintro teamed up with on difficult hunts. Their relationship was limited in its trust, but their shared interest in good business practices kept their guns in their holsters. Five years passed since their first hunt together, and so far the relationship proved to be beneficial.

"The whereabouts of your target," the boy said, lifting his chin in pride.

"We have no target," Kintro replied.

The human's nose scrunched in confusion, and as if a light clicked on, he smiled. "Oh, I see. Hush, hush, right?"

Dunch stared at the human for a moment. "Go home."

The kid ignored him. "The Tishta apartments on the other side of the Leo'Li crossing. They're in number six."

Kintro and Dunch both paused and looked at one another, communicating through expression. Over the years, Kintro learned to read his obese orange partner like a book, and his interest appeared piqued.

"Whose apartment is that?" Kintro asked, his voice quiet.

The human looked around for a moment and replied in a hushed tone matching Kintro's. "Dorian and Kalista's. Your targets. Hell, everyone's targets at the moment. My uncle owns the apartment complex. See, I live with him, and he's going to kick me out soon because I'm turning eighteen. The old grouch doesn't even pay attention to the people he puts up in his place, but I keep the books. If you guys can show me the first step to becoming a bounty hunter, I can walk out of my uncle's and have an adventure. C'mon, help me out."

Dunch actually smiled. "Think he's telling the truth, Kintro?"

"It's more than probable," Kintro said.

"Okay, kid," Dunch said. "We'll check out your lead. If it's true, you come back to this bar tomorrow night and one of us will be here to tell you where to go to get your start as a hunter with our blessing. If it's not true, you better believe that we'll kill you the next time we see you."

"Okay, deal."

Dunch stared him down for a few more seconds, no doubt trying to reinforce intimidation. "Scram."

The human didn't say another word, thankfully, and ran out

of the bar. Kintro ordered another round of drinks, and he and Dunch huddled over the plans on how to kill their newly discovered targets.

///

I scrubbed the last of the makeup off my face, avoided the mirror as soon as possible, and strolled down the ship's hall to my quarters. A quick input into the computer dimmed the lights, and I flopped onto the bed as if my spine disappeared. I needed rest.

Well, that was easy.

Bounty hunters were not the hardest people to fool. They were blinded by greed. I pulled the "kid off the street" act on them with ease. It was an overdone routine, and one that most people fell for. But in the profession of bounty hunting, a cousin of sorts to a mercenary, one had to keep vigilant for suspect behavior.

Like a tip coming in at just the right moment.

The term "there are no coincidences" was a lie, but it was the best damn lie to live by. Bounty hunters did not follow such rules. They followed the path given to them, and I was happy to be their captain.

I don't understand how someone can be so easily fooled.

Some people want to be fooled, Coyote.

You sentient beings are difficult to figure out. Seekers of truth, but purposely blinded to it. How does that make sense?

It doesn't.

Perhaps I should try to do the next performance. You seemed off, tonight.

I always do the street kid performance. You know that. I did fine.

Meh. If you say so.

72

The Coyote performed as well as I did, though, his acts were different than mine. There were certain roles that required my reserve to win out over his hyper-commitment. Street kids, barkeeps, and businessmen required a certain composure. The routines needed to fool the subject into believing he or she could relate to me. The Coyote was many things, but he could not be related to. He was the insane scientist, the drug abuser, the serial killer. All characters suffering from a type of madness.

"Madness" is the experience all self-aware beings are either uncomfortable expressing, or fear revealing. It is a completely understandable outgrowth of the psyche. That is why it exists, and why it will continue to exist.

You are not a product of madness, Coyote.

We held these debates at times. The Coyote seemed to prefer the idea that he was biological and psychological in nature. A natural madness. I didn't think he was that simple, and my own theory was that he was an experiment performed on me at a young age. One that perhaps they thought failed, but instead, blossomed.

I don't feel . . . artificial.

What is artificial? What is the difference between a computer and myself?

Biology.

Biological or not, we are all atomically a part of the same family. Don't be afraid, Coyote.

The Coyote feared that he was an artificial intelligence. He was conscious, after all. If he was a computer, did that mean he was fake? Or that his existence was not existence as he thought of it? A part of me? A part of a living, breathing being?

I think I am alive.

9

THE local town markets of all the planets I visited always made for an interesting time. The aroma of exotic foods being fried, baked, and boiled filled the air. The voices of many beings speaking many languages created a rumbling, bustling sound that made me think of a chaotic beehive.

Above the voices of shoppers, the trumpeting sales pitches of sellers was even louder, promising the latest and greatest at half the cost. And among such bustling chaos, my targets were hiding. My tracking system was still fully functional. Dorian was out for a very nervous stroll with his sister, purchasing the few supplies they needed to travel with. No doubt they were planning to leave the whole system, not just the planet.

I didn't get too close, even allowing them to stray out of eyesight. Dorian was observant, his mind trained to recognize the signs of trackers, and I couldn't afford to arouse his suspicions.

However, I was tracking two other individuals by eyesight. Kintro and Dunch. They, no doubt, were up all night observing their targets and formulating a plan. The two of them looked quite casual, but I knew Dorian would detect them soon, and when that happened, my own formulated plan would come to fruition. There was no doubt in my mind Dorian had an escape route in place, and it likely involved the abandoned buildings to my left.

This section of Morkal was run down; one of the few places on the planet that was. To my right was the bustling market, and to my left were condemned store fronts. The buildings were more like office cubicles, made of three walls. Two sides to separate them from one another, and one in the back to keep product stored. The fronts were completely opened, with only a few scattered signs warning market patrons to keep out. From my quick glances, the condemned buildings appeared to have many a hole in the walls, enough for someone to find cover and move quickly in any desired direction. It was a perfect escape route.

If everything went as I wanted, my plan would blossom without a hitch. Of course, there were always variables, but I was flexible, able to adapt to the situation. The Coyote taught me to keep my eyes on the goal, and find the most efficient means of attaining it. If that meant changing plans halfway through, then so be it.

And although the ability to improvise is critical, make sure those around you don't see it.

Bluff.

Precisely.

Kintro and Dunch moved, and I made sure to follow, sifting through the crowds of people. When Dorian and Kalista came into view, I knew the bounty hunters would flank the two of them, preparing to strike. Kintro in particular was known to do his work in crowded places, where his target would never suspect him to. And although Kalista appeared not to notice their presence, Dorian was staring at the pair of them.

Showtime.

I found a new path. A path that would intercept the target.

///

"Run to Jorg's Bar," Dorian said.

"What?" Kalista asked.

"As fast as you can, Kalista. Now."

There were two of them. A yookallan and a deeshie, and both of their greedy eyes were focused on Kalista. Although his face was on the wanted posters, it was his sister's bounty that promised the big payday. Dorian was considered secondary, worthless without Kalista as part of the prize.

"Dorian, what's going on?" she asked, her eyes frantically scanning the crowd, trying to find the source of his concern.

He whispered a curse. "Kalista, we're blown. Run to Jorg's Bar and hide in the back. Just like we talked about. I'll be there as soon as I can. Go!"

She stopped hesitating and ran for the buildings. Dorian turned to view the reaction of his adversaries. As he expected, both hunters ran after her, eyes locked on their target. Dorian hung back long enough to follow the deeshie, who was nearest to him. The yookallan was in front, the swifter of the two. As the hunters ran, the crowd made a wide berth. Public denizens tended to give bounty hunters plenty of room.

Kalista was running at full speed toward the abandoned buildings they agreed to use in case of an emergency. There was only twenty meters that separated her from the lead bounty hunter. Dorian made his move. Waiting until the deeshie was in perfect range, he took three powerful strides and dove feet first at the deeshie's legs. Despite their impressive strength, the deeshie had a weakness at the knees, and Dorian exploited it to the fullest degree.

A muffled *pop* sounded, followed by a deep bellow of pain. Dorian and the deeshie fell to the ground together. Moving with precision, he snatched a pistol from the deeshie's belt. After rolling to his feet, he took aim at the yookallan, who halted his progress to check on his injured partner.

As Dorian fired, the deeshie kicked at him. His shot went wide, and the yookallan hunter drew his weapon. Dorian dove to the ground, behind the deeshie as the other hunter opened fire. He heard a sickening thud as three of the bullets pierced the thick hide of the big alien. The deeshie's already bulbous eyes grew even wider, and blood trickled from his mouth.

The yookallan screamed in outrage, and Dorian used the opportunity to sit up and return fire. His opponent ran into the old buildings, dodging the shots. Dorian was quick to follow. That was when he noticed a third hunter he was unaware of, a human, running in Kalista's direction. Dorian needed to be swift.

He ran to the first wall, next to a door and squatted down. His ears picked up quiet footsteps on the other side. The footsteps continued in a panicked sort of way. His enemy didn't know where he was. Dorian aimed the gun at the wall, waiting until the shuffling feet lined up. Without hesitation, he pulled the trigger.

Nothing happened.

He quickly looked down at the small screen on the side of the gun. It read in a language he didn't recognize, but he knew a countdown when he saw one. It was a deadman's switch attached to the deeshie's heartbeat, no doubt.

Dorian threw the pistol back into the open, where the yookallan would see it. It exploded into a cloud of bright blue just as it hit the ground, drawing the bounty hunter's attention. With two big steps, Dorian ran through the wall, made of fragile plaster, in a cloud of dust. The yookallan turned on him in surprise, but Dorian knocked the gun out of his hand with a downward chop. While the hunter's body turned with the momentum of losing his weapon, Dorian threw out a strong left hook. The punch connected cleanly, and his enemy stumbled back.

He didn't waste one second advancing on the yookallan, who attacked with a series of punches. Dorian bobbed his head out of the way with an ingrained fluidity, and jabbed with his hand opened stiffly. The tips of his rigid fingers collided with the throat of the hunter.

Just as his opponent started to choke from the blow, Dorian wrapped his arm around the alien's head, and with a violent and forceful twist, broke his neck. He was racing toward the third hunter and Kalista before the yookallan hit the floor.

///

Kalista sprinted with all her might, taking in panicked breaths with burning lungs. The worn, connected buildings were dark and confusing, but she was able to continue navigating her way through. She didn't look back. The bar was less than a hundred meters away.

Always running, always hiding. Always seeking refuge from the chaos.

Even now, the lines of poetry were brought to the surface of her mind. The plan was to hook a left at the end of the line of buildings. At that left, she would find Jorg's Bar, pay the bartender a substantial lump of money, which was at the ready in her pocket, and stow away in the back. Dorian would come.

She knew he would be alright. He was always alright. Over the past three months, she watched him do his fair share of killing to keep them safe. Soldiers, assassins, and now bounty hunters. They all ended up the same when faced with her brother. Dead.

Her thoughts drifted back to the present when she heard something behind her. Glancing back, she saw a young man rushing toward her at breakneck speed. He was only three meters behind her, but she didn't hear him until now.

Panic overrode her, and all thoughts of Dorian persevering left her mind. Her feet suddenly felt like lead. Tripping over a small pile of plaster she was too distracted to see, she tumbled to the floor, and the weight of the hunter's body soon joined hers. Screaming, she swung her arms and legs, but it was no use. Within a second, he was on top of her, and the eerily familiar prick of a needle stung her neck. And although her consciousness quickly faded fade, she was able to see his face before all became dark.

He was the young man who always hugged her. He was her poet.

"It's okay," he said. "Don't worry. I'm here now."

His voice faded with the light.

///

I sat up and pulled the needle from Kalista's neck as gingerly as possible. She was beautiful. I knew her beauty from memory, but laying eyes on her again captivated me. It was the first time I had seen her in three years. Far too long.

Focus.

Right. Focus. I checked her pulse; it was strong. The tranquilizer I used was safe and effective. All I needed to do was take care of

Dorian, and phase one would be complete.

I looked at my tracking screen, and to my dismay, discovered that the little white blip was moving toward me fast. After standing up, I changed out the cartridge of the tranquilizer, set it to shoot, which was not my preference as it wasn't very accurate, and braced myself for possible pain.

No, there's definitely going to be pain.

Dorian turned the corner, rushing me with fire in his eyes. He put on a last burst of speed just as I shot the non-lethal projectile. It hit him dead in the chest but didn't slow him down in the least. I might as well have shot a BB gun at a charging elephant. He shoulder charged into me, causing my body to fly back from the force and rebound off the near wall, sending loose plaster in all directions.

"A tranquilizer?" Dorian asked, pulling the dart from his chest. "The bounty is for death. Why are you using a tranquilizer?"

I expected him to fall flat on his face at any moment, but he remained standing. In fact, he didn't even sway.

His expression was grim. "They only sell two types of tranquilizers, and one of them is extremely hard to come by. I've built an immunity to both."

Crap.

I started to get up, and his hands helped me. He pinned me against the wall, his glare intense, but I could see the hesitation in his expression. While racing down here, he, no doubt, fully expected Kalista to be dead. He also expected the dart to kill him in the same fashion. Now, the relief of realizing that I merely knocked her out was making him hesitate in the action he should take with me.

His type aren't forced to think that often.

"What do you want?" he snarled.

"At the moment, I could go for an ale," I said. "It's been a hard week."

He slammed my head against the wall, causing bright specks to swim before my eyes. "I'm not going to ask you again."

"Maybe two ales."

Once again, the back of my precious brain shell found the wall, but this time I threw my head forward with the rebound. My forehead made hard contact with his, and he released his grip immediately. I was still seeing stars, but I lashed out anyway.

A hard kick to his midsection made him stumble back, and I surged forward with a punch. He recovered with incredible agility, however, and blocked my punch with the experience of an assassin. I never saw his exact retaliation, but something hard made contact with my jaw. Before I could consider any options, my feet were taken out from under me, and I was staring at Dorian from the flat of my back.

"Trust me when I say that you don't stand a chance," he snarled. "Now, if you don't start giving me real answers, I'm going to . . . going . . ."

The blood drained from Dorian's face. He took a few steps back and looked at me in confusion. I took my time getting up, dusting myself off as he slumped against a wall.

"I'm afraid that even immunizations can't get around the accelerator I put in that dose. It can only delay the inevitable," I said. "Sweet dreams, Dorian."

He crashed to the floor, unconscious. I didn't expect him to be immune, but I always had my backup plans. The accelerator in the tranquilizer found its way around any biological defenses, even if it did take some time.

And he's out for the count.

Brain beats brawn.

10

IT all went crazy from here. I knew that. Cayden knew that. And we planned for it; for years, in fact. Phase one was complete. Unfortunately, it was the easiest to plan for.

Now, onto the hard part, Coyote.

"She's cold," Dorian said.

I faced my hostages. We were back on my ship, drifting through the great black expanse of space. I already plotted most of our course to the next destination. We were in the cargo area, next to a few crates of supplies.

Dorian was in a chair, secured to a degree that made me comfortable. First, an electric harness that would put enough jolts through his body to knock him out for a week if he moved more than twelve inches in any direction. Second, fiber cord strategically knotted around his hands and feet so he couldn't move more than six anyway. Third, I was armed, and he wasn't.

Kalista was bound with the same chords in a similar chair across from her brother, though I left out the electric backup plan. Dorian was the one I was worried about, not her. Her skills were not physically threatening.

"It's warm in here," I answered.

Dorian stared daggers at me. "She gets spells."

The female *was* shaking. I initially thought it was panic or fear, but I could now see that she was indeed cold. I opened a drawer not too far away and pulled out a heating blanket. With a quick toss, I laid it across her shoulders and tucked it into the crooks of her arms. Her shaking died down, but she continued to avoid my gaze.

"What kind of 'spells' does she get?" I asked.

"I don't know," Dorian said.

"How often does she get them?"

He did not respond.

"Are you going to kill us?" Kalista asked, her voice soft and calm.

For the first time since I sedated her, she was looking at me. There was fear in her eyes, and a strange look of curiosity, which I considered more than a little off-putting. Why curious? Of all the appropriate expressions, why was curiosity displayed across her features? Fear, I understood. But that which kills many a cat, I did not.

Her skills could have affected the memory wipe. She may remember me, Coyote.

Would you like to question them, Cayden?

You know I can't be trusted to be around her without compromising us.

Cayden was quite insistent that I should be the one to question our guests. I did not understand the chemical and psychological connection that tethered him to the female, but then again, I considered myself chemically and psychologically independent of the rest of the universe. Still, despite my obvious evolutionary superiority, I acknowledged the flip side of my personality, Cayden, did share a connection with her. And he feared that if it were him asking the questions, he would betray our intent too soon and spoil well-construed planning. I, of course, came to the same conclusion.

"No, he's not going to kill us" Dorian said. "The bounty on our heads specified death only, and we're alive. He's not a hunter."

"My name is Cayden," I said, a smile on my face. I smiled because such an expression was meant to convey non-threatening intent. "Cayden the Coyote. Jack-of-all-trades for hire to the highest bidder."

"Then why keep us alive?" Kalista asked. "If you're a simple mercenary, why didn't you take the bounty?"

"Because he's not a simple mercenary," Dorian said. "I'm not sure what he is."

"Think a little," I said. "It's really not that hard to figure out if you put your mind to it. For what other reason could I possibly want you?"

"You didn't just want us," Dorian said, his eyes darting back and forth as he pieced together the puzzle I left them. "You wanted us alive, healthy, and with you. Why?"

I bounced on the balls of my feet. Such an action was to convey cheeriness. "Actually, my dear Dorian, the bounty stipulated that I deliver you alive. Kalista, however, was supposed to be killed. But I needed you both for my own reasons. We both share something."

Kalista's answer was soft, but loud enough to be heard. "Memory."

I matched her whisper. "The lack thereof, to be more accurate."

"You're one of us?" Dorian asked. "That's impossible. I could have easily killed you when we fought. We're much harder to kill."

I opened my hands theatrically. "And yet here I stand, and there you sit. But I suppose the end result doesn't compare to the possibilities, now does it? The group that is now being labeled 'us', my feisty friend, is not made up of people that all have talents in the same area. Still, your area is the majority. Luckily, if broken memories and hypotheses serve correctly, you are the best among your compatriots. My talents reside elsewhere, however, as do your sister's. I don't quite remember what they are, though."

I was lying, of course. I was fully aware of Kalista's talents. I was one of the few people who saw her ability as a talent and not a mistake. What she could do unnerved my previous employers so much, they needed her dead to ensure their security.

Dorian's mouth opened, but no sound came out. Kalista cocked her head to the side and gazed at me with that same strange look of curiosity. The fear that haunted her eyes was now absent, furthering my bafflement. Why curiosity? Where was the fear that usually accompanied such a predicament? Especially from her, whom I captured so easily. She possessed no physical defenses. Why was curiosity her most prevalent emotion at the moment?

She remembers. God, she remembers me.

Calm down, Cayden.

This is how she used to look at me. With no intimidation, with no fear of reprisal. I was the only one she looked at like that. She was so comfortable with me, with who I was, with my intentions.

"Neither of us know what her talents are." Dorian's voice snapped me out of my head, so to speak. "She only seems to have symptoms."

"What kind of symptoms?" I asked, pressing my fingertips together.

"Cold spells," Dorian said. "Sometimes they are frequent, and sometimes she goes days without them. The worst symptom is a seizure, that's only happened twice in the past three months."

"Why three months?" I asked. Again, I knew the answer, but I didn't want them to know that.

"Three months and eight days," Kalista said. "That's how long we've been running. That's how long we've been free."

"What other symptoms is she experiencing?" I asked.

"The cold spells are the worst. Sometimes she can't stop shaking," Dorian said.

Kalista interjected. "My fingers hurt."

"What?" I instinctively felt my own fingertips. They still ached sometimes.

"My fingers hurt," she repeated. "The tips of my fingers hurt, as if the nerves have been tampered with. The joints are sore on and off every day."

"Do you remember why?" I asked.

She nodded. "I remember. I remember a lot."

You heard that, right?

No, Cayden, I suddenly went deaf.

Was that sarcasm?

Yes. Did I do it right?

You did. Good job.

"I remember nothing." Dorian stated.

I squatted to look at the female more directly. "How much do you remember, Kalista?"

She smiled a little, though the look was more sad than happy. "How much do you?"

///

"I don't like this," Margaret said. She was speaking more to herself than to the asset that sat opposite her desk in the guest chair.

"It's too soon to tell," Jerry said. "You can't jump to conclusions."

Margaret's office was her castle. Here, she could purge her mind of the complexities of the day-to-day activities and think clearly about both the present and the future. The decor helped. Thin, basic furniture. Two guest chairs placed side-by-side, across from hers, which was much more extravagant. Covered in premium yookallan vresh, it was her most expensive purchase since the promotion. It was worth it. The chair made her feel truly in charge.

The desk situated between her chair and the guest seats was plain, much like the rest of the room. A frosted white top, with only basic instruments lying on its surface. Four thin, titanium legs held it stable. The walls and floor of her office were bare, allowing her nothing but uniformity to gaze upon. She breathed easier with no distractions. The open, empty space felt . . . precious. So much of her life was cramped.

"Two well-known bounty hunters are dead, and the siblings are missing," Margaret said, rubbing her temples. "Missing, mind you. Not dead."

"Dorian killed the bounty hunters, not Cayden," Jerry said, waving his hand in dismissal of her point. "That's what Dorian does. He's the best at it. As for our mysterious Coyote, it's too soon to tell what he has done."

"Why haven't we heard from him? Where is he?"

Jerry's face reddened with agitation. "All questions you knew were going to arise when you decided he was the backup plan. This was a mistake. I told you he would outmaneuver you. That is his gift."

Margaret took her fingers from her temples and gave Jerry an impatient look. "He hasn't outmaneuvered us. He hasn't moved at all."

"What are you?" Jerry asked, his face masked with a look of disgust. "A child?"

"Excuse me?" she demanded, her expression giving away her shock.

Jerry scooted to the edge of his seat. "You think if you close your eyes, then whoever is outside can't see you? You think that the tiger in the jungle isn't stalking you, watching you, just because you can't see it move?"

Margaret's reply got stuck somewhere between her lungs and brain, and her mouth gaped open without uttering a sound. She must have looked like a fish gasping for water but only finding air. Jerry, and all of the experiments like him, were supposed to have limited social interaction abilities. His conversations were supposed to be impersonal and to the point, not emotional.

Jerry and Cayden were part of the beta batch, and exhibited a few quirks the newer, more specific models lacked. Margaret couldn't get used to how normal they seemed. Unlike the more recent assets, they were fully capable of making up their own minds. Being angry and spiteful. They acted as equals to their makers. Something Margaret thought was a mistake from the beginning.

It was the chief reason why Bronx was demoted, and Margaret brought in to take his place. His methods were intriguing, but overambitious. If one failed the GS as badly as he, one was usually eliminated. But, though the initial assets such as Cayden and Jerry were ultimately deemed failures, the GS was able to cultivate new batches in a more straightforward manner because of Bronx's research and development of the original experiments. It was from his work that all others were made. So, they demoted him instead and charged him with the duty of trying to continue to cultivate Cayden, so that he might one day be used.

"You had better move, Margaret" Jerry warned. "He'll win."

Jerry turned out to be somewhat useful, though he skated on

thin ice. For all his positives, the GS was disappointed in the side effects. He was supposed to be a simple tool. Not a complex machine.

"What do you suggest?" she asked, finding her voice once again.

"You should have let me kill him." He paused for a moment to examine his fingernails. "You still should."

"You know that won't be authorized," she said. "We have to know he's a threat before acting out of turn. Cayden can be of great use to this organization."

"He's a threat as long as he's breathing," Jerry said, the anger in his voice evident.

"We have to know that he's turned on us," she said. "Then, I'll make sure you have the go ahead."

He shook his head, gritting his teeth, and stood up. His fists were clenched, and she could see a vein throbbing on his forehead. "You give him time, and you give him opportunity. With an inch, he will take a mile. With a match, he will set fire to your world. You are all damned fools."

Margaret considered him for a moment. "If we, with all of our resources and strength cannot stop him, what makes you think that you can?"

Jerry smiled, but not with his eyes. "When I am unrestrained, Cayden cannot plan for me. He's never been able to. Just let me go, Margaret. Let me have him."

11

I will admit, Cayden, I understand why you find her so interesting. At least to some degree. Don't expect me to understand the emotional side of your brain though. She's still just a person. A very confusing, irrational person not showing the correct emotional responses.

We are all just people, Coyote.

Speak for yourself.

"Well?" Kalista asked.

"Well what?" I retorted.

I did my best not to be annoyed with her. I knew what Cayden thought of her, and I needed to be mindful of his feelings. His health was my concern.

"What are you going to do?" Dorian asked. "Her memories are a mess, but they're still memories."

I paced, my footsteps echoing clearly in the empty hangar. "I don't want her memories."

"But they did it to you, too," she said, her voice trembling a bit. Desperation? "They wiped away your memory. You must want what I remember. I'll tell you everything I know."

"My dear, I *do* remember. The organization that did this to us forgot that I was more twisted and sick than they were. What they view as weakness in me is my greatest strength, and they reacted out of fear and ignorance. And believing their consistency was infallibility, they released me to the world, not knowing I would come back to destroy them. To break their perfection."

Waxing a bit poetic, are you not?

Shut up, I'm working.

"I am the monster to their doctor, the cancer to their addiction. They do not comprehend my threat, they cannot comprehend my threat, because they do not believe in my motivation. But it is two-fold, as I am two-fold, and together it is the greatest motivation in this universe, worthy of tales of old and new."

Dorian did not blink through my speech, and observed me with a kind of disgust. "What the hell is wrong with you?"

"You sound angrier than you used to," Kalista said, disregarding her brother's comment. "I wish you weren't angry."

I'm not.

Keep it together, Cayden.

"Do you wish to hear my plan?" I asked, looking at Dorian, and doing my best to ignore Kalista. Overexposure to her was not good for Cayden at the moment.

"I'm the brains, and you're the brawn," I explained. "Well, I'm not so bad myself, but you're quite incredible. Kalista is the bonus. It'll be nice to have her around, I suppose. She was always nice to me."

At this, her cheeks flushed red, and a tear crept down her cheek. She looked away, her breathing more erratic than it had been. Such actions suggested that she was feeling emotional pain.

Coyote, please.

Cayden's distress made me . . . feel, though I was not sure that I really did feel anything. What I knew was that I was selfish, and not a bit selfless, but Cayden was a part of my selfishness. His needs and wants were mine, in a way. It was through my own sense of self-preservation that I connected with Cayden's emotions, which urged me to act in favor of him.

"What makes you think I'm going to agree to whatever plan you have in place?" Dorian asked.

"Because you have no reason not to," Kalista answered, sniffing quietly.

I smiled. "She's right. Now you have two people protecting your darling sister, a load of weapons, a ship, access to money, and my plan to permanently fix both of our problems. Everything to gain and nothing to lose."

Dorian gave me the kind of hard stare that communicated a deal that need not be spoken. I knew he would kill me if I crossed him, and he knew that I knew that he could. But if he was smart, he knew that I knew that he knew that I was much smarter than he was, therefore countering his previous knowledge of my knowledge.

If you are an artificial intelligence, you're a twisted one.

"Fine," Dorian responded. "We'll work with you. But we discuss terms only when we're out of these . . . security measures."

"Fair enough," I replied, beginning to undue Kalista's restraints first. "But I do believe that you are going to love my terms. I'm going to give you guns. Lots and lots of guns."

///

Rymera's meditation was interrupted by a quiet buzz, which indicated there was an emergency call. Only eleven people knew how to contact her, all of whom she either worked for or with.

She was settled on a space station located in the orbit of Feshnil, a small moon of Crel. Crel was a gas giant and was the fifth planet in the yookallan solar system, her native system. Feshnil was abundantly rich in minerals, and her people had been tapping its resources for centuries. Rymera was working as an office assistant to one of the mining managers, awaiting orders.

"Kry'oom," she said, and the lights in the room restored to a comfortable dim. Her meditation required the nakedness of her body, so she quickly donned a pair of shorts and a shirt. Sitting cross-legged, she answered the call and the handsome face of Jerry appeared before her.

"Hello, Rymera," he said with a smug smile. "You're looking especially attractive this fine evening."

Jerry was an odd person to work with. He would always inter-act with her in a flirtatious manner, though she knew he was not attracted to her. His eyes read more like he would like to kill her as slowly as possible, cut her into pieces, and dispose of her in whatever sick manner he enjoyed most. He disguised his true desires with false ones, perhaps to elicit a reaction from her or in an attempt to behave like a normal person. She found his unnecessary mannerisms waste-ful.

"What is it?" she asked.

"All business and no pleasure, yes?" he prompted.

"Business is my pleasure."

"Then what must I do to be your business?" Jerry asked, his eyes lighting up.

"Commit an act of treason so the GS will send me to kill you," she said, cocking an eyebrow.

Jerry laughed a little. "Yookallans are a fascinating race of people. So human in appearance, yet completely different minds."

"My patience wears thin, Jerry. What do you want?"

He cleared his throat. "Of course. On to your pleasurable business. I'm calling to forewarn you."

Rymera tilted her head. "Warn me of what?"

Jerry sighed, and the previous appearance of happiness faded into one of annoyance. Humans were extremely obvious in their expressions.

"They employed Cayden," he said.

She paused and digested the information, taking into account that Cayden was Jerry's most hated rival. His only rival. If Jerry was passing her information about Cayden, she needed to take it with a grain of salt. Jerry's intentions could not be trusted, but she would play along.

"That was foolish," Rymera said. "I thought he was due for a final evaluation."

"They ran into a snag they needed an immediate fix for." Jerry rubbed his temples with his middle fingers. "Dorian and Kalista broke free and have been on the run. You were aware of this?"

The sound of Dorian's name may have caused a visible reaction in her, but she tried not to betray herself. "Correct."

"They believed that Cayden was their only chance at killing Kalista, because of Dorian's skills," he said. "Dorian eliminated three of us within the first three months of running."

She raised an eyebrow. "Which three?"

"Donye, Incerno, and Diego. Donye and Incerno tried to take him out together, and Dorian killed them, even though he wasn't armed. Then, the GS thought with Diego's preference to eliminate his adversaries from a distance, he could end it easily. We still haven't found his body."

Rymera nodded. All three of them were accomplished assassins, though she knew Dorian was the best among them. Still, he was on the run, confused, and protecting a girl that wouldn't know which end of a gun the bullet came out of. She hoped they would call her in to finish him off.

"Getting Cayden for the job was a mistake," she said. "That much is evident, isn't it? That's why you have called?"

Jerry nodded. "He still has three days to bring us Dorian and Kalista, dead or alive, but I already know that he's gotten to them. The only bodies we've found belong to two bounty hunters that were hot on the tail of the siblings. Mysteriously, Cayden dropped off the map. You and I both know he's going to be a big problem. He has Dorian with him."

"Why didn't they see this coming?" Rymera asked. "They should have known better."

"Remember, Bronx has been replaced because of Cayden," Jerry said. "The GS believes he is less of a threat than previously analyzed to be. They think that mixing the siblings with Cayden again is the best way to test him."

Rymera shook her head. "They're very short-sighted."

"Just be ready."

She cocked an eyebrow again. "Do you believe we will be asked to intervene soon?"

"Very soon. Be prepared to meet up with the rest of us the next time I call."

"How many of us will there be?" she asked.

Jerry paused for a moment. "As many as we can get."

12

MONEY. That was our current problem. Most of mine was depleted. However, I discovered long ago, that with my skill set, money could be obtained at will. And of all my options, only one place in the galaxy could bring in an income as fast as my needs demanded. The Edge. The absolute easiest place to earn money, get lost, stay lost, or get killed if you didn't know what you were doing. Of course, I always knew what I was doing.

Of course.

"The Edge isn't exactly safe," Dorian said, his voice wary. "I've heard of it, and I thought about going. But there's no place to hide. It's chaos."

He was sitting with me at my small dining table, drinking a blend of tea I recommended. It was a much more civilized conversation, and one ensured Dorian of his freedom. Kalista complained of a headache and fatigue, so I showed her the refreshing unit and her quarters. Dorian, though obviously tired, refused to rest before discussing my plans.

"The Edge is called the 'Edge' not because of where it lies in the galaxy, but because of its relation to a sword," I said. "A sword can, of course, be very dangerous. However, if you know how to use it, then it can keep you very safe. So, either it will be a place that will lead to our deaths, to our victory. It all depends on who's wielding this particular sword."

"Mind dropping the metaphors?" he asked, taking another sip of his tea.

"I'm saying that I've been there before, and I know exactly how to keep everyone safe while making the most profit," I said.

"How?"

"The raw basics?" I asked.

"For now."

I shrugged. "You go alone, and your sister and I will stick together."

Dorian's neutral expression turned stern, and the soft sound of sipping died away quite abruptly. I knew my plan needed to be sold to him with great care. He was not a trusting person by nature.

"I don't like this plan," Dorian said.

"Of course you don't," I said. "You haven't heard it yet."

"Kalista will stay with me."

Appeal to his mechanical side. Use the raw logic of the plan. It should work.

Cayden remained locked away inside our brain, content to coach instead of play. It made sense. Although my personality appeared to annoy Dorian to a greater degree than Cayden's, I was the more capable of relaying the plan's raw, irrefutable logic than him. And at the moment, hardcore logic was needed.

Dorian had been psychologically hardwired since birth to use unbiased reason in his decision making. Unlike myself, he was trained to be efficient, not creative or free-thinking. His unique mix of natural instincts and mechanical rationality was what made him so lethal. It also made him a conflicted soul, and if I could overload the logical side of his personality, I could influence the decisions he made.

"Don't be absurd," I said. "You are at your best when you're alone and you know it. If you were with me, you'd be even safer simply because I know what I'm doing. But Kalista is a liability. How you've managed to stay alive and free for this long is beyond me."

He shook his head. "They underestimated my abilities."

"Well, my dear Dorian, 'they' sent me, and I caught you," I said.

At this point, he quieted.

"Good," I said, continuing on. "If Kalista is with me, I can keep her safer than you could."

"How so?" he asked.

I spread my hands open on the table. "First, you'll both be away from one another. All of the bounty hunters out there know that they have one tracking system to find your sister. You. Because you are the only one who leaves behind any traces, as you are the only one to make any moves. They track you, and they get the bounty. However, if she's with me, all they're going to find is you. And, perhaps I'm overstating your abilities, but I do believe you can handle yourself. Especially without having to worry about the safety of your twin."

His eyebrows raised. "How did you know we were twins?"

"A guess," I said. "I'm good at guessing. You resemble one another, though not to the point of being identical. You appear to be the same age. And you have a link to her that keeps you closely attached. Often comes with twins."

He breathed in deep and rubbed his hands together. I could almost hear the wheels turning. "And what will I be doing to aid our campaign?"

"Have you ever heard of the Gladiator tournament?" I asked.

Dorian pressed his index finger to his head. "Memory problems."

"Naturally," I said. "The Gladiator tournament is the most

famous fighting tournament on Rome. Rome is the home of all fighting tournaments at the Edge. The event is only scheduled four times a standard year, and our arrival coincides perfectly. While you and Kalista were unconscious, I signed you up. Thankfully, I have a few contacts on Rome."

"How much money for winning?" he asked.

Good. He doesn't seem to care that we signed him up without asking.

I told you he wouldn't.

Yes, Coyote. You were right.

I smiled. "That's the best part. The winnings increase at each tournament. A considerable amount of people make bets; a considerable amount of people with a *lot* of money. The last winner took home over two million pounds. Dorian, that's more than enough money to hide you and Kalista forever."

"And I must kill?" he asked.

Uh oh.

The response was not what I expected. "Yes, Dorian, you must kill."

No, no, no. Don't do that. He knows he needs to kill. He wants to know why.

Dorian's eyes drew level with mine. "Why?"

Perhaps, you should take over, Cayden. I do not understand.

We made the switch, and I was once again inhabiting my own body. I knew what Dorian was asking, though I didn't plan for it. I had not anticipated him identifying any type of guilt.

"We all do what we have to do, Dorian," I said. "There's always a price."

I don't understand. He was made for one purpose. Killing. It's the reason for his existence. Why would he be questioning it?

We're all just people, Coyote.

"Do you ever wonder if you'll do this until you die?" Dorian asked. His gaze didn't waver.

"There is always that chance," I said with a sigh. "But it's not what I'm planning. People are capable of changing. And I plan to change."

Dorian took another sip of his tea. "Isn't that what you're supposed to do, though? Plan?"

I smiled. "Not exactly. I'm . . . different than you. And the rest like you."

"How so?" he asked.

"I was a part of the beta batch," I said. "In fact, that's what they called us. The Betas. The first successful string of experiments. I'm a couple of years older than you and Kalista. The GS designed your batch, and the other ones, with more specific purposes in mind. I belonged to a test group of sorts."

His brows scrunched in curiosity. "What did they want to use you for?"

A few fleeting memories flashed before my eyes, and I took a deep breath. "Everything."

You can say that again.

"Like what?" he asked.

I waved his question away. "It's not important. We can reminisce about these things later. We need to focus on the task at hand. In less than twenty-four hours, we will reach the Edge. Will you compete in this tournament?"

Dorian paused for moment. He sat back. He sipped his tea. I sipped mine. The Coyote panicked.

Say something, Cayden. This part of the plan is not optional.

Relax, Coyote.

Dorian leaned forward, propping his elbows on the table, cup still in hand. He separated his eyes from mine, instead choosing to look beyond me, down the hall. Nothing was there. He looked to the side, at a wall. He spun his cup slowly on the table. I said nothing. The Coyote went mental.

Have . . . you . . . lost it! Do something. Say something. Do something!

Keep calm.

Patience was not one of the Coyote's many virtues. But it was required in these instances. I understood why Dorian was pausing. But I could not relate. Since I was young, I never paused to think. I never needed to take time. When I did, it was intentional; a part of a play. I learned, through the years, that others did not see as far ahead as I did. For the Coyote, it was impossible to understand.

"I'll do it," Dorian whispered.

"Fantastic," I said, getting to my feet. "I have something to show you. I think you'll like it."

///

There were far more weapons than he expected. Dorian imagined that one day, perhaps after three or four years of effective hiding, he would be able to obtain weaponry like what he was seeing. Even then, it wouldn't have been as nice, nor as organized and well hidden. Cayden was serious about his plan.

"Can you handle any of these," Dorian asked, doing his best not to look surprised.

"I'm quite good with a gun," Cayden said. "Though, I'm sure you are better."

Yes, I am much better, Dorian thought.

The weapons compartment was hidden in the bulkhead of the ship, just before the kitchen area when walking out of the cockpit. Press a hand to what appeared to be a temperature control gauge, and the bulkhead split at the horizontal seem to reveal a case full of guns. To be more accurate, it was empty compared to the room it held, but there were sufficient weapons of all sorts for the both of them. Four pistols, two shotguns, four submachine guns, a very impressive looking sniper rifle, and a plethora of grenades. Not bad at all.

The disguised temperature gauge was a simple hand scanner. Cayden incorporated Dorian's hand print, along with his sister's, into the system while they were unconscious. That fact made Dorian throw out any preconceived notions he assumed about Cayden. He was serious.

Someone who trusted in their plan that much was one of two things. Stupid or smart. However odd he was, Cayden did not strike him as stupid.

Dorian knew he was a better killer than Cayden. He was faster, stronger, more talented, and more technical. In fact, he was better than anyone else he encountered. It's what kept him alive for the past three months. When he was in a combat situation, instinct took over. He automatically engaged in the most efficient method to eliminate the threat. Yet Cayden defeated him with relative ease. In fact, if he wanted to, Cayden could have killed both him and Kalista.

And now, he thrust Dorian into a reverse situation. Cayden loosed Dorian from his bonds and gave him access to all of the weapons under the terms of a simple, verbal agreement. Now, Dorian had control. To overpower Cayden, kill him, steal his ship, and go on living with more resources than he ever dreamed of.

But a small sense of danger lurked in the back of his mind that halted any action. What was his plan? Dorian could not see it, could not imagine it. The weapons were right there, not two feet away. What could Cayden do if he were to reach for the nearest and shoot his host in the head? It would only take half a second.

Cayden knew something. He must have had a contingency plan. It was the only thing that made sense. He was playing with Dorian's head. Dangling the possibility before him, almost daring him to make an attempt. But it wasn't meant as a temptation. Cayden wanted him to know. To know that he was still a step ahead.

"I think I'm gonna catch some sleep," Cayden said. "Feel free to examine them, if you so wish. I'm particularly fond of the Viper pistols."

Dorian nodded as the mystery walked away. It was aggravating to let another person control his fate. Extremely aggravating. But Cayden was better than him. Perhaps not in the middle of a gunfight, but he was the man who controlled the gunfight. A dangerous man to trust.

A dangerous man to cross.

///

Kalista fought the pain inside her head. Migraine again. Just behind her eyes. She tried to place what it was that caused these problems. Perhaps it was the memories themselves. Like shards of glass rattling around in her brain. What was once a whole picture was now broken and tearing her to shreds inside.

Her memories were a joke. The GS blended them with their splicers to such a degree that she only remembered bits and pieces of what happened. On top of that, she filtered those memories through the illusions and hallucinations her mind created when trying to fill in gaps that made no sense.

Kalista walked out of the bathroom, wrapped only in a towel, her hair dripping cold water down her bare skin. She ran smack into Cayden, and nearly fell.

"Sorry about that," he said, his hand taking hold of her arm to steady her. "I thought you had already gone to bed."

She was careful to notice that his grip was weak, and his palm sweaty. His words were rushed as well, as if nervous, which didn't fit his character. When her brother was around, he acted as if her presence was an annoyance. However, now that it was just the two of them, he seemed to be caught off balance. Not that she could say anything herself, as she found his presence off-putting.

She saw him in the present, and then imagined him in the past holding her in the dark, whispering poems in her ear. It was comforting, and at the same time . . . not right. The memories felt peaceful, but she was overcome with sadness when they flashed before her eyes.

"I brought you some clothes," he said, holding them out to her. "It's nothing special or anything. Just some cotton pants and a T-shirt, but they're clean and should make good pajamas. Not that you have to wear them if you don't want to, and that's not a suggestion that you sleep naked, although there's nothing wrong with that in any way. In fact, some people prefer to . . . um . . . . here, take them."

"Thanks," she said, accepting them from his arms and feeling a grin tug at her lips. It was funny to see him so unprepared.

"Yeah, after we get some more money, I'll be sure to let you and Dorian shop for more clothes," he went on. "But . . . uh . . . get some rest. Big day tomorrow."

He walked off, and she had no doubt he was chiding himself.

///

What was that?

I ignored him. I could do that. Our relationship was one-sided in many ways. Not that I was in complete control. It was within the Coyote's means to make my life a living hell if he wanted to. However, I was in control of . . . us. He couldn't take control of my body when I didn't want him to. And if I wished to keep my thoughts to myself, I could do so.

I'm not mad, Cayden. You just have to remain in control. Soon enough, you will have to interact with her on your own, and I won't be able to help you.

I opened the door to my quarters and stepped into the dark, continuing to ignore the Coyote. After taking off my shirt and pants, I crawled into the bed. I needed rest in the worst possible way.

I don't like it when you go silent. You know that.

It made him nervous when I didn't communicate back to him. I knew it was unfair. The Coyote only had me. His interactions with others were meaningless to him. I was the only intelligence that counted to him.

I swear, I'll talk all night.

I'm fine, Coyote. I just need time.

Now you're starting to sound human. Have a good rest, Cayden. This is going to work. I promise.

I closed my eyes. Upon the back of my eyelids, I found Kalista. My memory flashed to when we were younger. Then, to the last moment I saw her. Tears welled in my eyes.

This has to work.

13

NOSTALGIA was the only thing I hated about having Dorian and Kalista around. Memory could be a funny thing. I thought I lost mine, only to find it again through the Coyote, and then wished ninety percent of it stayed lost. I tried to forget some of the darker moments in my past. But what if in trying to forget the bad memories, I unintentionally forget the good ones? The ones with Kalista. Aren't all memories tied together like a looping, twisted rope?

I don't think your head is full of ropes, Cayden.

I halted my efforts to forget and found ways to manage living with them. Small steps, like avoiding mirrors. Mirrors were a trigger, so I stayed away from them as much as possible. This was an inconvenience, but not one that I couldn't cope with.

What is with the mirrors, anyway?

The Coyote knew more about me than anyone else, but he couldn't understand this side of me. He didn't understand trauma. For him, actions were actions. What happened was what happened. Significant moments were no different than other moments. Nothing was special or horrible or joyous. All things were identical.

I understand trauma. A mental injury occurring from extreme events one is a part of.

Do you understand that trauma leaves lasting marks on the individual affected?

Yes.

Do you understand how those marks work?

No. But my highly evolved intellect tells me that your aversion to mirrors has something to do with it.

I let my eyes drift across the ship's controls, triple-checking our arrival time for no particular reason. We would reach the Edge in another three hours. I slept, I ate, and now I waited.

It's the bane of a linear existence. Waiting.

Dorian retired to his assigned quarters. I hadn't seen Kalista since our run in with the towel, and the nakedness underneath the towel. Could a distraction be both welcome and unwelcome at the same time?

Mirrors, Cayden. Your balance is disrupted with Kalista and Dorian here. Tell me about the mirrors, and maybe it will help.

I breathed deep and closed my eyes. I knew he was right. Being in the presence of the twins removed me from the norm and put me into the past. Every time I had nothing else to do, my thoughts drifted to my childhood. This was not how I usually operated. I tended to be focused on the future; on the next move in the game. But that focus was disrupted by ghosts of the past, and all of my previous experiences haunted my thoughts.

Moments of goodness were fleeting.

Bronx called us the Betas. By "Beta" he meant we were the second batch of freak experiments. If an "Alpha" batch existed, I knew nothing of them or their fate. I didn't think I wanted to know. We were all nearly the same age, born within five weeks of one another. Our group consisted of thirteen individuals. Jerry and I were the only two left alive from the testing phase.

My knowledge of the "why" was a puzzle pieced together with facts, theories, and guesses. Bronx was the lead researcher for the GS on experimental cognitive assets. What we were meant for, I do not know. Other batches were made after us, and they were much more precise. Dorian and Kalista were part of the assassin batch, which was cultivated three years after my birth. Many of their group survived, and their collective purpose was much more direct.

Myself, Jerry, and our now dead compatriots were more like multi-tools. We could kill. Not as well as the assassins, but we were skilled. We were intelligent, but not as much as the Brains; a group of unfortunate souls that were physically disabled to the greatest degree and whose only cultivation involved matters of the mind. All they did was think, their physical bodies atrophied to the brink of death.

The Actors were undercover specialists, able to be placed in any situation and blend in for years. Their information gathering abil-ities were unrivaled. We were not as good as the Actors, but our Beta batch could go undercover in most operations and blend into the background long enough to get the job done. We could do many things, though not one thing as well as the specialists.

After I was sent packing by the GS, I was able to reconnect with Bronx. He was punished for not making the Betas to the satisfac-tion of the GS. According to him, that was why belonging to the Betas turned out to be so fatal. The GS decided to make the Betas an extreme test group. One upon which they could wreak havoc and record the results.

The Assassins consisted of twenty original members. Eigh-teen made it through the testing phase. Only one member of the Brains died due to an embolism. All forty-three Actors survived the testing.

When I was fourteen, the cruelty stepped up a notch. Eleven of us were still alive. Two died from complications during the starva-tion and sleep deprivation phases. Once we half-recovered our strength, they began to pit us against one another. At first, it was only fights. No weapons were allowed in the caged matches, and the battle ended when one combatant became unconscious.

I wasn't the best fighter among the group to begin with, but at the suggestion of the Coyote, I purposefully lost each battle. It was the first test of trust between us. He had a plan, he said. He could foresee that the situation would only elevate in its danger. I fought seven times over the course of a month. I lost each fight, fighting back only enough to make my opponents and the GS believe I was doing all I could.

It was after my seventh fight, during my recovery of a dislocated shoulder, they turned a cruel test into a lethal one. I was pushed into one of the combat rooms, a perfect square space, and I found myself looking at multiple reflections.

It was dizzying. The room was made entirely of mirrors, save for the dull gray, metal floor. I was looking at hundreds of myself in every direction, and I breathed deep to regain my composure.

The sound of a door opening broke the silence, and across the vertigo-inducing room, Inq'lu entered. A yookallan boy, considered by us to be the most talented of the Betas. I'd heard he'd won all of his fights, even the fight against Jerry. He was tall, strong, and always tested above everyone else in athletics.

We got along well enough up to that point, though we were not friends. Most of us realized that making friends was a mistake. He nodded at me grimly as the door behind him closed, the seams of it disappearing into the perfect reflection of the mirror wall.

Our gazes drifted downward at the same time, and our eyes fell on the same object. In the middle of the room, unsheathed and glittering in the pristine light of the death chamber, was a dagger long enough to run its blade through the chest of a full-grown deeshie. The surge of fear that went through me was paralyzing. I thought the Coyote's plan was blowing up in my face. They were pitting the weakest fighter against the strongest. They were trimming the fat.

A woman's voice sounded from hidden speakers. "In ten minutes, we will flood this room with a deadly gas unless one of you is dead."

Good, this is what we wanted.

What the hell are you talking about? He's going to kill me!

He knows you've lost all seven of your fights. He knows he's won all seven of his. His overconfidence is what's going to help you win.

I remember hearing that word and wanting to cry. Win? No one was going to win. One of us was going to kill the other. But those types of scenarios, as I would come to find out over the years, didn't matter to the Coyote. He didn't understand the emotional experience. He only understood the puzzle before him. As I listened his plan, he sounded cheery. Almost giddy. Everything was happening just the way he wanted it.

When the fight begins, do not go for the knife. He's faster than you, and he will kill you in short order if you're too close.

What am I supposed to do? Wait for him to bring the knife to me?

Do exactly what you see.

What?

Like a film in my head, I saw myself exactly where I was standing from a third person's point of view. I watched as Inq'lu charged for the knife in slow motion. One could walk the distance of the room in any direction within ten paces. The young yookallan warrior would have his weapon in two athletic bounds, and it would be tearing through my gullet in another two.

I took a step away, my right hand reaching to my left shoulder, and with a violent pull, tearing the sleeve off. The sewing loosened months ago. Inq'lu held the knife in hand as I wrapped the ends of the cloth around my knuckles and stretched it taut, keeping it low.

My opponent continued his charge, bringing the knife over his head. I would be dead in the next step. As he brought it down, I threw my hands up, intercepting his arm at the wrist with the sleeve. Once the blow lost some of its energy, I stepped to the side and wrapped the cloth around his wrist once, pulled and twisted it toward me so that his arm bent backward. The knife fell from his grip and into my outstretched hand. I stabbed directly into his heart, and he fell backward, dead as space.

Easy, right?

What the hell was that?

A simulation.

"Begin," the woman's voice said over the speakers.

I locked wide eyes with Inq'lu for half a second, and then he charged for the blade, exactly as the Coyote played it out in my head. I hastily reached my right hand up to my shoulder and tore the sleeve as hard as I could. Inq'lu had the knife, and his determined eyes were on me.

Focus.

I wrapped the ends of cloth around my hands as my foe brought the knife over his head and swung down with lethal force. I stepped slightly to my left, held the taut cloth up and intercepted his strike just as I had seen before. Inq'lu was strong, and his arm bent the cloth inward, the tip of the blade just missing my right shoulder. With a quick twist, I wrapped the torn sleeve around his wrist and pulled up and inward, extending his arm. Switching my grip so that both ends of the cloth were in my left hand, I ducked under his extended arm and then pulled with the cloth, leaning my head back simultaneously so my neck put pressure on his elbow.

Catch the knife.

The weapon dropped from his grip, and I reached for it in midair with my right hand, but that was when the plan changed. My knuckles knocked into the handle, and the blade skittered across the room.

What now, genius?

Plan B.

Before I could ask, Inq'lu's fist crashed into my side, causing me to release his other arm. I turned in time to throw my arms up and partially intercept two of his punches, but not the knee he threw into my abdomen. My breath left in a *whoosh*, and I doubled over in pain. Inq'lu took advantage of the moment and charged past me for the knife.

He's focused on the weapon. Tunnel vision. Take advantage. Grab his left leg, lift, and use your weight to drive his knee into the floor.

I didn't know what to do, and it seemed like the Coyote knew exactly how to proceed. Inq'lu was almost at the knife, and I followed the Coyote's instructions. I was able to catch his left pant leg at the ankle, lift it high, and my shoulder drove it into the floor. I heard a *pop* followed by a scream of pain from my adversary. And then, my scream joined his.

While I successfully immobilized Inq'lu, that did not prevent him from reaching the knife, which was now four inches deep into my shoulder. I pushed his hand off the handle and backpedaled with the weapon still stuck in my arm.

Good, you have the knife.

Because he stabbed me, you prick!

You have to get it out, but not yet. You only have five min-utes to kill him before you pass out from blood loss.

I was able to get to my feet, clutching the knife with my right hand. It hurt like hell, and the sight of blood droplets on the floor made my stomach lurch. Inq'lu stood, gingerly, favoring his right leg. We were seven paces apart.

Time to put on a performance. You have to act as if the knife is stuck in you shoulder, and wait until he is almost on top of you before you remove it.

Inq'lu limped toward me, and I, for better or worse, did as the voice in my head instructed. I did my best "pull the knife out of your shoulder" routine, and the sight of it being stuck added urgency to my enemy's gimpy walk.

Not yet. He has to be closer.

If it weren't for his injured leg, he would have been within striking range. I tightened my grip on the handle of the knife, my blood making it slick. Inq'lu telegraphed his move, his eyes focused on the weapon.

He's going to try and push the knife deeper into your shoul-der, and then rip it out and kill you. Lift your left arm, then pull the blade out, and swing your right arm low and up into his chest. You'll stab directly into his heart and kill him instantly.

Inq'lu did exactly as the Coyote foresaw, swinging his arm for the protruding knife. I gritted my teeth as tight as I could and lifted my left arm and used my right hand to rip the knife out of my shoul-der. Inq'lu's hand slapped harmlessly into my side as I brought the freed knife from high to low and shoved upward. Inq'lu's other arm hit my wrist enough to throw off my aim, but not enough to stop the blade from plunging to the hilt into his abdomen.

He's still dangerous. Charge forward, and trip him onto his back. Do not let go of the knife.

I screamed at the top of my lungs, hooking my right leg around his left. He fell onto his back, his left hand gripping my wrist, trying desperately to pull the knife from his gut. But he lost leverage when I fell on top of him, my weight holding the weapon in place.

You missed his heart by three inches. It's going to take him too long to die. Pull down as hard as you can. The internal damage will kill him quickly.

I didn't know why, but my vision was blurred. I did as I was told though, pulling downward with the knife. It was a sickening sound and blood sprayed my face. The sound and splatter reminded me of biting into an overripe fruit. Inq'lu's eyes widened to an almost impossible degree, and his grip on my wrist loosened. His breath came in shallow gasps. I wiped my blurred eyes with the back of my wrist, and I realized it had been tears interfering with my vision.

Pull the knife out. He'll bleed out faster. He's in shock.

With a quick pull, I removed the knife and tossed it behind me. I rolled to my knees beside my vanquished foe, breathing hard. A familiar tingle spiked at the back of my tongue, and I vomited.

How long before he dies?

Two minutes.

Why does he look like that?

Inq'lu was staring upward, his face almost serene. If it wasn't for the blood pooring out of his mouth and the gaping gash down his stomach, one might think he was resting. But he looked focused . . . fascinated.

He's watching himself die.

I looked at the ceiling to see that he was indeed staring at himself, watching the life leave his body. This triggered something in me. I crawled over to the dying boy, and shouted "no" as loud as I could. I didn't know why I was saying it. I cupped his face in my palms, trying to pry his stare away from his reflection. He paid me no mind. His breathing was irregular.

I pushed him to his side, forcing his head to turn, but he only encountered another mirror. Large portions of his intestines spilled onto the metal floor from the move. Inq'lu didn't seem to mind. He didn't even look. I shoveled his torn guts back into his abdomen, but every time I did, more would spill out. I was still shouting, but it sounded muffled.

I gave up on the intestines, and looked up only to see my own reflection. I was covered in blood and gruel; some of it mine, but most of it his. The wound to my shoulder was still bleeding heavily, but I felt no pain. My face didn't look like mine anymore. My features were contorted in a grotesque fashion. When my eyes moved to the left, they found Inq'lu's gaze. I wanted to say something, but my mouth was still busy screaming.

I watched as his eyes turned to glass, the intestines continuing to spill out, smelling of sewage. I realized I was standing and staring at a closer reflection. I spun, but only saw another me. I did this several times, always encountering myself everywhere I looked. I panicked. My heart felt like it was going to beat out of my chest.

You're having an adrenaline rush. It will pass.

The latch on the door behind me echoed loudly throughout the room, interrupting my moment of insanity. One thought dominated my mind, and without hesitation, my body obeyed. I sprinted for the knife as the soldiers came into the room to restrain me. Sliding on my knees, I collected it expertly from the floor and bounced back up, charging for the entrance.

Cayden, no!

I wasn't listening to him anymore. The door opened, revealing three heavily armored guards, stun guns in hand. I pounced. They were not expecting it. I swung down hard with the blade, lopping off the first guard's hand at the wrist. At the same time, I kicked into the chest of the guard to my right. Just as the wounded guard screamed behind his visor, I pushed the knife under his chin, and the protective helmet, killing him on the spot.

When I turned in an effort to continue my assault, everything went black. The third guard apparently managed to use his weapon and rendered me unconscious.

After that moment, weeks of silence passed. I don't remember much of it. Bronx would arrange time for me to talk to Kalista in an attempt to help me. I wouldn't talk, but it helped being there.

Kalista was a natural caretaker, and even at that young age, she understood what comfort a simple touch could offer. Some days, I would lay on the floor and stare at the ceiling for hours. Other days, I would cry until my whole body ached. Kalista would sit and hug my shoulders, whether I was silent or weeping. She gave me something no one else could.

"Cayden?"

I nearly jumped out of my chair, yanked back to the present as if I suddenly departed a time machine. I looked up to see Kalista standing in the doorway, a worried expression on her face.

What happened?

I've been trying to shake you out of it for the past ten minutes. I just wanted to know why you hated mirrors, and then you went into some kind of trance.

I was covered in sweat, so much so my shirt stuck to my back and front. Moisture sprayed angrily into the air as I rubbed a hand through my short-cropped hair. I never remembered those events in that detail before. The memories were there, but I never entertained them.

"Are you okay?" Kalista asked.

I looked at her. She appeared nervous. "Yes. Why are you here?"

She shuffled her feet a bit and stammered. "D-Dorian said that . . . we would be racing?"

"Ah, yes," I said, trying to sound casual.

Standing up, I commanded my muscles to relax. They felt as tight as springs, and my heart was pounding. It was like I was back at that moment. I looked at my hands to assure myself there was no blood on them.

Clearing my throat, I said, "If you will meet me in the cargo bay in ten minutes, I can show you the racer we'll be using. I'll answer all of your questions there."

Kalista nodded and gave me one last nervous look before exiting the room. I breathed deep, doing my best to come back to a relaxed state. My heart still felt like it would burst through my rib cage and bounce down the hall at any minute. The beating almost hurt. I put my hand to my chest and breathed deep again.

Let's not do that again.

Agreed.

14

KALISTA navigated the ship well enough. It was a simple design. The cockpit, where she found a very disheveled Cayden, was located at the nose of the craft. From there, a short hallway led her to the kitchen and dining area. Everything was basic but functional. It was a design meant to keep oneself, and perhaps a few others, comfortable for a long time. The living area across from the kitchen housed two compact couches and a chair that faced a large viewing screen. A table in the middle held a small screen, from which games could be played.

She was unsure of the details of his plan, but it was obvious he intended to live here. The spaces were well-designed, comfortable, and thoughtful. It was hard not to be impressed.

The kitchen/dining/living area led to another hallway. After exiting, a path to the left went to Cayden's room. The path to the right housed Kalista's and Dorian's rooms. The walkway straight ahead took her to the cargo bay.

The floor sounded hollow as her feet struck its metal surface, and she noticed a large hatch in the middle of the hall. If she were to hazard a guess, it led to the engine room. Through one more doorway, and she was in the cargo bay. It was spacious, and for the most part, empty. She was on the second level, looking down into a spacious bay that could hold whatever Cayden wanted.

Kalista descended the steps, the sound of her shoes echoing

loud against the walls. A single crate on the far side of the bay was the only thing other than her that occupied the space. It wasn't an overly large containment vessel. Perhaps four meters long by two meters wide.

She reached out, touching its cold metal surface, breathing deep, while closing her eyes. This ship felt familiar somehow. All of it felt familiar. She was too comfortable around Cayden. Far more comfortable than she was around other strangers. The more time she spent on the ship and around him, the more at ease she felt.

But nagging at the back of her mind was an incredible sadness. As if she were only in a hallucination, and none of this existed. Not the ship, not Cayden, nor her comfort. It all seemed like a lie.

Cayden was honest, though. That much she knew for sure. He had yet to tell her a lie that she could detect. And she could always detect lies.

"I see you've found my racer," a smooth voice said from above her.

Kalista looked up to see the enigmatic young man strolling down the stairs. He looked to be much more composed than he was a few minutes ago. He changed his dull gray, sweat-soaked shirt for a more fitted black one. His old white pants exchanged for a magenta pair. He walked toward her with the confidence of man who had no troubles. Kalista knew that was a lie, and yet she could not sense it.

"She is beautiful," he said, eyes on locked on her, and not the crate.

Cayden came to stand next to her, though he kept a comfortable distance of a few feet between them, and finally broke his gaze from her to look at the storage unit. A smile tugged at his lips as his hand caressed its side. Kalista said nothing.

"I built her after the GS dropped me off at the Edge," he said.

"She doesn't look like much, but she's got the goods on the inside. I made sure of that."

"Should I assume your racer has something to do with the activity you have planned for us?" Kalista asked.

"Oh yes," he said, while unfastening the lock on the front of the crate. Cayden pushed the handle and pulled the door toward him and away. A low hum could be heard inside the storage unit, and he smiled again. "Hello, Matilda."

"Matilda?" Kalista asked.

Cayden ignored her and stepped inside the container, extending his hands to grab hold of a dark metal frame. He pulled, and the low hum increased in volume by a few decibels as the racer floated out of its cage.

Kalista stepped out of the way as he guided it out. It was long, nearly the full four meters of its container, but only about one meter wide. It floated lazily above the ground, waist high. Kalista cautioned a glance underneath the racer to see several metal semicircles the size of melons placed strategically from front to back. They must have been what made it hover.

A taut fabric cover was clipped around most of the frame, hiding much of it from view. Just as she thought to ask to see what it looked like, Cayden unhooked the clips. He tossed the fabric to the side.

"It's been too long," he said, running a hand over one of the frame's bars.

Kalista didn't know what racers were supposed to look like, but it was more than likely they didn't look like Matilda. Everything on the racer was visible. There were no coverings that would hide any of the components. Only a black frame that offered little in the way of shielding.

As if he were reading her mind, Cayden spoke up. "Most pilots use body panels to give the racers sleeker looks. Plus, they can attach sponsor images to those panels and earn a little extra cash. I found it useless."

Kalista meandered around the racer. The nose of the vehicle was its longest and thinnest feature, housing some type of device down its middle that was visible through the cylindrical bars of the frame. The pilot's seat was located in the center of the cockpit. Just behind the first seat was another, but much smaller, with only two diminutive cushions for the butt and the back. Directly behind and below the second seat was what had to be the engine. A complex conglomerate of metallic blocks, plastic hose lines, and exhaust pipes looked to be a tight fit into the back of the vehicle. All of these details were clearly visible, because Cayden was apparently content to let the universe see every component. She found the choice curious.

"Don't you have to worry about something getting into the engine or objects flying at you while you're racing?" Kalista asked.

He shook his head and pointed at the device in the nose of the craft. "Racers all have shield generators. Can't race without them. Like I said, the body panels are useless."

"Other racers can see you, though," she said.

He smiled. "It's been my experience that this unnerves them more than it does me."

"I assume you've entered a significant amount of races," Kalista said.

He nodded. "Won most of them."

"How many, exactly?"

"Eighty-seven out of eighty-eight," he said, his voice nonchalant.

"You only lost one race?"

"Yeah, my shield generator overheated halfway through the race, so I had to drop out," Cayden said. "But after I fixed it, I went on a bit of a roll. I hold most of the records on Rome."

Kalista raised her eyebrows. "And those were all single-pilot races?"

"Of course," Cayden said, buffing out a spot she couldn't see on the racer's frame. "I've always handled my business solo until now, but involving you shouldn't be a problem."

"You want me to race?" Kalista asked.

Cayden winced, as if the very thought scared him. "No, you won't be racing. But you will be my guide."

"How will that work?"

Cayden leaned against the racer. "In single-pilot races, I have control of everything. I'm able to see a digital map that will guide me through the course. The safe, intermediate, and dangerous courses will be highlighted for me, along with the locations of the other racers. The two-seater races make things a lot more interesting."

Kalista ran a hand over the frame, the cold metal tingling her skin. "How so?"

"Well, the passenger becomes the guide," he said. "I won't be allowed to see the map while we're racing. That will be your responsibility."

Now Kalista winced. "You think it's a good idea for me to have that type of control?"

Cayden waved away her concerns. "It's really not that bad. The two-seater racers aren't as talented as the single-pilot racers. I'll still be able to see everything in front of me as we go, and after eighty-eight races, I know their courses and tactics well enough."

"If you say so," Kalista said, the nervousness in her voice evident.

"Come on," he said, gesturing for her to join him near the vehicle. "I have a couple of training visors in the cockpit we can use. We've got a few hours to kill, and it'll give you an opportunity to get accustomed to what it will feel like. I'll give you a boost. Take the back seat."

Kalista approached with caution as Cayden cupped his hands at knee level. She placed a hand on his shoulder as she slid her right foot into his grip. He lifted her with ease, and she swung herself into the back seat without too much difficulty.

It wasn't exactly roomy. She was forced to maneuver her left foot around a rod coming through the floor. At the end of the rod, at eye level, was a small display screen. She guessed it would be for her map. Her leg room was limited as well. The back of Cayden's seat was between her knees.

Cayden swung himself into the seat in front of her with a well-practiced hop. She imagined that he'd gotten used to the racer's awkward height a long time ago.

"I didn't really design the racer for two people," he said, leaning forward to pull out strange looking visors from a small compartment. "Sorry if it's a bit uncomfortable. The rules on racers require a second seat, but I never really planned on having a guide, so I made it about as small as possible. Think you'll be okay?"

"Yes," she said.

Kalista wasn't really listening to him as he handed her the visor and began explaining how it worked. She was too busy lost in her own thoughts. As Cayden leaned back against his seat, Kalista fought an incredible urge to reach down and run her fingers through his hair. To caress his face.

To kiss him.

It wasn't that she felt a deep desire to do any of those things.

She felt like she was supposed to. It was natural. Almost as if she was looking at instructions on how to act when Cayden was around. Like there was a script she was supposed to follow.

Kalista wiped away a tear creeping down her left cheek. What was real? Why was she here? Why was he sitting in front of her acting as if none of this mattered?

She just wanted to know what was real.

///

"We'll try out a simulation. Give you a taste of racing," I said.

Kalista turned quiet abruptly, opting for one-word answers while I talked her through what the simulation would do. I looked back every once in awhile to make sure she was paying attention, and she seemed to be. She would nod her head or give short responses to affirm that she understood. She even answered a few review questions correctly. By all means, the girl was ready. But the spark of curiosity she displayed earlier was gone, and a kind of sadness took over.

Sort of bipolar, isn't she?

The Coyote insisted that I walk her through the introductions of the racer. I would be the one competing, after all. And so far, I surprised even myself. As intoxicating as I found her presence to be, I retained my composure.

"You'll need this out-dated headgear," I said, holding up the training visor. Her delicate hands took the equipment from me. "They're old but the simulations they give are dead on. I'll link my pair to yours, and we'll be fake racing in no time."

Kalista asked softly, "How do I put it on?"

No. Don't, Cayden. That's a trap.

I turned around, placing my knees on the seat, raising myself

124

to her level. Only the cushion separated us from a full lover's embrace. I looked down at her, my arms braced on either side of her delicate frame, and tried desperately to figure out those gems that she called eyes. What was she thinking? How could she not figure out how to put on a visor?

You know this is a trap. Just turn around and start the training.

Kalista's hands reached forward and grabbed a hold of my shirt, pulling me down hard. I could have let my chin hit hers awkwardly, or turned to the side, or resisted her pull, or done a lot of things to completely ruin the moment. But I was barely able to hold back my desires as it was, and her move was like breaking a dam holding back an army of emotions. Our lips met, and I kissed her with all the passion I contained. She returned the favor.

We soared on clouds. We crossed over into heaven in that brief time, kissing and caressing one another. Her arms wrapped around my neck and held me close. I pulled her up so that I could hold her, just like I used to, and mentally cursed the cushion that blocked the rest of our bodies from making contact.

I know it's tough, but you have to come back to reality. You have to stop.

My lips wreaked havoc on her neck, and the sound of her breath in my ear drove me crazy. We kissed again, and I felt the wetness of tears on her cheeks. Or were they my tears?

Cayden, you have to stop. I'm sorry, but you have to.

I pulled away first with the greatest reluctance. Never before had I wanted to hold on so hard to anything. I could've stayed there for eternity, cushion and all.

Cayden . . .

I just want to hold her. That's all I've ever wanted.

Stick to the plan.

"Okay," I said, and before she could respond, I positioned the visor on top of her head. "Remember it's a simulation and do your best to keep up."

I didn't dare look into those eyes while I readjusted myself into the proper sitting position. I didn't dare think or ponder. Return to void all who are burdened and bask in the peace of nothingness.

A bit of dark poetry fits quite nicely.

Isn't poetry supposed to rhyme?

Rhyming is too cliché for me.

Many things are too cliché for you.

I pulled the visor over my eyes, and linked to hers with the push of a button. A backward glance confirmed that she too had shielded herself from the world with the opaque lenses. Soon, we were immersed in the thrill of a simulated race. Perhaps that's all life was. An imitation.

That's all it ever felt like without her.

15

RULES were for children. Rymera was not a child. She was a professional assassin who deserved more notice. Yes, there were three days left. Nearly two, now. However, if she were to set out for the Edge now, she would make it there in time to make the quickest approved kill. Or perhaps she wouldn't make it to the approval part and just kill them anyway.

"Are you sure he is going to the Edge?" Rymera asked over the viz-comm.

"Trust me," the morkallian woman, Neg'stella said. "Cayden's going to the Edge. He bought enough weapons to start a rebellion on a small planet. He's got plans, but he needs more money. He practically spent a fortune at my shop. The Edge is the best place to make the big bucks and stay hidden at the same time."

Neg'stella was one of theirs. Not an assassin like Rymera. She was a plant. A professional actress that could fit into any walk of life at any time by the order of their commanders. She was planted in Cayden's life after his memory wipe with a promised expiration date of three years. Those three years were up, and she wanted out. Rymera was quite happy to do her this service.

"Not even Cayden will be able to plan for this," Rymera whispered.

"Don't fool yourself," the morkallian said. "You're going to need backup. Lots of it. He has Dorian with him, and from what I understand, he is the best of your kind. After three years of life with Cayden, I can tell you the only way you will beat him is to catch him off guard. Trap him."

"He doesn't suspect us," Rymera said. "He believes he has at least two days left before being hunted. If we get to him even a day beforehand, he will be caught completely by surprise. And my guess is that he and Dorian will not be together at all times. Seclude the two of them, and we have victory."

"Remain negative," Neg'stella said, almost cutting her off from her last sentence. "Don't give any hope to your plan, assume you are the one being hunted, and be prepared for an attack."

"Why do you say this?" Rymera asked.

Neg'stella sighed. "Because that kind of mindset is what you will need to beat Cayden. It's the kind of mindset you will need to even play in his game."

///

That was a very stupid thing to do.

I know.

Don't do it again.

I was back in my quarters, trying to get ready for our arrival to the Edge. We would be there in twenty minutes, and I needed to be prepared. My focus was crucial, and the plan could ill-afford screwups.

What do you need?

Nothing.

You need something.

I said, nothing.

I turned the light on in my bathroom. The mirror reflected my presence, and I didn't turn away. Harder tests than a reflection were in my near future. I couldn't let anything take me out of the game. Anything.

And by anything, I assume you mean Kalista as well?

I recovered, didn't I?

Only after twenty seconds of engaging her in a tongue-wrestling match.

Whatever semblance of control I maintained was destroyed in the recent memory of our kiss. I shattered the mirror, and shards of my image cascaded to the floor. A primal, wordless scream erupted from my mouth, as I withdrew my bleeding fists and drove my knee as hard as I could into the wall of the bathroom.

My hands found the frame of the mirror, and I ripped it off the wall, throwing it behind me. My elbows struck into the wall, my fists again, my knees, my feet. I saved only my head, though I would have liked very much to throw it into the unforgiving wall as well. Perhaps knock myself unconscious.

The pounding of my heart slowed, and I examined my shaking, bleeding hands. There were a few cuts, but they were all shallow. I didn't feel any of them.

"Damn it," I said, picking out a piece of mirror from one of the wounds.

And you said you didn't need anything.

I kicked the frame of the mirror in anger, ignoring the Coyote's barb. He wasn't trying to goad me, but just about anything would goad me now. My impatience and passion almost ruined the plan.

You're only human, Cayden. We're back on track.

"Damn it."

///

Jerry knew that Rymera would chase Dorian. His knowing was confirmed by fact not too long ago. Rymera was the perfect candidate for his little plan. He actually hated plans. No matter how thorough he was, Cayden always outperformed him in that area. But Jerry didn't let his hatred defeat his ability to learn.

If Cayden taught him anything, it was to study everyone in great detail. Know everything. Make as many conclusions as possible about what they would do when presented with words, actions, or thoughts. Then, plan around it. Cayden was the master, and he seemed to be perfect in his area of expertise. No matter what happened, Cayden was prepared.

Jerry tried to borrow that mentality as much as possible. Contact Rymera under the false pretense that he was trying to warn her of an upcoming mission, but give her conflicting information. She knew as well as all the rest of the assassins that one couldn't track, chase, or hunt Cayden. His plans would kill them all, especially with an asset like Dorian at his side. They had to get ahead of him. They had to disobey orders.

They had to kill him.

Rymera managed to contact all of the assassins, which now numbered thirty-two. Only eight of those contacted consented to go with her, which was a hopeful number. The nine of them stood a chance, especially if Cayden and Dorian were separated. It would be better for them if Jerry came in with reinforcements to surprise Cayden a second time. Perhaps an unexpected attack on two fronts would be too much.

Perhaps not.

"I don't want him dead," the man sitting across from Jerry said. Bronx was a complicated man with complicated motives. Jerry did not care.

"Fine," Jerry said, lying with practiced efficiency. He could never lie as well as Cayden.

The GS probed Cayden's mind while he told lies, and even the most state-of-the-art technology couldn't separate the lies from the truth. They deduced that the man literally tricked himself into believing his lies so well that they became real in his mind. How he managed to not go insane while doing so was still a mystery.

"He'll come to no harm?" Bronx asked, though the question sounded more like an answer.

Jerry raised an eyebrow in amusement. "You do understand there are no promises, don't you?"

"Unfortunately, I understand completely. Not a word of this to Margaret," Bronx said, holding up a thick index finger.

"I dislike her more than you," Jerry said. "No, I will not tell her of this meeting or of anything else. She obviously isn't capable of handling Cayden."

Bronx nodded. "Nobody is. We're just hoping to get lucky."

"I happen to agree with Margaret on one issue," Jerry said, taking a good look at the burly man across from him. He was nearly as much a mystery as Cayden.

"Oh, and what's that?" Bronx asked.

"You're too sure of him," Jerry said.

Bronx brushed the comment aside with a subtle roll of his eyes. "You know as well as I what Cayden is capable of."

"Of course," Jerry said. "I've rivaled him since birth. We were bred to the same litter. You know this, Bronx."

"And you still doubt?" Bronx asked, his eyebrows raised.

Jerry leaned forward. "All of your attention to him has blinded you to the capabilities of the rest of us. Don't be fooled. He is only a man, and he will fail."

Bronx shook his head and let out a sigh. "We all have our flaws, I'll give you that. It's useless to argue the point further. But tell me something, Jerry."

"Yes?"

"Why do you hate him?" Bronx asked.

And the chord was struck. There were so many reasons why, all of which were private to him. Very private. Hatred was a funny thing. A funny thing that was uncomfortable to talk about.

"Do you know the feeling of falling in love?" Jerry asked.

The corners of Bronx's lips tugged slightly upward, as if recalling an amusing story. "To an extent, I think."

"Love has no reason," Jerry said. "It just is. Hatred, being the opposite of love, functions under nearly the same parameters. My hatred just is. And I hate Cayden with all of my heart."

16

MY bandaged hands were the first thing Kalista noticed upon entering the bridge of the ship. Her voice was filled with worry when she asked me what happened. I brushed off her concern, but when Dorian joined her, his focus was on the same thing.

"Will you be able to race with that wound?" he asked.

"It's superficial," I said. "I'm fine."

Dorian appeared to be satisfied with the answer and took a seat in the copilot's chair, facing the colorless expanse before us. Wormhole travel offered no exciting visuals. Only oblivion.

Though her twin was happy enough to let the subject go, Kalista didn't seem to want to. She stood between us, and her eyes didn't leave my bandaged hands. Still, she said nothing.

I didn't lie to them. It could have been worse. The mirror shards only gave my hands shallow cuts, and the bandages were there simply to stop the bleeding.

And that's why you don't lose control of your emotions.

Easy for you to say.

True. I have no emotions.

Although I would have liked nothing more than to retreat inside my own mind and allow the Coyote to take over, it just wasn't an option. Despite all of his positive attributes, he simply exhibited no feel for flying.

Or racing for that matter.

Which was why I currently resided in the cockpit, and would reside in the racer's seat when Kalista and I entered the tournament. The Edge was not an easy place, and I would need my skills as a pilot to navigate us safely through.

The Edge was well hidden in a cloud of asteroids. The locations themselves were simply hollowed out bits of rock. Magnificent planets and moons were now broken and shattered by a war long forgotten. It took nearly a hundred years for a society to start. New technology offered artificial atmospheres that added to the largest chunks of earth to once again host life. It was almost like a space archipelago. Personally, I've been to seven of the eighty-two islands that formed the Edge.

Our first stop was to an island I was familiar with, though it wasn't my favorite. It was simply referred to as Rome, in honor of the human history of gladiator battles. The tournaments ranged from fully padded fighting competitions to weapon-wielding bouts to the death. Dorian would be competing in the latter.

Hopefully. Dorian sounded hesitant.

He'll do it.

Once he was set, and once I enacted part of my backup plan, Kalista and I would travel six islands down from Rome to the races. That chunk of moon had a less creative moniker. It was known only as the Racing Moon.

"Hold onto something," I said, shutting off the alarm warning us that the wormhole was near its end. "I'm coming out hot, and the ride might be bumpy."

Dorian fastened his shoulder strap restraints and motioned for Kalista to take a seat behind him at one of the control panels. She did so without hesitation and secured herself as her brother did.

My ship rocketed out of the pure blackness of the wormhole into normal space with a rude jerk. Dorian's hand shot instinctively to hold the console in front of him as we sped directly for an asteroid twice the size of our ship.

What, he thinks he can stop the ship by having his hand on the dash?

Instinct, Coyote. Can't help it.

My heart didn't skip a beat as I guided my vehicle around the giant space rock, missing it by less than a hundred meters. I pushed the accelerator forward, rocketing around the asteroid and flying like a bat out of hell toward the main archipelago of the Edge.

"Is it necessary to get as close to these objects as possible?" Dorian asked, his hands back in his lap, but clenched into tight fists.

I didn't lose focus from navigating, as I needed all of it to weave our way through the field of unforgiving rocks and the corpses of random spaceships. Although most of the objects fell into a somewhat predictable orbit, there were always recent collisions that set other objects to travel at different velocities. One needed to achieve the perfect speed to avoid both the predictable and unpredictable. Perhaps it appeared reckless, but it was not.

"How about you let me take care of the flying part," I said, without looking at Dorian.

He is a bit jumpy, isn't he?

He doesn't like the lack of control.

Well, jumpy assassins aren't exactly a good thing, so perhaps you should try and slow down a bit.

Really?

"I'm sure Cayden knows what he's doing," Kalista said, though the tone of her voice did not carry much confidence.

Dorian and the Coyote would be able to relax soon enough as

the tense navigating approached its end, and the islands came into unhindered sight. Rome was one of the smaller islands, and the parking docks were always packed. The fighting tournaments were very popular. All beings in the galaxy seemed to have a special appreciation for violence.

I do find it fascinating that every variety of sentient being in this galaxy will pay to watch people brutalize other people.

We all die, and we all compete in this life. The evolutionary processes of all species in all the systems demanded that from us. We fight to survive. It follows that we would be fascinated watching people die during the ultimate competition.

Why would you be fascinated by the worst things in life?

It's called a cruel irony.

"I bid you a warm welcome to Rome," I told Dorian. "It will be your stop."

"We'll be on different planets?" Dorian asked.

"They aren't planets," I said. "We'll basically be next door, on the Racing Moon. Relax."

"You can't simply wait for my fight to be over and then have all of us leave for your races?" Dorian asked.

I set my course for Rome as we cleared the most dangerous of the debris. "We already discussed this. The bounty hunters after Kalista track her through you. If she's with me, she'll be safer. And the Edge is filled with bounty hunters. They will all be on the lookout. None of them suspect she will be with me."

Dorian didn't respond, and it was obvious why. I was right, and he knew it. Kalista would be in far less danger with me, and the bounty on Dorian's head was worthless without his sister. Both siblings would be safer, especially Kalista.

Even though she'll be strapped to the back of a tiny vehicle racing through a course of death traps at hundred of kilometers per hour?

You're doubting my skills as a racer?

I doubt your skills when she's there. You may not take the necessary risks needed.

Thanks for the boost of confidence. I can always count on you.

Don't get cute. One wrong move on that racer and you're vaporized. One hesitation, and we don't get the funds we need to pull off the final act.

I'm well aware, thank you.

I know. Just remember that when you have to risk her life on a hairpin turn.

Despite the crowded settings, it didn't take long to get a dock number once out of the field and then to park my beautiful ship between a pair of pirate junkers. It comforted me that my baby wouldn't be here very long. Parking at the Racing Moon was much better. I shut her off, and silence reigned, save for the noise of me flipping a few last switches.

"Ready to rock and roll?" I asked the twins.

///

Nine assassins against two former colleagues and a helpless human girl. Their odds weren't too bad. Rymera couldn't help but smile at the chance to go head to head with Dorian again. They were two of a kind once inside an arena, with nothing but themselves and whatever was of use. Warriors bred to deal death.

It was as it was meant to be.

During their years of training, she rivaled Dorian. He earned the unofficial rank of being the best among them. She earned second. Rymera's record against him was a losing one, but at least she was capable of putting a dent in any streak he made.

With the help of her eight colleagues, she knew she could win. She hoped for more, but eight was enough. They all trained with Dorian at some point, so they knew what they were getting into. But they were going in well-armed and prepared.

"My informant on Rome just sent me a message," Monfri, a sturdy yellow deeshie, said.

"What is it?" Rymera asked, looking up from the screen plotting their course. They would be there within the hour.

"Dorian is entering a gladiatorial tournament," he said, mild surprise in his voice. "That doesn't seem like him."

"That sounds like something Cayden would do," Vi said, bringing her tall morkallian figure into eyesight.

"A trap?" Ru'eld asked. Another morkallian, but male.

Rymera shook her head. "They don't know we're coming. Cayden believes he has time to enact a plan. The reasons behind the tournament are simpler than that."

"Money," Monfri stated.

"Exactly," Rymera said. "Cayden needs money to continue his plan."

"And just what is his plan?" Vi asked.

"What if it's to lure us there?" Ru'eld asked. "What if he knows we're watching?"

Rymera shut her eyes and rubbed her temples with her fingertips. She was not a planner. Neither were those who joined her. They were all assassins, like Dorian. People of action.

If there was a target that required a quiet kill, they would observe, study, and formulate the best way to do their job. But, outside of those uncommon circumstances, the shortest distance between two points was a straight line. And Dorian was waiting, unprepared.

"Cayden's not one of us," Monfri said.

Vi looked at him with a confused expression. "Yes, he is."

"No," Monfri said. "He's a Beta. Not an assassin. His combat skills are significantly worse than ours."

"Yes, well, there is the small matter of Dorian, whose skills surpass all of ours," Ru'eld said.

Rymera clenched her fists in frustration. Dorian was good, but she was not far behind. And with her colleagues' help, Dorian wouldn't stand a chance.

"There are no projectile weapons allowed in the gladiatorial battles," Monfri said. "Dorian won't be armed with anything that can contend with us."

"And without Dorian, Cayden will have no help," Rymera said. "Any more problems?"

"It still feels too convenient," Vi said.

"There are eight of us," Monfri said. "If Cayden has something planned, we'll be able to see it."

"Agreed," Ru'eld said.

"Make your plans," Rymera told Monfri. "Inform the others. I'm going to get ready."

She walked away without waiting for them to respond. They didn't need her help. They were a different breed of assassin than her. Let them make their plans. Let them think. All she wanted was Dorian, one on one. One more battle. One more fight.

Let death decide.

17

ROME was not a nice place. I visited on occasion and entered some of the safer fighting tournaments in my earlier years of freedom. I won, but not without physical cost I considered too high. Once, a separated shoulder, and another time, a few ribs. The downtime required to recover from the injuries and the relatively low pay for winning made me lose interest.

High cost, low pay.

The real pay came with the riskier fights. There were the "no rules" fights, in which death was not required but acceptable. These paid better. And better still were the weapons matches, the most famous of which, Dorian was about to enter.

Just walking around Rome was risky. The place was notorious for its lawlessness. Instead of a police force, Rome retained privately funded security, who were there only to protect certain wealthy fight managers. During every single stay on Rome, I was the victim of an attempted mugging. No help was given to me, and when I overpowered the criminal, no one bothered to hand him over to any kind of authority.

"Dorian says he wants enough time to scout the arena and his opponents," Kalista said, walking into the kitchen area, where I was double checking the ship's security measures.

"I'll be there in two minutes," I said. Kalista nodded, and I watched her walk away.

Why are your eyes focused on her gluteus maximus?

You mean her ass?

Yes.

It's a sex thing, Coyote. You wouldn't understand.

Oh. It does appear to be a healthy gluteus maximus, as far as shape is concerned. Is that why you were watching?

Sure. Are we set on the plan? Do you foresee any complications?

So far, so good. Are you sure using Bronx is a good idea? We could try this without him.

We need him, and you know it. The risk of doing this without his help is far too great.

Maybe for others, but not for us. We could just adjust the timeline.

That's not acceptable.

I waited for him to argue more as I booted the security systems into active status, but he said nothing. I knew he didn't like involving Bronx in our plans. I didn't either. If one could accomplish the task alone, then that was the best method. Trusting others was a sure way to complicate otherwise simple matters.

But sometimes it was the only way. Bronx's position inside the GS offered invaluable advantages. The more I trusted and depended upon him, the better my plans would go. However, I would also lose more and more control. The key was using his services when I absolutely needed to, but making sure not to put too many eggs in that one particular basket.

I strode away from the kitchen and toward the dock as the ship powered down. My heart raced as the goal grew closer.

Patience.

Easier said than done.

///

"Quite frankly, I'm tired," Margaret said, alone in her office with Jerry and Bronx.

"Tired of what, Margaret?" Bronx asked, folding his hands and giving her a condescending look.

Jerry stood at one corner of the room, laughing softly after Bronx finished his question. "I think she's beginning to catch on."

"I do my mandatory check on our assets, and nine of them are missing," she said. "Rumors of the two of you meeting more and more often in private reach my ears. Maybe one of you should fill me in on what's going on with *my* operation."

"Your operation," Bronx repeated, his voice quiet. He looked like a hulking gargoyle seated in her guest chair.

"Yes, my operation," she said, hoping her harsh tone bit hard into Bronx's overgrown ego. "The one recently given to me due to the incompetence of its former manager."

"May I remind you that I am still here, Margaret? Incompetent or not," Bronx said.

"A shame, really," Margaret said, staring him in the eyes without blinking. "From the investigations, I would have deduced that you almost willfully helped Dorian and Kalista escape."

Bronx paused, and gave her a hard look. "He had a gun to my skull. You know as well as I, even after I gave him the access codes, that I only had a small chance of coming out of the situation alive."

She raised her eyebrows in an unimpressed expression. "And yet here you are."

There was a long pause, and she exchanged glares with the

former manager. Bronx was a complicated man. She couldn't begin to figure out why he did what he did, and why their superiors kept him around. He was the leading expert on Cayden and seemed to be the only person able to get close to him.

"Should I leave and let the two of you continue the cat fight?" Jerry asked. She'd nearly forgotten about him.

"No, Jerry. You will now tell me exactly what's going on," Margaret said, letting the impatience in her voice become as evident as possible.

The Beta project survivor smiled at her, proving once again he was borderline insane. Or maybe not borderline at all. Margaret was warned about him, and those who gave her the warnings were quite right about Jerry. Despite never being first place in any one area among their assets, he fought his way to the top. He was just as special as Cayden and Dorian.

"Rymera and a team of eight other assassins are on their way to the Edge to intercept Dorian, Kalista, and then Cayden," Jerry said, his voice cool and even.

Margaret's nostrils flared. "Despite my orders to do no such thing?"

The corner of Jerry's mouth upturned in an unmistakable grin. "Oops."

She clenched her teeth, and the familiar heat of anger tingled at the base of her neck. "Would you mind telling me why you disobeyed me?"

"Because you're incompetent, Margaret," Bronx answered. "I know you think I am, but try to look at your position from a third perspective. I advise you to chase him. Jerry advises you to do the same. Nine assets are willing to disobey their orders and follow Jerry's rumor despite possibly suffering termination for doing so. You're the one that's new to this operation, but you still think that somehow your opinion is more important than the experience around you simply because of our failures in the past. You'll only make the same mistakes that we did if you don't heed what we have to say. So, for the good of the cause, we went behind your back."

The anger made its way from her neck to her cheeks, and she could feel them flush. The blatant disrespect shown by the two of them was unbearable. How they operated with that kind of a mindset was beyond her. She resided in her current position because the heads of the organization wanted someone fresh in command.

"You're reckless, Bronx. But unfortunately, there's nothing I can do about that," Margaret said. "You, however, Jerry are quite exposed to punishment. Pack your bags. You're off this operation."

Things happened so fast that she couldn't recall just how she was pinned with her back to the wall. Jerry held her there by her throat with a vice-like grip. His other hand held a gun to her temple. There was no shake in his hands, no nervous sweat beading on his brown, and no fear or doubt in his eyes. In fact, he looked eager.

"You may want to reconsider this decision, Margaret," Jerry said, his voice steady and relaxed. Bronx watched from his seat, a slight smile tugging at his lips.

"Okay," she said, her voice coming out in what seemed like a squeak.

Jerry smiled, closing his eyes, but the gun remained pinned to her head. "You see . . . Cayden belongs to me. He will die by my hand, and it will be like the poetry he used to write and the pictures I used to paint. You've already interfered with my plans, but I've been patient. Now, however, you've stepped too far. If you get in my way again, I will end you. Do we have an understanding?"

Margaret nodded, and to her great surprise, a tear slipped

from her eye. The fear of dying gripped her heart much like Jerry's hand gripped her throat. All the fear she thought she forgot long ago was now brought to the surface, and it was all she could do not to have a breakdown.

"Good," he said, lowering his hands and holstering the gun. He walked out with a nod to Bronx as he left.

"I noticed something, Margaret," Bronx said, as he stood up and she sunk to the floor. "You and I aren't so different. You just had a killing machine hold a gun to your head and make a demand. Like I, you complied without hesitation. Like I, you had a very slim chance of coming out of the situation alive, as the monsters we've created kill without much thought and no regret. And yet here you are."

Margaret could say nothing as he left.

///

The arena in which Dorian would be competing was massive, with enough seats to fit at least one hundred thousand observers. I stood with the twins at the entrance to the combatant chambers. It was awkward. Kalista was wringing her hands, Dorian was staring at the arena, and I tried to put a little distance between myself and the siblings, hoping to give them a bit of privacy.

Thank you. Move farther away if you can. I despise these awkward social interactions.

On that, we agree, Coyote.

Though it shouldn't have surprised me, neither Kalista or Dorian appeared to know how to say goodbye. Kalista looked at her brother more than he looked at her, trying to find the words to say, no doubt, but without success.

Finally, and to my relief, she stepped forward and hugged

him. Dorian returned the embrace with one arm, but the other hung awkwardly at his side. Kalista whispered something in his ear that I couldn't make out, then let him go, and moved stoically toward me.

"Wait here," I told her, as I walked to Dorian.

He turned to me as I approached. He looked grim. Solemn. Like a man condemned to death. Somewhere inside my chest, I felt a pang of guilt. Beyond the brainwashing, the programming, the training, and the fractured innocence, Dorian was just a person.

I still don't get it. He's about to do something he's really good at. Something he was bred for. And this time, he'll actually get a reward out of it.

But that's what is causing him discomfort. When he kills, he sees it as a necessity. Either someone else is giving him a command that he must follow, or he is defending himself. He's never volunteered to deal death for money. It's a moral crisis for him.

Has he ever had one of those?

Probably not. The conditioning runs too deep, and now that he's alone, making his own decisions, he's lost his reason to kill. That's what's causing him concern.

"Give me your hand," I said, pulling out a white plastic card from my pocket.

Dorian looked at me with a curious expression but did as I requested, lifting his left hand, palm up. I pressed the card to his thumb, and a small red light appeared appeared on its seam after about three seconds.

"Give this to the entrant guard," I said, moving the card from his thumb to his palm. "It the key to our joint account. When you win, the prize money will be transferred there. You'll now have access to the account with your thumbprint and DNA."

He nodded, pocketing the key card. "Do I need to collect it

after the competition?"

"No, it's disposable. You're now half-owner of the account," I said.

Dorian nodded again but did not make eye contact. The swell of guilt in my chest was getting more intense. I wanted to ignore it, to justify it somehow, but my sympathies were becoming overpowering. I felt like the GS. Manipulating people into doing horrible things.

Do not waver from the plan. This is for a greater good, even for him.

Some of the most unspeakable atrocities were committed in the name of the greater good.

Do not waver.

"You don't have to kill," I said. The statement drew his immediate attention.

What are you doing?

"Death isn't a requirement to win the battle," I said, looking the assassin in the eyes. "You can incapacitate your competitors. You're good enough to do that, but don't hesitate to use lethal measures. Many of those you face are bloodthirsty killers that are there because they *want* to be there. They want to kill. They like it."

"But some are not there for that?" he asked.

I shrugged. "Some, I'm sure, are there in desperation. Perhaps, because of unpaid debts. Some may be thrill seekers after the ultimate competition."

"How can I tell?" he asked.

"You'll know," I said. "Just don't let mercy kill you. Win this. Win this, and it's the last time anyone will ask you to kill again. You'll be free to make your own choices."

Dorian appeared a bit less crestfallen. Perhaps giving him an option to save lives from his skill was a bad idea. Then again, perhaps it would aid his determination. It was a toss up.

I just hope you chose the right side of the coin.

Dorian turned and walked through the entrance and did not look back. I joined Kalista's side, and her eyes lingered on the door her brother walked through.

"There's one more thing we have to do before we can leave," I said.

"And what's that?" she asked, a slight tremble in her voice.

"Let's call it a security measure," I said, grabbing her hand and turning us back in the direction docking port. "Dorian may need some extra protection."

18

ATTEMPTING to casually conceal a high-powered sniper rifle in a carrying case was not easy. It was strapped to my back, disguised well enough to look like a weapon used in one of the tournaments. Kalista followed me all the way to the ship and then back into town. There were moments she ran to keep up with my pace. Time was not on my side.

"Where are we going?" she asked.

"Less talk, more follow," I said.

I turned at an alley, making my way past multiple market-square bums trying to sell assortments of food and jewelry. My destination was one more turn to the right, and then up the third building to the roof. Kalista stayed silent, but grabbed a hold of my hand as the crowd thickened.

Does she honestly think she's going to get lost?

I'll never lose her.

We made the next turn, and I found my building. It was a whorehouse, so the doors were wide open. We strode through the entryway, and I was amazed at how fast the residents were able to fondle the more private areas of my body. I was forced to literally push past them in order to find the stairs. It was hard, but I did my best to ignore the strange sounds coming from behind closed doors.

What the hell is going on in room twenty-four?

Something so pleasing that it's painful or so painful that it's pleasing.

Strange how it can work that way.

One of the secrets to being stealthy was knowing when to move. Another secret when having to use it in plain sight was moving around like you owned the place. So, we opened the doors in our way without pause and ascended the small staircase to the roof.

"Lock the door," I said, and I unzipped the bag.

"Why are you setting up a gun here?" she asked, obeying my command.

I extracted the rifle and assembled the tripod it would rest on. "Extra protection for your brother. And it's part of the plan. Well, it's part of the backup plan that I have in place, though I fear that it will have to become the real plan instead of the backup plan. And really, the backup plan is just a shortcut to the real plan."

Why do you jumble your words like an idiot when she's around? Your grammar is abysmal.

You know why.

I chambered a round in the rifle, and then loaded the full magazine. "This rooftop directly overlooks the arena for Dorian's tournament. It's at just the right elevation to have clear aim over the stands."

Kalista's voice, normally soft and unassuming, turned stern. "They're coming, aren't they? You know they're coming, and you're letting him do this anyway."

I set the rifle on the tripod, and screwed it into place. It would soon become a functioning automatic turret. Kalista appeared to be unimpressed.

"It's not about knowing anything," I said, rotating the weapon to face the arena. Its motion was appropriately smooth.

"You obviously know something," she said. "Otherwise, why go to all this trouble?"

I shook my head. "I don't know what's going to happen next. I can't predict anything. I'm just extremely good at planning for all possible pathways. Which is why I'm planting this high-powered, third-person controlled, sniper rifle here."

"Third person?" she asked.

"Yes," I said, reaching down and grabbing a palm-sized screen from the side of the gun. "I can control the gun via the camera scope and shoot from afar. It works within a fifty kilometer range."

I tossed her the semi-transparent screen, which she caught with fumbling hands. While she looked at it, I withdrew a set of thin poles from the case that held the rifle and tripod. Connecting the poles was a shimmering, silver cloth.

"What's that?" Kalista asked.

"Camouflage," I said. "Here, help me put it up."

She pocketed the screen and aided me in stretching the poles out around the gun, until we successfully made a tent-like structure over the weapon. Only the business end of the rifle remained uncovered. We pulled the shimmering cloth taut, and I withdrew from my pocket a finger-sized remote. I pressed its lone button, and the surface of the cloth surrounding the gun mirrored its surroundings, all but making the entire setup invisible. It wasn't perfectly hidden, but it would be effective enough.

"Come on," I said, folding the empty carrying case into something that resembled a pack. "We need to fuse the seams of that door to make sure no one can get up here."

"I already locked it," she said, following me to the lone door on the rooftop from which we had come.

"Someone's bound to have a key," I said, withdrawing five

thin green sticks of thermal fusing from the inside pocket of my jacket.

"Do you just carry this sort of stuff with you all the time?" she asked, taking two of the sticks from me and pressing them into the right side seams of the door.

"I only carry what I know I'll need," I said, jamming the other three sticks into the left side and top of the door's seams. I pulled another small remote from the opposite jacket pocket and pressed the button.

Kalista and I shielded our eyes from the violent sparks that erupted from the thermal sticks as they welded the door shut. I pulled her to the edge of the roof on the opposite side.

"Time to make our exit," I said, working an ancient-looking control panel that brought a crude, rusted ladder to our level. "Just don't look down."

The formidable height and steep angle of the ladder didn't faze Kalista as she swung her leg over and climbed down at an impressive pace. I followed her without pause, shouldering the now empty case.

When we reached the bottom, I stopped at the ground control panel. After lifting the ladder back to its full height, I withdrew my pistol, quickly slid a silencer into place, and fired two rounds into the screen. No one would be able to make repairs.

No, I'd say you've definitely killed it.

"What if someone saw you?" Kalista hissed.

"This is Rome," I said, detaching the silencer and holstering the pistol. "No one cares. Stay close to me."

I grabbed her hand, but as I tried to walk forward, she pulled away. When I turned to see what the problem was, tears were floating in her eyes, but her expression was as hard as steel.

"Are you going to kill him?" she asked, her voice angry.

"Who?" I asked.

Kalista's arms shot out fast and pushed me hard in the chest. "Dorian! You're going to kill him!"

"Whoa, hey," I said, grabbing her by the wrists and walking us to the wall of the building. "I'm not going to kill him. I swear."

Tears were falling from her eyes, and her chest heaved in hard shudders. I wanted to hold her, but I knew it wouldn't be a good idea. We had to move. Fast.

Dramatic gesture to instill trust?

Yes.

I let go of her wrists, reached into my jacket, withdrew the pistol and flipped the safety off. Kalista, shocked at the gesture, began to retreat, but before she was out of arm's reach, I held the gun out to her, barrel facing my chest.

"Take it," I said, as she paused in her backward retreat. "Take the gun."

Although Kalista hesitated for a moment, she did just that. First with one hand, and then with the other as I relinquished control of the weapon. She did not keep it aimed at my chest, instead slowly lowering it as she stared at me.

"I'm going to get us out of this," I said, raising my hands in surrender. "You have to trust me. I've been planning this for a long time. I will get us out. All of us."

Kalista nodded, wiping the tears from her cheeks with one hand. She walked forward and pressed the gun back into my hands. "Do what you say you're going to do. Be who I want you to be. Please."

I holstered the gun, took her by the hand, and walked us out of the alley. On to the Racing Moon.

On to freedom.

///

In a small way, being a gladiator felt right. There was something about the arena that brought the word "home" to the surface of his brain. And despite his conflicted feelings over what he was about to do, Dorian could not deny his comfort level was increasing with each passing minute.

He was quite aware it was all an overdone spectacle to make the competitors feel like they traveled back to a more brutal time, but he didn't mind letting their deception take over his senses. It was an intoxication that he could deal with.

I belong here.

Everything looked as if it were thousands of years old, save for a few surprises here and there. The arena was gigantic. The builders based their blueprints off the original Coliseum, built by the real Rome. It was just as big as the original, and styled in much the same fashion, down to the dirt.

The gladiators' armor and weapons gave away some of the futuristic feel. All of the armor was made of blue-colored metals, which were much lighter than the originals, and worn over the current style of dress. It was the same with the weapons. They were light, and nearly unbreakable according to the guide, who was a stocky, pasty-skinned human male with an affinity for talking. He must have known that none of the competitors were there to learn about ancient Rome and how it compared to their version, but he continued to drag on about it for several minutes.

Only medieval weapons were allowed, which limited most to swords, spears, and shields. A few chose axes and maces. Unless they were well trained with such weapons, they would be the first to die.

Dorian performed warm-up exercises to prepare himself for the battle. Twenty-five beings, all competing for the ultimate prize, and only one attained it. They were to begin in seven minutes, and the competitors were crammed in a waiting area just outside of the arena.

Although there wasn't much room, the others allowed him space to exercise. There was a certain respect among most of them. Some tasted battle before, but the ones who saw very little death were either wetting themselves, or jumping up and down with excitement. If they survived, they would forever regret entering the tournament. Those who were skilled fighters were sure to have their reasons. Apparently, those reasons were worth the very real chance of death. Dorian could respect that.

Chained animals were visible from their waiting area, outside of the arena. A male tiger on the right, standing tall and ferocious. Dorian guessed it to be well over two hundred kilograms. Unlike in ancient times, the people that set up this tournament kept their animals well fed. Instead of using starvation techniques, they trained the beasts from birth to kill anything in sight. The chains gave them about ten meters of reach in every direction.

Across from the tiger and on the left was a male lion. At first glance, the lion looked to be the bigger animal, but its size was deceiving. The lion's immense brown mane made it appear larger than it was. The two cats looked like they wanted to kill each other more than anything else.

An eschule stood chained on the same side as the tiger, another ten meters down. The two animals were only just out of reach of one another. The eschule, which was native to the planet Morkal, had a troll-like appearance. Three eyes, no nose, a gaping maw for a mouth with spaced and uneven pointed teeth, and hardly any neck. It stood on two feet, but could easily transition to four since its arms were twice as long as its hind legs. It resembled a primate in its stance, except it was completely bald, ugly, and as mean as could be. The eschule probably weighed twice as much as the tiger or the lion.

A rayh'va from the planet Deeshie was next to the lion in the same fashion that the eschule was to the tiger. The rayh'va was all blue fur, yellow teeth, and black claws. With six legs, a forked tongue, and the ability to climb up most flat surfaces, it resembled a lizard in many ways. The worst part of the beast was at the end of its tail, which was over half of the creature's length. A pale blue stinger, which was about as long as Dorian's arm, acted like a spear. The monster wielded it quite well.

The four animals were chained to large, stone columns. The slack in the chains allowed the animals to reach out almost ten meters in every direction. Only the very middle and outer edges of the arena were free from the beast's reach.

The twenty-five competitors would be split into five groups of five. Two groups would be placed on opposite sides at the south of the arena. Two more groups would do the same on the north. The remaining group of five would be placed at the very middle.

Unlike what many thought, the event wasn't at all unorganized. There were guidelines to follow, though they weren't enforced. The idea behind the guidelines was to allow one winner to each group. The individual victors would proceed to the very center, where the final showdown would begin. However, the winners were free to go to an unfinished group and fight there if he or she wished to do so. Then, there would be a final four instead of five. It didn't matter. It was unlikely to have a final five simply because of the animals. They would be released one by one every three minutes.

The fat little historian informed them that there were a few battles in the past where no one was announced the victor because of the beasts. His advice was that the finalists should work together to kill the animals before proceeding to kill one another. Dorian couldn't have cared less. As long as he was the final one standing.

The opening of the gate and the eruption of excited screams from the crowd interrupted Dorian's workout. The emotion of the moment washed over him, but he forced himself to stay calm. Emotions, no matter what they were, lent themselves to disorganization and ineffectiveness. He could afford neither.

The organizers of the event sorted the groups by color-coded wristbands. He was blue. Dorian allowed himself to be ushered forward with the rest of the competitors. He allowed himself to let go of his moral hesitations. He allowed himself to let go of his humanity.

It would not aid him now.

///

Dorian's fight would be starting any minute. Our race would be a shorter event. The plan was to win, obviously, and then rush back to Rome. I would be prepared for a fight, if one was to come.

I'm betting on the fight.

Unfortunately, so am I.

Bronx would have communicated with us by now if nothing was going to happen.

I agree.

"Card?" an old male morkallian asked. He was seated behind a well-secured booth. Two menacing deeshies, cradling massive stun guns, flanked his booth as guards.

I handed him my keycard, identical to the one I gave to Dorian. He took it, jammed it into a machine, and when a pleasant *ding* sounded, his toothless mouth upturned into a disturbing smile.

"The race will begin in five minutes," he said, his raspy voice carrying a forced politeness. "Please be prompt. The Racing Moon waits for no one."

A booming announcement of the countdown echoed over the viewing center, causing the fans to cheer. I did my best to block out the noise, and walked to my racer. Kalista was in the copilot seat, a worried expression on her face.

Is she nervous?

Aren't you?

I don't get nervous, Cayden.

How would you describe your worry when I race?

I'm not worried. I'm . . . concerned that my existence will be snuffed out in a brief explosion.

Ah.

What?

You could have just said you're nervous.

That's what that is?

Yes.

Huh.

"Try not to worry too much," I said, climbing into the racer in front of her. "I know what I'm doing."

"I know you do," she said. "How long do these races usually take?"

"About fifteen to twenty minutes," I said, powering up Matilda and running the standard preflight diagnostics.

"All of these people are here to watch?" Kalista asked, craning her neck to view the audience behind us.

"To watch and to gamble," I said.

At least five thousand filled the crude bleachers. Even more were watching from their homes or expensive press boxes. Gigantic screens hovered in front of the crowded seats. Drone cameras would follow each racer, giving the audience, no matter where they were, a live view of each pilot.

Who would want to miss such fine entertainment?

"The competition looks fierce," Kalista said.

I glanced to my left. We were all the way on the right end, the last entrants into the competition. Twelve other racers were spaced apart on the track at five meter intervals. Each one had body panels and enclosed cockpits, hiding the pilots and their navigators from the prying eyes of their competitors. Multi-colored, mismatching, tacky advertisements covered their crafts from nose to tail.

So unoriginal.

It's a way to guarantee an income if you can't win the race.

Then are they actually racing to win?

No idea.

"Are any of them good?" Kalista asked.

"I don't recognize any of them," I said, revving Matilda's engine.

"None of them?" she asked.

"Nope."

Kalista sounded nervous. "I thought you would have known some of them."

Should you tell her that racers tend to have short life expectancies?

Probably not a good idea.

"Most racers don't stay in the game too long," I said. "If they get a few wins, they tend to retire early or take on safer occupations."

Well, that's one way of putting it.

A voice boomed over the speakers to announce the race would begin in two minutes. I took a deep breath that turned into a yawn. Some people threw up before the big moment. I yawned.

Hardly the strangest thing about you.

I just find it ironic.

"Are you tired?" Kalista asked, attempting to lean forward in her seat.

"I'm fine," I replied, stifling another yawn. "Do you remember what to do?"

"The map will become available as soon as the race begins," she said.

"And what will you do then?" I asked.

"Ignore it. Brace for acceleration," she recited.

"Good."

"Once I've acclimated to the speed, I'll try to find a course," she continued.

"And what do we want to avoid?" I asked.

"The other racers because they will either be on the safest course or the most dangerous."

"Excellent," I said. "Are you ready?"

The thunderous announcement called for the one minute mark. A floating clock, counting down from sixty seconds, appeared at the middle of the starting line. The racers around me fired their engines in earnest.

"As ready as I'll ever be," Kalista said, her voice somewhat breathless.

I turned on Matilda's shield generator, surrounding our vehicle in a barely visible, violet bubble that muffled the sound of the other racers' engines. I inched us to the very edge of the starting line as the clock ticked down to the thirty second mark.

"Cayden?" Kalista asked, her voice barely audible.

"Yes?"

"We're going to live, right?"

I smiled. "Oh, how we will."

19

JERRY took a regiment of twenty soldiers to the Edge by the order of Margaret. She didn't mention their tense confrontation, and neither did he. In fact, he looked completely at ease when she talked to him, if not a little entertained by her nervousness.

Madman.

The two surviving Betas weren't . . . normal. Margaret knew about Jerry's violent mood swings. She just didn't expected him to act them out on her since she was his superior in every way. Margaret was supposed to be untouchable. The GS gave her complete authority and autonomy.

The look in Jerry's eyes still made her stomach turn. He wanted to do it. He wanted to kill her. She realized at that very moment that he *liked* killing. If the GS turned him loose instead of Cayden, it would not have surprised her if Jerry became a serial killer.

Cayden, on the other hand, was nothing like Jerry. He never liked killing, and from the results she saw in the tests of the Betas, he only killed when necessary. But he won. Despite the early signs that he was one of the weaker candidates, Cayden always found a way to win.

Margaret studied both of their files to an extensive degree. Bronx was cunning enough to see that they were natural enemies. Jerry's obsessive nature made Cayden a target. Cayden's nonchalance only fueled the fire.

Jerry was the oldest of his litter. His parents made a deal with one of the many satellite operations the GS operated around the galaxy. An adoption facility took children from parents that didn't want them and gave them to waiting families. At least, that's what the parents thought.

First, strict genetic requirements were to be met. Once the genetic matches were made, the pregnant mother began receiving treatments to improve the child. The mother thought this was all normal procedure, of course. The adoption facility was state of the art. It functioned as a hospital that kept tight tabs on its contributing parents, and their "concern" helped sell the idea that the shots and extra medications were health benefits for the children and mothers.

Unknown to the parents, the fetus was receiving dangerous and experimental treatments from the earliest possible stages of pregnancy that affected a wide range of areas. Brain growth, intelligence levels, reaction times, nerve sensitivity, and such were all tampered with in an effort to improve the final product. Only seventeen percent of the children chosen to undergo the treatments made it to birth. Less than half survived the first two weeks after birth. After that, their likelihood of living improved.

The GS sent pairs of Actors to play the part of the adoptive couple, making sure to leave the donating mother no doubt that their child was going to be well taken care of. Once secured, the GS sent the infant back to headquarters to begin the true experimentation.

Both Cayden and Jerry came from the same adoption facility, only a week apart from one another. They seemed like they had been pitted against each other since birth. From the very beginning, they bickered with one another, and Bronx was wise enough to set the two up as rivals in their training. The natural competition between them might have produced a friendship if not for the external interference of the GS. Instead of friendship, hatred was born.

By the time the two entered puberty, they became bitter enemies. Jerry would always try to exploit Cayden's weaknesses with cruelty and theatrics. The GS could have stepped in to control the situation, but it became quite clear that Cayden's and Jerry's private war was driving them to become better.

Jerry was the more physically gifted of the two. He was stronger, faster, and superior in a fight. He would often use his physical superiority to try and punish Cayden. But Cayden was smart. Too smart for Jerry.

Cayden knew the long game was to win. Not every fight and small test required victory. Cayden's focus was to stay in position to win the war. Jerry, on the other hand, had tunnel vision, and his only goal was to hurt his rival. Cayden found ways to exploit this. Often, and sometimes to the detriment of his own health, Cayden would goad Jerry. Bait him into deeper waters.

Jerry fell for it every time. His shortsightedness would allow Cayden to emerge test after test the victor. It became clear that whatever Cayden lacked in raw physical talent, he more than made up for in the brains department. His strategic skills were unrivaled.

It would seem that Cayden was untouchable, the perfect protege for the GS. However, what attracted the GS to Jerry was his cold-blooded behavior. As the tests became more intricate, Jerry would enter Cayden's world knowing he would lose. Instead of trying to reverse this outcome, he abandoned it completely, opting for a different tactic.

Jerry told Bronx that he would only focus on hurting Cayden, competition be damned. He would even say what he was going to hurt.

It became impossible for Cayden to defend. Jerry would focus only on what he had in his mind. Break Cayden's wrist. Dislocate Cayden's shoulder. Crack Cayden's ribs. And though Cayden always won the competition, Jerry always succeeded in his goals. The single-minded obsessive drive of Jerry's actions won him many admirers, despite Bronx's disapproval.

The characteristics that made the GS despise Cayden were his free will, secretive nature, and inexplicable behaviors. Though she hated to admit it, Margaret knew the organization decided on Cayden's memory wipe and three year ban because they feared his potential. Compared to the appeal of Jerry, the dull instrument, Cayden's sharp mind made the GS nervous. No matter how much Bronx protested, the GS felt threatened.

Jerry was chosen over Cayden. However, due in large part to Bronx's insistence, the GS did not exterminate Cayden. Instead, they gave him one more test. One more chance to show what he could do. And this time, there would be no boundaries on his potential.

With their standard memory wipe, Cayden would wake up knowing his name, and the general attributes of his personality. He would know nothing of his past and nothing of the GS. It was a controlled amnesia, so as not to ruin the individual's potential.

Bronx volunteered to be the chief observer of Cayden. He was well known in the pirating business, and so it was easy for him slip into Cayden's life. The GS demoted Bronx because of Cayden's failure, but his performance, much like Cayden's, saved him from extermination. The organization felt he posed no threat by keeping track of his former protege, at least as long as he was observed and made regular reports on Cayden's progress.

Then, there was Neg'stella, one of their finest plants. Between Bronx, Neg'stella, and the multiple spies unknown to Cayden, very tight tabs were kept on his life. He'd done very well, though the organization didn't perceive one of their subjects ever living a life like the one he did.

Dorian was their greatest success and greatest failure. Dorian and Kalista were twins, and so the GS cultivated them both in hopes of breeding two great assets. Instead, they got one incredible asset, and one incredible pain.

Dorian excelled in every way imaginable. He became the ultimate assassin. The yookallan, Rymera, could only give him small challenges in his areas of expertise. But Dorian was their best talent. And unlike Jerry and Cayden, his personality showed no strange side effects. He was exactly what the GS was looking for. A specific, precise, and effective tool.

Kalista was a different story. While all of the injections and medications did affect her in some way before and after birth, the outcome was problematic. Instead of developing skills, she developed defects. Disabilities instead of abilities. Essentially, she became the opposite of Dorian. Every positive outcome of the organization's experimental methods was reaped upon Dorian, while Kalista received everything that was negative.

The only things that kept Kalista alive through the years were the abnormalities. She was a human lie detector. The GS was fascinated by the ability, but disappointed that she showed no other effects from the medications. They tried to correct her through additional medications as she aged, but they only weakened her more. And when they put her through the typical assassin training, she nearly died on several occasions.

Still, Kalista's telepathic abilities were enough of a curiosity to warrant further study. It turned out that detecting lies was not her only gift. Kalista was also quite sensitive to the emotions of people around her. From this, the GS found a useful role for her to fill.

Assets often experienced mental breakdowns. The GS had, of course, expected this, and they did their best to work around it. So, they allowed Kalista to become a counselor of sorts to the assets. She would know what they were going through, the emotions they were experiencing, and when they were lying.

Cayden talked to her more often than all the others, and the GS suspected that their relationship was growing romantic. Although Kalista was able to serve a small purpose, it also became evident that her presence contributed to some of Cayden's less desirable character traits. And after Cayden's expulsion from the GS, Kalista became more of a liability than a useful tool.

The only thing that stood against their plans to terminate Kalista was her much more valuable brother. Dorian's relationship with her was complex. From their extensive observations, the two of them did not seem close. Yet, Dorian did have a well-defined protective nature over his sister.

It was their own fault for trying to foster a bond between the twins. Basic biology and psychology prepped them to lean on one another. The GS encouraged this at first, hoping to reap a positive result. How could they have foreseen that the female would become so problematic?

Dorian was too valuable to lose, but Kalista was too useless, and perhaps dangerous, to keep. Her ability to detect the truth became more powerful as she aged. The GS had many secrets, and they preferred to keep it that way. Despite the low possibility of someone so weak doing them any real harm, the GS decided to play it as safe as possible.

It was supposed to be a fool-proof plan. With their advanced memory modification procedures, they would implant a fake memory in Kalista that would make her believe she was dying of a fast-acting brain cancer. It was a tricky operation to perform. They'd never done something so exact without modifying the whole memory of the subject. Trying to splice in a fake memory, while keeping her other memories in tact, was new ground. But, considering her value to be low, the GS decided the risk of experimentation would be worth it. If there were negative side effects, they could use their brain cancer story as a cover.

Everything seemed to work. Kalista's operation was performed without a hitch, though she lost much of her memory in the process. When Dorian questioned what was wrong with her, the GS used their brain cancer story as an explanation. Kalista needed an operation, but something went wrong. The GS convinced Dorian they were trying to save her life.

But Kalista knew. Despite her deteriorated mental state. Despite her weakness. She still knew.

"You're lying," she said.

They were lucky that Dorian didn't become violent. Belligerent. More so than he had ever been. They were able to calm him down by convincing him that she wasn't in her right mind. The brain cancer was affecting her abilities.

He bought the story, but for how long? An executive decision was made to wipe Dorian's memory and terminate Kalista immediately. The wipe would shelve Dorian for several months, but he would recover. It was an unfortunate, but necessary action.

By what appeared to be sheer luck, as Bronx was escorting Kalista to her death, they passed the memory-less Dorian. Margaret reviewed the security footage a hundred times. Dorian's face showed no recognition of Kalista. He almost didn't noticed her at all. But when she spoke, everything changed.

"They're going to kill me," she said.

Dorian took action too fast for anyone else to react. He killed two guards, dislocated Bronx's shoulder, and had a gun to his head in seven seconds. Using Bronx as a hostage, Dorian was able navigate his way through their facility to a small jump ship. Then, he and Kalista were gone.

The prize of the GS was gone.

Although the GS anticipated Kalista's memory wipe presenting complications, they could never have foreseen Dorian's actions. Margaret viewed the data from his memory modification. It was perfect. No mistakes. Why did he react to Kalista's voice?

It was a mystery, and the worst mistake in the history of the GS. Not only had they lost their most prized assassin, but when they attempted to recover him, they lost even more assets. Dorian killed three talented assassins and an entire squad of soldiers. All dead because of a weak, failed experiment that just so happened to be his sister.

Which is where Cayden came in. For three years, he was observed. And an entertaining show it was. The GS dropped him, unconscious, at a seedy motel at the Edge, on Rome, with nothing but the clothes on his back and the room paid for a night. Cayden did not waste any time.

His success in the fighting tournaments couldn't be ignored, though he only won enough to buy himself a ticket to the Racing Moon. Using a cheap rental, he won his first five races in as many days. With the money, he was able to lease a small apartment with a serviceable garage attached and afford a better rental racer.

All of Cayden's time was either spent on the track or in his garage. By the time competition number thirty came, Cayden emerged with his own hand-built, and quite recognizable, racer.

Bronx reported to the GS that he christened it as *Matilda*. With it, he went on to win every race but one, due to a mechanical failure.

It seemed, however, that after about six months of racing, Cayden grew bored. He searched for opportunities to join a pirating fleet. Recognizing a natural way to have Bronx enter Cayden's life, the GS allowed Bronx to make contact with one of his old pirating friends.

Bronx joined the crew as the second mate, and with his recommendation, they hired Cayden as a deckhand. Cayden stayed on for a year, illegally salvaging junk ships from planetary government docks and running drugs across the galaxy. During that year, Cayden elevated himself from mere deckhand to the rank of Captain.

Cayden struck a natural friendship with Bronx, which was exactly what the GS was hoping for. After his year-long contract expired, Cayden decided to leave the pirating life, and Bronx joined him. They were dropped off on the planet Deeshie.

Using a couple of Bronx's contacts, Cayden started his life as a professional mercenary. It didn't take long for him to build a reputation, and he was soon known as Cayden the Coyote. After very little time, he was taking jobs from only the highest paying clients.

While doing this, Cayden built an incredible ship. The GS was actually examining Cayden's blueprints so they could copy his work. They had no idea how he was able to construct it all by himself.

Cayden lived a more than impressive life. The possibilities spread before the organization when controlling a man who could do anything, were far too attractive. He was exactly what the GS wanted and needed. His work as a mercenary proved to them that he was the perfect candidate. It was what they were bred to do, and Cayden did it without flaw.

One final test was devised that would take care of all the organization's problems. Kill Dorian and Kalista. Not only would it prove to the GS that no bond remained between Cayden and Kalista, but it would also further prove that Cayden was their greatest success. Everyone they sent after Dorian died. If Cayden could beat their most talented assassin, he would be someone the GS could build their plans around.

Although they left the option to capture Dorian alive, they never expected him to do so. But before their excitement over his success could reach its peak, the GS learned he captured Kalista alive. It was a worrying development. What was he thinking? Why was he taking them to the Edge?

All of this was coming to a wonderful crescendo, with Margaret riding the wave. Cayden had Kalista and Dorian with him. So far, they'd heard nothing from him. The danger he posed with Dorian at his side was downright scary. Jerry wanted him dead, and now he possessed the go ahead from Margaret. But only if Cayden posed a threat.

Margaret got the funny feeling that Cayden somehow knew he was being tested. That he had a plan in place, and he wasn't going to reveal it until he was ready to make his move. That was what he was so good at. And if so, was she playing into it? Was she supposed to? Was Cayden trying to prove something?

Nine assassins, some of them the best of their litters, were about to converge on Dorian and take him out of the picture. Jerry and a squadron of soldiers were on their way to kill Kalista and secure Cayden. At least, they were supposed to secure Cayden. Margaret did not doubt the loyalty of her soldiers, but there was no predicting Jerry and his ego.

Margaret let out a small sigh and rubbed her neck. It was going to be an interesting day.

20

THE siren wailed a cold song across the stadium, and the battle began. Dorian's group of five included two other humans, one male and one female. A male deeshie and a female yookallan completed the number. They were positioned on the left side of the Coliseum, directly behind the chained lion. He hoped it would not be the first beast released.

All, including Dorian, were armed with the same weapons, save for the tank-sized deeshie. Instead of a short sword and shield, the deeshie carried a battle axe. The light blue colored weapons gleamed under the intense lighting of the stadium.

The human male to Dorian's right looked as if he'd never thrown a punch in his life, much less engaged in serious battle. He was terrified, sweat dripping from his long brown hair. In contrast, the blonde human female next to him looked quite capable of killing. The two of them turned on one another, ready to fight. Dorian picked the woman to win.

The yookallan female held her stance like a warrior, but she stepped back to watch Dorian and the deeshie battle. Dorian made it quite clear with his body language and hard stare that he wanted the deeshie first. It would be a quick, good example of his skill. Kill the biggest and most intimidating.

The sound of metal against metal sounded to his right as the human man and woman entered battle. The stadium erupted in cheers as the five groups everywhere began their quest for survival. A roar sounded from the deeshie's bloated throat, and he charged Dorian, his axe pulled back far behind his thick, yellow head.

During battle, Dorian possessed a sort of premonition. Despite his hampered memory, Dorian knew about his fighting foresight like he knew his ability to run ten kilometers in thirty minutes. It was just something he could do. And that premonition was telling him the axe was going to swing down and across in an attempt to cut him from his left shoulder through to his right hip.

Most would have ducked or jumped back. Dorian charged, leaning forward instead of ducking down. The axe *whooshed* by his head as he ran past, missing only by inches. Dorian's sword came up and slashed hard against the arm that he ran under, cutting deep into the muscle that connected the pectoral to the shoulder. Greenish-black blood splashed warm against his face as the sword broke free from flesh.

Dorian turned around, rushing to finish the job. His counter disabled the deeshie's muscles in his right arm, and the alien was therefore unable to lift his weapon. The massive deeshie wasn't able to turn around before Dorian was on top of him. Leaving his feet, he planted his knees on the shoulder blades of his hunched adversary, and stabbed to sever the spinal cord from the brain stem. The deeshie died immediately, falling to the ground. Maintaining his balance, Dorian extended his legs so that he was standing on top of his foe. He was careful to observe the three fighters that remained.

The yookallan stood three meters away, ready and content for him to make the first move after seeing his ability to counter. He glanced at the other two, and his prediction was correct. The woman was too experienced for her foe.

173

Her male enemy was lying flat on his back. He appeared to be dazed, no doubt the after effect of being knocked in the skull by a shield. The woman wore a vicious smile as she sat astride his waist. She plunged her sword directly into his heart. Because of the specific placement of her blow, it only took a second or so for him to die. She was quick to get up, holding her weapon towards Dorian.

The two warrior women were on either side of him, and both appeared to want to terminate him before taking each other on. After all, he was the one who killed the only formidable opponent in their group so far. Dorian was ready to kill more.

The human female charged, screaming like a banshee, and swung for his head. Dorian used his shield to block and spun behind her so that he could face the two head on. The yookallan rushed towards him, no doubt hoping to catch him off guard by her sudden offensive.

Weapon met weapon over their heads, and Dorian used his shield to bash forward into her gut. She stumbled back, stunned by the blow, but not injured. Now the human female charged again. Dorian spun around to gain momentum and kicked hard into the yookallan's midsection. She flew backward off her feet, just as the human female pressed forward. The human's sword thrust towards Dorian's midsection.

He sidestepped and swept upward with his weapon in a manner that betrayed the speed with which he moved. Her arm was lopped off a few inches below the elbow. Before there was time for her to scream, Dorian carried his sword from an upward motion to a downward one, relieving the woman's head from her shoulders. The corpse collapsed to the ground as the yookallan warrior recovered.

"Dorian" was being chanted from the crowd in his section of the stadium. He'd underestimated the power a crowd held over the people whom performed for them. Hearing his name being cheered was invigorating.

The yookallan woman stood ready, waiting for Dorian's attack. He didn't disappoint her. The tiger was the first to be released, and busy bothering the group across from them. The other three animals were still chained, and Dorian made a quick scan of the Coliseum to confirm it was just the two of them within their area. He could let her live now.

Dorian's sword swung for her neck, and the yookallan leaned back out of the way. Before she could attack, his blade came back for another pass, but her shield intercepted it. At the same time, she lunged with her weapon, aiming for his heart. It was exactly the attack he wanted. He swept his shield sideways so that it hit the inside of her extended arm, and its motion caught the butt of her sword, sending it flying from her grip.

The shock of losing her weapon so quickly allowed him to slide his sword over her shield and bring it down in a brutal plunge. The blade buried itself in her torso, just above and to the left of her lung, but below the shoulder. It was an effective enough wound to take her out of the battle, but not enough to kill her anytime soon. A grunt of pain proceeded from her lips as he pulled his weapon from her flesh. She collapsed to the ground, and it was no secret that she was giving up the fight.

Dorian knelt beside her, and she closed her eyes, waiting for her impending doom. "Put pressure on the wound, and you may survive long enough to get to a medic."

He twirled the short sword in his hand, taking off at full speed for the group across from his being harassed by the tiger. The sound of a chain releasing preceded by a roar quickened his steps.

The lion was free and hot on his heels.

///

Rymera watched in fascination as Dorian demolished his group. She almost missed watching him. Every time she did, she sharpened and honed her own skills. There was no doubt in her mind that if not for her rival, she would be half the fighter she turned out to be. Dorian pushed her to greatness.

All eight of Rymera's companions were at strategic points among the crowd of the Coliseum. They were going to strike after the competition ended for two specific reasons. First, it was entirely possible that Dorian could be killed in the battle, and there was no sense in bypassing the wisdom of patience. It would take an enormous stroke of luck, but it was possible. The other reason was that if he won, he would be exhausted after the present ordeal and more vulnerable to attack. Rymera didn't see how it was conceivable that one man could escape nine heavily armed assassins ready for battle, but she wouldn't underestimate his raw talent. Dorian was capable of pulling off amazing stunts, and if she wasn't sharp, he would continue to do so.

Rymera's fingers slipped across the hilt of the sword at her waist. It was an ancient weapon, first formed by a group of warriors known as the Samurai from the human world. It was called a katana, and it was a favorite of Rymera's. She'd made adjustments to it, of course, so that it was a more formidable weapon, even against guns.

There was a light purple glow about the blade because of the plasma-echo infusion the was crafted into it. If it was swung with any significant force behind it, an echo of the blade would fly in that direction, giving the weapon an effective distance and a most confusing attribute. The plasma echo was sharper than any metal, and it could

176

travel up to ten meters before dissipating.

It was with this blade that Rymera would kill Dorian. She knew, even with her superior weapon, that he could possibly defeat her. There were no odds, no percentages, and no capable ways of knowing who would come out on top. That was the beauty of fighting to the death. You could be as prepared, trained, and talented as possible, and you would still be as vulnerable to a lethal attack as anyone else.

Rymera wanted to take that chance with Dorian. If he died by another hand, she could deal with it in time. But if the opportunity to do something legendary arose, what kind of coward would turn down that chance? He was her rival, the one who always beat her, and if not for a combination of unlikely events, he would have been the organization's lead assassin.

The opportunity to prove once and for all that she was indeed the best was presented to her on a silver platter. The true time came for her to step out. Only those who were afraid of making history would back away.

If she died, then she died.

21

THE most exhilarating part of the race was the very beginning. It mirrored the effect of some drugs on the market. A high that rushed you to its peak with such intensity that all you could do was hold on. That high was upon us, and I was ready. My guest, however, was shaking like a leaf caught in a hurricane.

Is she shaking or seizing?

"You doing okay back there, Kalista?" I asked, as the countdown hit the twenty-second mark.

"I'm f-fine," she said.

"Don't bite your tongue," I said. Ten seconds remained. "And maybe close your eyes."

I hate this part.

Perhaps you should close your eyes, too.

Don't be ridiculous. I have no eyes.

I'd been here before. Watching that clock tick to zero nearly a hundred times. My left hand, tight on the accelerator, retained muscle memory from this.

Two seconds.

Matilda growled with the pent-up impatience of a hunting dog, and I sympathized. It had been far too long. Adrenaline was coursing through my veins, my heart was racing, and my lungs were pumping. I was born for this. For this moment.

The clock struck zero and at the same instant a great horn sounded throughout the stadium, loud enough to be heard through Matilda's shield. My left hand thrust the accelerator forward, and we roared into the race.

Kalista's shriek of terror and my scream of exhilaration combined to form a short symphony of opposites. Our velocity plastered me to my seat, and we, along with the eleven other racers, quickly reached top speed.

I took the front position, as I always did in the past. Racers were required to have speed caps to ensure fair competition, but there were no such restrictions on initial acceleration. Matilda was a work of genius engineering, and I had yet to encounter another racer that could beat her off the starting line.

The first stretch of track was wide and free of obstacles. I switched on the comm system, and I could instantly hear Kalista's panicked breathing in my right ear.

"Hey, are you okay back there?" I asked. We weren't able to hear one another without the headsets.

She didn't answer, but her breathing continued unabated, so I knew she was alive. I checked Matilda's gauges, ensuring that everything was in proper condition. So far, she was responding as well as I could have imagined.

Why do you refer to your machines with feminine names?

Perhaps the echoes of a more chauvinistic era cloud my vision.

You don't refer to me in a feminine context.

You're not a machine.

I'm not?

"This . . . is . . . so . . . fast," Kalista said, her voice crackling loud in my right ear.

"You'd better get used to it," I said. "We've only got a few more kilometers before starting the first obstacle course. Why don't you try bringing up your map?"

"Okay," she said, and I heard her maneuvering the tablet in front of her. "I've got it."

"Good. Can you see the other racers?"

After a moment, she responded. "Yes."

"Do you remember what to do?" I asked.

"We want a different path than the ones they take," she said.

"Excellent," I said. "I suggest you find it quick. We don't have a lot of time left."

"Okay," she said, and I could hear the worry in her voice despite the poor quality of speaker in my ear.

"Don't worry," I said. "We're going to be fine. It's going to be a lot of fun."

"Okay," Kalista said. She did not sound convinced.

Am I not a machine? And if I'm not, then what am I?

Not now, Coyote.

///

Jerry breathed deep. He wanted to savor the smell of the air. The taste of it. Could he smell Cayden in that air? Kalista? Though it was impossible from this distance, he liked to believe he could. Yes, he could smell them. Could smell the romance, and it made him want to tear into flesh. Any flesh would do. Something alive and warm. Something he could sink his teeth into.

Jerry wanted to hurt Cayden. He wanted to make him suffer. He always wanted this, and there was no point in denying his obsession. He hated the bastard. Everything about him.

The emphatic roar of the surrounding crowd shook him out of his reverie. The race began, and Jerry watched as Cayden and Kalista disappeared down the track.

Let them have their fun. It would be the last time they would have such an experience together. The more they enjoyed it, the more hope they would have. And then, he would feast on that hope as he killed them both. Slowly. Painfully. He would take his time with them and savor every drop of blood.

"Sir, should we move to the finish line?"

Jerry turned to see the captain of the regiment that accompanied him. The GS was a complicated organization, and they created many uses for a diversity of people. The captain was raised as a soldier from birth, just as the other men and women with him. They were simple gun hands, whose loyalty and bravery couldn't be matched. Good for missions like this. They didn't question, they didn't think, and they didn't have dreams or aspirations. During action, the regiment would act as one living organism, following his commands.

"Yes, I do believe so," Jerry said, standing from his seat in the bleachers and stretching.

"Will we set up our attack there?" the captain asked. Jerry couldn't remember his name. Frank? Fred? No, no, no. It started with a "F", though. He knew that much.

"No. I alone will be responsible for killing them. I need you and your squadron to chase them to the docks, where I will be waiting at Cayden's ship," Jerry said. "It's Francis, isn't it?"

"Reginald, sir," the captain said, unfazed by Jerry's incorrect guess. "And how should we chase them, sir?"

Jerry smiled. "Let them collect their winnings after the race, Reginald. Make yourselves visible. He'll figure it out from there. All you'll need to do is chase him, and the rest will take care of itself. Don't kill him or the girl."

"No guns, then?" the captain asked.

Jerry gave the captain a startled look. "And why wouldn't you want your guns?"

Reginald looked confused. "You want them alive, yes?"

Jerry laughed, his voice loud and mocking. "I love the confidence, Reginald, but don't be an idiot. You'll need your guns to get him to the docks."

Reginald did not look pleased, but said nothing back to Jerry. He placed the back of his wrist to his mouth and whispered several commands. He gave Jerry a respectful nod of salute, but Jerry laughed at him more.

"Just make sure you funnel him back to his ship, Reginald," Jerry called as the soldier walked away. "Don't fail me on this, or I'll have to find new ways to laugh at you."

Jerry wanted to be at the start of the race to ensure that the ever so tricky Coyote wouldn't try anything too crafty. It should have been safe to assume he had no clue Jerry was present on the Racing Moon. But that was only what the naked eye revealed. A life pitted against Cayden taught him the senses were stubborn things.

What appeared to be never was. Not with Cayden.

22

THE growling of the lion hot at his heels didn't deter Dorian. What he was planning would require perfect timing. Because when the lion let out a particularly vicious growl after being released, the tiger's attention shifted. The striped cat ran toward him at full speed, his yellow eyes intent not on Dorian, but on its feline cousin.

Dorian pumped his legs as hard as he could, his focus on the two warriors that remained in the group across from his. One was a hulking deeshie wielding a mace, and the other, a lanky morkallian, armed with the ever popular sword and shield. The two of them were working together to fight off the tiger, but now they turned their eyes toward the speeding Dorian.

If two more seconds passed, the lion would have sunk its teeth into Dorian's neck. But the tiger pounced in one. Dorian ducked under the tiger's leap, and the two beasts collided with what sounded like bone-crushing force. As the cats rolled, a part of one of them caught the back of Dorian's leg. He stumbled in his run as he neared the mace-wielding deeshie.

The alien let out a roar almost as vicious as the lion's, and swung down with his hulking weapon, intending to crush his human opponent's skull. Dorian dove, throwing his shield over his head, and spread his legs. The mace hit the ground between his lower limbs as the momentum of his leap carried him to safety. By pulling his legs up, he was able to slide onto his knees, and then move his shield out of the way. Dorian's sword shot upward in a perfectly placed thrust that pierced the deeshie's heart.

After dumping the monstrous being off him and retrieving his weapon from the deeshie's chest, Dorian faced his next opponent. The morkallian charged, and Dorian saw an opportunity.

With a powerful heave, he swung his left arm and released the shield. The defensive weapon proved quite offensive as it spun like a discus and made heavy contact with his enemy. The morkallian raised his shield in time to deflect the blow, but it was the surprise that Dorian was looking for. As shield hit shield, it created an opening, and he threw his sword the moment that opening presented itself. The weapon spun through the air and buried itself into the throat of his opponent. The morkallian crumpled into a dying heap, blue blood gushing from his mouth and the vicious wound beneath it.

Dorian jogged, and ripped his weapon out of the flesh of his dying enemy. He turned only to come face to face with the yellow eyes of the tiger. A quick glance past the beast, a mere five meters away, revealed a dead lion. The tiger must have caught the lion by surprise, and used its powerful bite to break the cat's neck. Dorian was hoping for a little more time.

The bloody muzzle of the beast growled at him, and there was little damage to it that could be seen. Dorian's sword was at the ready, but his shield was at least ten meters to his left. The tiger appeared content to walk a slow circle around him, perhaps wondering how it would kill him without harming itself. The crowd cheered loud, and Dorian could still hear chants of his name.

Two groups were still fighting on the opposite side of the stadium. Only two beings remained in the right group, and three in the left. The center group was finished, with a yookallan male standing tall as the sole survivor. He was watching Dorian's encounter with the tiger with what appeared to be mild entertainment. The sound of a chain breaking far behind him caught his attention. The troll-like eschule was released, and it lumbered toward the left group of three. The yookallan was safe, and the tiger remained Dorian's only problem.

He was forced to think fast. The big cat growled low in its throat. It stopped prowling, and instead crouched low, yellow eyes focused only on Dorian. It was ready to spring.

Dorian did exactly what one wasn't supposed to do when facing a mean, angry, hungry predator. He ran. As fast as his feet would carry him, he ran and switched from holding the sword in his right to gripping it with his left. The tiger sprinted after him, and Dorian kept his head turned to watch its progress. It would have him in no time, and he was counting on its natural inclinations to become an advantage.

Pounce. Come on, pounce.

It did just that. With about four meters between them, the cat pounced. Its front legs extended, claws clearly visible as it reached for its prey. Dorian planted his feet and turned to face his much larger enemy. Everything happened in an instant.

Simultaneously, Dorian hooked his weaponless right arm around the extended front left leg of the cat and thrust with the sword in his other hand. The weapon plunged between the cat's two forelegs, going through the chest cavity. The claws of the tiger's free paw dug in behind his left shoulder, colliding two hundred kilograms of muscle and fur with about eighty or so of human flesh.

The impact was dizzying, and the two combatants tumbled to the Coliseum floor. The tiger was as dead, and Dorian still drew breath. He was lying on his back, and consciousness was loose within his grasp. He could feel vibrations in the floor. Each shake grew in intensity. Adrenaline pumped through Dorian's body as he realized what the vibrations were.

A lone figure was nearly on top of him. The sole survivor of the center group. The male yookallan sprung into action, trying to take Dorian out at the opportune time. Reinvigorated, Dorian got to his feet and jumped back to avoid the first sword swing, but his own weapon was stuck in the chest of the tiger.

The yookallan pressed his advantage. His blade swung sideways, down, up, then sideways again in well-executed slashes. Dorian stayed a step ahead by ducking and sidestepping to avoid the blue-tinted metal. The yookallan was good and left little room for an opening.

His enemy advanced with precise attacks, and Dorian moved backward, aiming where he wanted to go. After a failed attempt at decapitation, Dorian ducked and used the opportunity to dive into the arms of the dead, mace-wielding deeshie. His opponent charged, as he anticipated. Dorian jumped to his feet, swinging upward with his newly acquired mace.

The yookallan barely avoided losing his chin from the upper-cut motion of the heavy weapon, and Dorian continued his attack. If he halted his momentum, the yookallan could once again return to offense. His opponent's weapon was lighter and easier to handle, but Dorian used the energy of each swing to continue new attacks. He swept across, up, and down, continuing to gain speed and accuracy every time. Their roles were now reversed, with Dorian performing well-practiced sweeps with his mace, and the yookallan forced to duck, dive, and dodge out of the way. Trying to block such a weapon with a short sword was foolish, and he showed no confidence in his shield.

Finally, the yookallan made a mistake and the mace collided with his right shoulder. The impact was accompanied by a crunching sound. The yookallan was a lefty, so his sword was still in hand, but the shield dropped from his grip.

Dorian's foe grunted with pain as he attempted a last ditch effort to win the face-off. He lunged, but Dorian already dropped the mace and grabbed the sword-wielding arm of his enemy. With expert motion, he lifted the arm, then twisted it with his hand planted at the elbow. The limb snapped, releasing the weapon into Dorian's hand, and he swept over and down to sever the yookallan's head before he could feel an ounce more pain.

Blood splattered his torso as the headless warrior collapsed to the ground. Dorian took a moment to breathe. The sting of the tiger's claws on his left shoulder blade sang with renewed vigor. The scratches were deep. Not deep enough to affect muscle movement, but enough to cause pain to shoot through his body with each motion. Pain he could deal with. Muscle damage he could not.

The crowd was louder than ever, and the stadium was cheering his name. It was an intoxicating feeling that threatened his calm, but Dorian beat its pull through willpower. It was water, and he was oil. He needed to stay as cold and calculated as possible.

After collecting his shield, Dorian marched, moving toward the center of the Coliseum. The eschule was stalking the left group of gladiators. Before the beast approached the group, there were three fighters. Two remained. A bloody and grotesquely broken body was near them, and Dorian assumed the corpse was the victim of the eschule's enormous strength. The two that remained in the right group were moving toward the left, no doubt planning to assist in killing the eschule before each other.

The rayh'va was still chained, but as Dorian decided to move back, the animal was released. Dorian was now nearest to the beast, and it scuttled toward him like a lizard. Its long snout was open, and a horrendous hissing sound escaped from its throat. To complement the maw full of teeth and feet full of claws, the tail was curled with the stinger pointed at Dorian.

He raised his sword and shield, ready to kill again.

23

SPEED was my home. Everything about racing enthralled me. The difference one second could make, the quick instinct that told me to turn left instead of right, the rush of adrenaline that fueled my reflexes, the freedom I had with my own life, the exhilaration of moving this fast over a hard and unforgiving surface. All of it. It was all part of what made it home for me.

Truly, you are insane, Cayden.

You would know.

I was familiar with the race track. Each major race was unique, but there was always a familiar pattern. Every track was made up of three sections. A Tube Chute, an abandoned city, and the barren surface of the Racing Moon itself. The order of the three sections was always random, and each presented unique challenges.

As we rounded a soft corner, I could see the first section of course would be the city. Wide streets, ancient moon-dust covered vehicles, and crumbling skyscrapers stretched for kilometers. Once, a long time ago, it had been a real city. After a long forgotten war, it was abandoned. The overseers of the Racing Moon took advantage of its somewhat solid condition to use it as a unique track.

There were no rules on how to get through the city, but the map Kalista was reading would highlight both the safe and more dangerous courses. If one was daring, as I had been on a few occasions, one could abandon the map and forge an uncharted path.

"Take the left trail!" Kalista shouted, as my earpiece crackled from the volume.

"No yelling," I said.

"Sorry," came the quiet response.

I didn't ask why we were going left, or why she thought that it was the best way. As we neared the first course, the other racers leaned off to the right or stayed straight, and we alone went left.

That's what we wanted, right?

Well, I thought there would be one or two racers that followed me.

Since none did, is that bad?

Maybe.

How bad?

Nothing I can't handle.

We entered the first course, streaking by empty metal containers, old rusted vehicles, and damaged ships. Soon, we would be flying through the abandoned city, cramming ourselves between gigantic buildings and old train ways that once served as public transport.

"This path is just as short as the others," Kalista said. "But there are less turns, and no one was going this way. That's what you wanted, right?"

There was a sinking feeling in the pit of my stomach. Why didn't I remember? The one thing I needed to remember, and I completely forgot.

What is it?

"Right, Cayden?" Kalista asked again.

"Is there a flashing red light at the end of our path on your map screen?" I asked.

"Yes," she said. "But you didn't say anything about flashing lights. All the other paths had flashing yellow lights, and this one has a red light. What does it mean?"

"Ramp," I said, as I swerved to the right to avoid colliding with an ancient vehicle.

Ramp?

Big ramp.

"Ramp?" she asked, echoing the Coyote.

"Big ramp," I said.

Wait . . . which ramp?

You know which one.

The End-Maker.

The one and only.

"How big of a ramp?" Kalista asked, her voice filled with worry.

"Don't worry," I said, bending my arm awkwardly to pat her knee. "I've jumped it before."

Once.

We lived.

By sheer luck.

Each plotted course through the city ended with a ramp, which would propel you into the next course. However, there was one ramp more famous than all the others. One responsible for hundreds of deaths.

It was nicknamed the "End-Maker" a long time ago. Only three pilots survived her, and I was one of them. And though the Coyote's statement about luck was inaccurate, I never planned on testing the End-Maker again.

Because no one has survived a second attempt?

No one has tried twice.

I manipulated the controls, avoiding a plethora of obstacles at an incredulous speed. If we did survive the flight, we would comfortably be in first place. Our course allowed me to push Matilda to her limits because there were no harsh turns to worry about. Just large objects that would obliterate us if we made contact with them, instead of smaller, more subtle obstacles capable of catching a pilot by surprise.

After dodging a pile of concrete that once was a part of a building, the End-Maker came into view. It was enormous, and there was no escaping it. It was as wide as the street we were racing along, at least forty meters high, and with a nasty upward curve at the end that assured whatever vehicle it propelled would fly high.

"That's the ramp?" Kalista asked, her voice shrill.

"That's it," I said.

The problem with the End-Maker was that it launched racers too high. The ramps on the other paths did not not have this problem, because the hover spheres on the bottom of the racers would be able to "catch" the craft before it hit the ground. Unfortunately, the End-Maker's immense height did not allow for this.

You have a plan?

I'm liking the look of that building to the right of us.

You mean the building with a vertical surface that will do nothing to safely deposit us to the ground?

I'm thinking it will.

How?

Theoretically, the hover spheres will help.

The hover technology affixed to the bottom of my racer worked in two ways. It used anti-gravity principles to repel the vehicle from the ground, but it also employed electron adhesion to keep the racer attached to whatever surface it was on. This was so that in the micro-gravity of the moon, the racer wouldn't float away from the surface. If that surface was a vertical building, then the hover spheres should let me adhere to it, despite the artificial gravity of the abandoned city trying to pull me down.

Theoretically.

You've got a better idea?

I wish I did.

So do I.

"This is crazy," Kalista said.

"No," I said, "this is racing."

"Racing is crazy," she retorted.

Can't argue with that.

I probably shouldn't.

I punched the accelerator to its maximum limits, and we gained speed at a steady rate. The obstacles we dodged thinned out as the distance between the End-Maker and us shrank.

Why do unnecessary risks always get added to our plans?

No one lives forever, Coyote.

Speak for yourself.

"Cayden . . ." Kalista said, her voice weak and panicked.

"Take a deep breath," I said. "We're going to survive this."

We were at max speed, as the very base of the ramp changed our position from flat to angled. I aimed Matilda toward the sky-scraper.

This is going to work.

I hope so.

24

RAYH'VAS were notoriously hard to kill. With the tiger's marks stinging his back and the exhaustion nipping at his heels, Dorian decided it
was best not to fight the rayh'va face to face, but to enact a new strategy.

The eschule was a hulking, lumbering beast. A thick hide and
devastating strength were its allies. The four competitors left in the
tournament were holding it off, stabbing with spears and swords but
only succeeding in angering the animal. Idiots. If any of them were
smart, they would use two to distract it, and the other two to go for its
throat. Luckily for Dorian, they weren't smart.

He ran as fast as he could, breathing heavy. The exertion of
the tournament was taking its tole. The rayh'va chased after him with
a hiss. The lizard-like creature wasn't nearly as fast as the lion or
tiger. The animal's legs were designed for climbing, so they possessed
no lethal leap, and their strange waddle of a run reduced their speed.

However, the rayh'va had one very redeeming quality about
them. They feared nothing. Whether it was a man with a gun, or a
hulking eschule four times its size, they never backed down from a
fight. Unlike most predators from other worlds, the rayh'va also contained no respect for other hunters, and fought anything they saw, no
matter the odds. This fearlessness gave them an advantage over
even the largest enemies.

As Dorian neared the eschule, its back turned to him, he once more threw his shield like a discus. The weapon struck the beast in the back of the head. It was a blow that would have knocked out just about anything, even a large deeshie, but it merely caught the attention of the eschule. As it lumbered around, it swept its hand sideways in order to catch Dorian, but he proved too fast. Instead, it caught the rayh'va, which by the sound of it, was all too happy to change its attack target.

Vicious hissing mixed with deep roaring as the two beasts tore into one another, but Dorian didn't bother to see which was winning. Instead, he took advantage of the momentary shock the other four contestants were showing and charged. The nearest target was a slack-jawed human male with a spear.

Dorian jumped with a battle cry, and the startled human thrust his weapon in an attempt to impale Dorian, but the move was sloppy. Dorian turned sideways in the air, allowing the shaft of the spear to brush past his abdomen. With a circular motion of his right arm, he swung down hard with the sword and split the skull of his opponent.

Continuing to take advantage of the surprise, he left his weapon buried in the head of enemy, and instead, picked up the spear. Aiming only for moment, he threw the weapon at the unprepared morkallian female across from him. The spear impacted itself into the middle of her chest, and the force of the projectile knocked her off her feet. The male deeshie and female yookallan that remained turned to him, their weapons ready.

The surprise was over, but they wouldn't dare attack him, even though Dorian was weaponless at the moment. Keeping his eyes trained on them, and glancing toward the eschule and rayh'va as well, he unhinged his sword from the skull of the human.

Dorian kept his distance, as did the other two. They stood about seven paces away from one another. The deeshie and yookallan were the elite of the group. While making his surprise attack, he noticed that both of them stayed alert the entire time.

It didn't need to be said that the fighting between the combatants would wait until the beasts were finished with one another. They watched as the troll-like eschule and lizard-like rayh'va battled it out. There was already a lot of blood, all of it coming from the eschule.

The rayh'va was fast and relentless, climbing the much bigger eschule like a tree. It was biting, scratching, and stinging with its vicious tail. The eschule was trying to grab the lethal pest, but every time it reached with its hands, the lizard beast would bite its fingers. In fact, the eschule was already missing a couple of them.

The enormous arms of the eschule were swinging in desperation, but the swift rayh'va clamped its jaws onto the eschule's throat, stabbing mercilessly into its torso with its stinging tail. Just as it appeared the three competitors would be facing the quick and lethal rayh'va, the eschule made one final move.

Perhaps, the lumbering eschule knew it was losing the fight. Perhaps, it knew it was dying. Without hesitation, it grabbed the rayh'va by the back of the neck, pulling it off itself, ripping out a large chunk from its own throat in the process. Blood spilled from the gaping wound, but neither that nor the scratching claws or stinging tail of the rayh'va deterred the eschule from its intent. With a loud and broken roar, it slammed the furry lizard face first into the ground, crushing its skull in that single blow.

The eschule stood upright for a moment, and then stumbled to the ground, dying from its many wounds. The rayh'va twitched wildly, but it was as dead as all the other beasts and beings on the ground of the Coliseum.

Dorian, the mace-wielding deeshie, and the female yookallan all stared at one another as the crowd cheered in an uproarious fervor. The deeshie pointed towards the center of the chamber, and each of them began their short journey to the destination.

As they walked, Dorian took a chance to scan the crowd. To the right, seated on the front row of the crowd, he found someone. Dorian's heart raced.

Staring back at him, waving with an evil smile lighting her face, was someone he recognized. He didn't know who she was, but if it was a face that his memory was blocking, then it was a dangerous one. A quick look around confirmed that she brought help with her. They were easy to spot. They were the only people that weren't showing any emotion. And they were all staring at him.

Cayden betrayed him.

///

Rymera relished in the surprised look on Dorian's face. The color in his face drained the moment he saw her. She couldn't stop the smile that spread across her face as she watched her nemesis walk to the center of the Coliseum, preparing to kill the two competitors that remained.

"He has seen us," one of her comrades spoke over the comm unit.

"Relax," Rymera said. "He has nowhere to go, no way of escaping, and no one to trust anymore. We have beaten him already."

"When should we enter the ring?" another asked.

"As soon as the fight is over," she said. "But remember, I battle him first. If I lose, be sure to kill him."

"The wound he has sustained doesn't seem to be slowing him

down," yet another said. His tone carried worry.

"It's a surface wound," she said, rolling her eyes. "Don't you people know who you are dealing with? Dorian is the best fighter to come out of our organization. You're supposed to be impressed."

"How do we know you haven't led us to our deaths?" one asked.

Rymera sighed loud enough for the sound to be carried over the comm units. It was always this way. Dorian was the best, more impressive than any other competitor. Those who were in awe of him were blinded by their admiration.

"You have guns, you idiot," she shot back. "Shoot him if he kills me. Is he impressive enough to be bulletproof?"

25

MATILDA rocketed up the long ramp, and I braced myself for the feeling of what would feel like angry, steroid-induced butterflies in my stomach.

I hope this works.

So do I.

We flew off the ramp, which angled sharply upward toward the end, traveling just shy of our limit of six hundred kilometers per hour. The sudden loss of a solid surface beneath our vehicle could be felt in the gut-wrenching shudder that rocked my racer. The only thing between us and the ground was the building I was going to use to get us out of this mess.

Your trajectory looks good. Start tilting.

Our airborne flight only lasted a few seconds, but that felt long enough. I fired a thruster for a moment, angling the racer sideways, as we made contact with the skyscraper.

What would you call this?

Surfing?

Thanks to our trajectory and mid-air realignment, Matilda was "surfing" along the side of the building. A combination of our forward momentum and the hover sphere's adhesion fought off gravity's downward pull.

Kalista screamed. I couldn't blame her. It was intense. Each glass pane we passed, burst from the pressure of our hover spheres. Matilda rocked dangerously with each rupture, and I needed to keep us moving at full speed to avoid plummeting to our deaths. Unfortunately, the end of the building was fast approaching.

The railing, down and out fifty meters. Punch it, and we'll be able to stick the landing.

I didn't pause to think. I didn't doubt. As soon as I visually confirmed the distance of the railing, I went for it. It was an old public transport system that used to carry trolleys through the interior of the once great city. It was wide enough to accommodate Matilda's girth.

It's going to be close, but it will work.

I know.

"Cayden, what are you . . ." Kalista began, but she didn't have time to finish.

"Hang on!" I shouted, gritting my teeth.

Angling Matilda's nose toward the rail, I pushed the accelerator to its max, and we once again became airborne. I fired the thruster with more vigor this to time to level us out. My stomach lurched as we fell, but as we picked up significant downward speed, Matilda came in contact with the railing.

The hover spheres groaned under the pressure, and the bottom of Matilda scraped into the metal surface of the railing, but we made it unscathed. Our velocity carried us forward, and I turned hard to avoid flying off the rail.

We're still too high to make a drop to the ground.

Racers could handle jumps and drops, but if the height was too high for the hover spheres to make an effective catch, then they would crash and burn. I needed to find a low point for us to leave the railing and get back on course.

"Is this taking us in the right direction?" I asked.

"What?" Kalista said, her voice full of shock and confusion.

"The map, Kalista," I said.

"Oh. Yes, we're still on course. And we're ahead of the competition."

I maintained our velocity, but was cautious on the sharp turns as the railing wound its way through the dilapidated metropolis. Despite my near reckless speed, I was not traveling fast enough to stay ahead of the other pilots for long.

There's a boarding station ahead.

That going to have to work.

That stairway looks awfully thin.

I was thinking the same thing, but I didn't voice it. It had to work. Because after the station, the rail took a sharp turn upward, which would only increase our predicament.

"This might get tight," I said.

"Just get us back to the ground," Kalista said, sounding exasperated.

I believe she's had enough of this adventure.

We're not even through the first course yet.

Why do you level complaints at me? She's your girlfriend.

I slowed us down, which was not my preference, but I needed time to adjust our trajectory through the stairwell. Two sturdy walls were on either side of the staircase, and Matilda was going to fit with less than a meter of room to spare.

The shields aren't going to like it.

I know.

The truth was, the shields were going to be damaged by the maneuver, but there was no other option. Racer shields would flex before breaking, but not without putting an uncomfortable strain on the shield generator. We would be temporarily traveling with weakened shields, and would need to remain vigilant of even the slightest danger until they regained their strength.

I pulled us off the rail, and for a brief moment, we raced along the flat flooring of the boarding station, but the staircase was upon us within a second. A strangled cry escaped from Kalista's mouth as I guided us like a speeding missile between the formidable walls surrounding the stairs.

Electric blue light danced in front of us as the shields groaned like a wounded animal, compressing against the steel of the walls. I smelled a sickly sweet odor from the shield generator as we made a quick descent, but it was all over in a moment. We shot from the staircase like a bullet, safely back on the ground once again.

"Straight ahead," Kalista said, and I could hear her taking deep breaths over the headset. "Course two is straight ahead."

I could see it. The Tube Chute. We were in perfect position. Our path would take us straight into the tunnel without a need to turn. We would be able to make our approach at full speed.

"Where are the others?" I asked.

I could hear her fingers fiddle with the map screen as she checked the locations of the other racers. "They're a lot closer now. We're about even with their approach."

"No, they're going to have to slow down," I said.

We were approaching from the west, while our competition jostled for position from the east. They would have to either slow down or make a long loop in order to enter the Tube Chute. Unless they were suicidal.

One of them is suicidal.

It sure as hell looks like it.

While most of the pilots slowed to make the turn without incident, one broke away from the pack, racing ahead at full speed.

There was a difference between boldness and stupidity.

If you don't slow down, you may get caught in the explosion.

If I slow down, then I'll bottleneck with the other racers and there might be more explosions. I have to try and beat him.

Your shields are still weakened.

No real choice here, Coyote.

"Are we going to collide?" Kalista asked.

"No," I said. "But we might get scorched up bit."

"Scorched?" she asked. "As in burned?"

"Yeah. The jackass racing us to the entrance isn't going to make that turn, and whoever is piloting is going to explode," I said.

A spectacular explosion.

Indeed.

I pushed the accelerator to the limit, and we once again capped on our speed. We were ahead of the aforementioned jackass by a hair. He or she wasn't backing off their suicide mission. We would cross the threshold into the Tube Chute in twenty seconds.

"Is this ever going to get easier?" Kalista asked.

"I never said racing was easy," I replied, my muscles tensing for the explosion to come.

///

Cayden's ship was parked near an exit. Not a surprising maneuver. Jerry's first move was to block him in. He parked his dull-looking freighter catercorner behind Cayden's. Despite this maneuver, Jerry knew that Cayden may still get away. He always could surprise.

Always.

Humility was not Jerry's forte, but he had to admit that Cayden might know exactly what he was doing. All of Jerry's plans could already be accounted for by Cayden. Jerry knew this was a strong possibility, but he didn't care. He was here to kill Cayden. And if not kill, then maim him so he could kill him later.

A pistol twirled in Jerry's hand as he paced back and forth on the dock. The silence surrounded him like a blanket, and he could hear every little move, from the echoing sounds of his steps to the low hum of the generator by the left wall. The shine of Cayden's ship and the dull magenta color of his angered Jerry. Actually, everything about Cayden, near him, or even related to him angered Jerry.

That part of his personality would forever remain with him as long as Cayden drew breath. The hate that drove him took over. There was no denying it, fighting it, wishing it away, or hoping for a life-altering event to save him from it. It was part of him now. It was his heart.

Jerry did not consider himself philosophical, and perhaps someone who cared to think deeper on such matters, would question the hatred. Jerry did not want to question it. He liked it. He wanted it. He needed it.

Everyone needed a drive. A reason to live. And destroying Cayden was Jerry's purpose. He simply had to do it. Was it destiny? Maybe. Was it his deepest desire? Yes.

Jerry wanted Cayden's blood more than he wanted life. More than sex, food, or friendship. He wanted to feel Cayden's beating heart in his hand, and he wanted to bite into it. To rip it to shreds.

Jerry placed the barrel of the pistol behind his right ear and scratched an annoying itch. His finger played with the trigger while the end of the gun pointed at his skull. He applied a light pressure, teetering on the edge of pulling it all the way.

He thought about suicide on many occasions. Perhaps one

day, he would ponder the action again. After he ripped Cayden's heart apart. Maybe then.

26

THERE was a role for Bronx to play. Cayden had plans for him, just as Bronx had plans for Cayden. Bronx, of course, was aware of Cayden's plans. He knew what his protege was after, what he wanted, and his plan to get it.

He knew Cayden's weakness.

Bronx was a complicated man. He didn't like to be thought of as a pawn by anyone. But he knew when to take on the pawn's duties, and Cayden's game gave him ample opportunity to disguise himself in such a base role. A more prideful man would have thought such illusions beneath himself. But pride was a powerful man's worst weakness. The only weakness that ever defeated such men.

Bronx would not be such a fool. He could play the part for as long as necessary in Cayden's plans. As long as they didn't interfere with his own, because he did have plans for Cayden. Many, many plans.

Their paths were intertwined in knots that could not be undone. Bronx made sure of it. Cayden was his greatest accomplishment, and he was meant for great things.

He took Cayden under his wing and guided him through the years. Bronx would visit the boy when unfriendly eyes weren't watching, just to talk. He became a father figure of sorts, and so he earned the trust of Cayden at an early age. It required hard work, but Bronx was successful in this first phase.

"A man like you needs a new coat," a sleazy looking human dealer said. Unidentifiable crumbs were trapped in the scraggly hairs of his beard.

"No," Bronx said, passing him by without pause.

"Sir," said the seller, and he reached out his right hand.

A tourist would think the hand was reaching for his arm, but Bronx knew better. He felt the man's hand tap his elbow, and then felt it slide into his jacket, toward his wallet.

Bronx's reaction was without hesitation. Grabbing the seller's hand, he twisted the outreaching arm hard. Before the man could scream in pain, Bronx's free hand punched the criminal's throat.

The seller choked as he tried to inhale. Bronx did not bother to do anything further and walked away, leaving the gasping scum behind. Rome always proved to be an interesting visit.

In his youth, Bronx traveled the galaxy, and during that time, he wore many masks. Conman. Pirate. Mercenary. Philosophy professor. Scientist. Operations manager. Hell, he lived on Rome for over two years and fought his way to a small fortune as a young man. But he never found his equal.

Never.

People were stupid. Even the smart ones. They were subject to petty emotions that made them easy to manipulate. They lacked ambition, commitment, and vision. They struggled with the vague concepts and misconceptions of ethics and morality.

But not Cayden. He was different, and just as Bronx intended him to be. If one could find no equal, then one was forced into the position of making an equal. So that's what Bronx did.

The Betas were supposed to be his equals, but such daring plans were never perfect. Bronx knew the margin for error was great, and that he indeed might fail on all fronts. But, with no other option left, there was little to lose.

Jerry became a psychopath, and the others succumbed to the wasteful competition the GS implemented after their obvious dissatisfaction with the experiment. Bronx didn't much care for the GS and its obsession with what it deemed to be power, but he did respect their ruthlessness. Most did not have the willpower needed to act as they did.

But the GS was blinded by delusions of their own making. They desired universal domination. An ambitious idea, though not an original one. With every culture and subculture in the galaxy there was a history of desiring total rule. It was an evolutionary byproduct shared by all dominant beings that helped to propel them to the top of the food chain.

Not only was Bronx not interested in allowing himself to follow such base instincts, but he also knew they were impossible goals to achieve. It wasn't a matter of determination or intelligence. Universal domination would never work. It never worked before in any history of any people, no matter the time period.

"Hot sandwich, sir?" a yookallan girl no older than eleven said, holding up a platter of square-shaped food.

Bronx ignored her, continuing on his way toward the Coliseum. The roar of the crowd grew louder as he approached. Rome never disappointed. The blood lust here was so primal that it was hard not to get caught up in it.

Of course, some of his affinity for the place came from finding Cayden here after his memory was erased. It was a good moment. It was the first time Bronx realized he succeeded.

He created his equal.

When the GS, to the great dismay of Bronx, gave Cayden the

memory wipe and sent him on his way, Bronx followed. He convinced his superiors to allow him to be one of the pawns in Cayden's life. After all, they concluded that Cayden was his failure. They allowed the fallen man to make a miracle effort to clean up his mess.

Cayden made his start in the Edge, competing in some of the fighting and racing tournaments. He earned money fast and became a superstar in the racing world.

Bronx watched him for a few weeks, and it didn't take long for him to realize the memory wipe hadn't worked on Cayden. Though he wanted to make his presence known as soon as he discovered this, Bronx exercised patience. It would've looked suspicious for him to make contact so early.

He allowed a few weeks to pass, only observing and reporting his findings, before sending the young man a cryptic message that contained instructions on how to meet in secret. Their meeting took place at a spaceport between Rome and the Racing Moon at a crowded bar. When he sat across from Cayden, Bronx knew his suspicions were correct.

Cayden remembered nearly everything. A few holes in his recollection of events remained, but Bronx updated him. It worked.

Bronx staged the game.

He could still remember the exultation washing over him as Cayden outlined his intentions. Finally, Bronx could begin what he set out to do. It was like he had been whittling away at a sculpture for over two decades and was finally showing it at an art show.

Formulating his plans around Cayden's plans was easy. Cayden was ambitious and determined. He wanted to build a name, make strategic contacts, and establish a career. All of that would allow him to amass a decent amount of money, purchase weapons, hone his skills, and even build a ship. It would mean years before getting to spring his real plan into action. Only the most dedicated would take his path.

Bronx created a worthy opponent. One with the will to do what was necessary. But even though Cayden showed all the promise in the world, he was still holding onto the pathetic strings most people grasped for. Romance, happiness, peace.

Delusions of the idealist.

Bronx strolled through the entrance of the Coliseum, breathing the air in deep. He competed in this very same tournament, long ago, in another life. He won, of course, but not without paying a price. He'd nearly bled out from his wounds.

He still pondered whether or not it was a mistake to enter the competition. Being young, bold, and overconfident led to a six-day stay in the hospital, and a permanent pain in his right knee. But it secured him a lot of money and valuable experience.

Sometimes, there was a price for following your ambitions. Bronx learned that. Cayden would, too.

27

I'D been in a lot of close calls before. There was an exhilaration to near-death experiences that couldn't be replicated in any other way. The feeling of your stomach disappearing, your heart beating so fast it felt like it stopped. Nothing else like it.

These are feelings I'd rather you avoid. Why must you almost die to feel alive?

Kalista's shrill scream pierced my ears as we entered the Tube Chute in front of the suicidal pilot. Our angle allowed us to jump into the course unimpeded, and we kept our speed at maximum. The unfortunate soul that almost collided with us did not have the same fate.

The pilot was green. He didn't slow down one bit upon his entrance to the second course, perhaps thinking the angled walls of the Tube Chute would propel his momentum sideways. But the hover spheres wouldn't be able to handle his speed. He might as well have taken a nosedive off the building we skated across.

We were so close to the concussive blast that I felt it in my chest. And with our shields still weak, the heat wave of the explosion washed over us. Large chunks of shrapnel flew by, with one fiery piece landing in my path. I jerked Matilda out of the way, and then we were clear. The heat dissipated, and the sound of wreckage became distant.

"Are you okay?" I asked into the comm set.

There was no response, but I could hear her quick, shuddering breaths. I performed a silent five-count in my head to calm myself. She was probably just in shock.

Names often snap people out of these types of moments. Try saying her name.

"Kalista," I said.

No response.

Louder.

"Kalista!" I shouted.

"Yes?"

"Are you okay?"

"Yes," she said. "How are you?"

"Did anything hit you?" I asked, ignoring her question. "Are you bleeding anywhere?"

I heard her shuffling around, which put me at ease. Moving was always a good thing, and the fact that she was responding to my questions was encouraging.

"No, I'm okay," she said. "Are you okay?"

I smiled. "I'm fine, thanks. Listen, don't fixate on the lights in here. They will disorient you, and I need you to plot our course for the final stage."

The Tube Chute was quite literally a tube. It was like being on the inside of a giant, curving straw. Strobe lights lined the floor, walls, and ceiling in twisting patterns. If one wasn't careful, one could begin to follow those patterns into a very dangerous spin.

The Tube Chute itself appeared to be the safest course in the race. There were no obstacles to avoid or ramps to jump. The purpose was to disorient the racers. Many a pilot would spin inside the tube without knowing it, and upon exit, they would crash and burn because they couldn't adjust their racer in time.

"What does the third course look like?" I asked.

"How are you not getting dizzy?" Kalista asked.

"I keep my eyes focused on a point ahead," I said. "And I ignore all of the lights. If you follow them, you'll get vertigo. What does the third course look like?"

Instead of a worded response, I heard something to the effect of *urgh* come through my headset. She must have been staring at the lights.

Vomiting would not be constructive to what we're trying to accomplish here.

"Keep your eyes locked on the map screen," I said. "Just focus on that, and you'll be fine."

"Okay," Kalista said, her voice shaky.

"How far ahead of the competition are we?" I asked.

"Six seconds," she said. "And it looks like two other pilots are out of the race."

Excellent.

"Indeed," I said.

"What?" Kalista asked.

"The third course," I said, ignoring her query. "What do the available paths looks like?"

I could hear the tapping of her fingers on the map screen, pulling up the information. Sometimes, it was hard to remember not to respond to the Coyote out loud, especially when I was holding a conversation with someone in real life.

I'm not a real life person?

No, that's not what I meant.

Please explain, then.

Really? You're going to get a bruised ego now?

"There are three paths," Kalista said. "One to the left, one to the right, and one straight ahead."

"What color are the paths on your map?" I asked.

"The one straight ahead is red, and the other two are yellow," she said.

If I'm not real life, then what am I?

Can we do this some other time, please?

"Red is our path," I said.

"What does red mean?" she asked.

"It means it's the fastest way," I said.

And?

"The most dangerous, as well," I said.

"And that's . . . good?" Kalista asked.

I banked the racer to the left as the tunnel shifted to the right. I didn't necessarily want to take the most dangerous path, but the other pilots were going to get desperate as the race came to a close. I would need to take whatever steps necessary to keep my lead.

"We're about to find out," I said.

///

It was impossible the group of assassins found them without Cayden's help. Dorian and Kalista were hidden better with the mercenary than they ever were by themselves, and yet within one day, they were trapped. Cayden betrayed them.

He killed them.

Dorian didn't need to know how. How and why were not important. Only the result mattered. Dorian made the wrong choice in trusting Cayden. He should have killed him when he had the chance, because now, the odds were stacked against him.

He would have to take his time and think of something. Or

perhaps just take enough time to see if Cayden would show his face. Dorian would only need a minute to dispose of him. Then, at least, he could obtain vengeance.

The yookallan and deeshie stood ready at the center, as did he. He was left solely with the short sword. With the throbbing wounds from the tiger on his shoulder, wielding the shield would be more problematic than beneficial. Dorian would not let this hinder him.

He was going to use his speed to kill the deeshie and his superior strength to kill the yookallan. He was capable of ending them within two minutes. But doing that would only accelerate his own death. He needed to extend the fight while also doing his best to conserve energy.

Dorian took a deep breath as the deeshie charged him with a guttural roar.

///

"What a lovely day," a deep voice said, close to Rymera's ear. "A good day to die, I think."

"Bronx," Rymera said, gritting her teeth in anger.

His presence was not a good sign. He wasn't supposed to know her location, and even though she couldn't perceive any immediate threat by his arrival, she knew he was there for a purpose. The man didn't do random.

Rymera was no Beta, but that didn't mean Bronx wasn't an infection in her life. He was an integral part in all of their lives, though the Betas bore the worst of his . . . insanity. He was a genius, no doubt. But an insane genius.

"Still believe you can kill Dorian, I see," Bronx said. "I'm sure it's a lovely thought for you. A delusional thought, but a lovely one."

Rymera didn't look at him. Some of her comrades stirred once they realized Bronx was present, but they didn't move from their posts. Her eyes remained on Dorian, who was employing only evasive techniques to avoid the attacks of his two final opponents.

"I would ask why you are here, but I have no doubt that you would lie to me," she said.

"Very good, Rymera," Bronx said, his voice dripping with sarcasm. "You should use that deductive reasoning more often. It could have saved your life and all the others you've brought. The GS will lose many assets today."

"I don't care if I die. Our mission will still succeed," she said.

"Well, of course *you* are going to die," Bronx said. "Instead of just shooting Dorian, you're going to try and fight him. That's because you're an idiot. And idiots like you die. But that's no reason to have all of these other assets die with you."

Rymera did not take her eyes from Dorian. "What are you talking about?"

"What about Cayden?" Bronx asked.

"Jerry is taking care of Cayden," Rymera said.

"Yes, I'm sure that will work out well," Bronx said.

"Cayden doesn't know we are here," Rymera said. "He doesn't know Jerry is here."

Bronx let out an exasperated sigh. "When has Jerry ever controlled him? When has Jerry ever overcome Cayden?"

"This is different."

"Oh, it's always different, and it's always special," Bronx said. "This time, we have him. This time, he can't get away. This time, he won't succeed. So while you and all the others blindly believe in your pathetic excuse for a plan, he takes full advantage of the elements you've given him."

Rymera still kept her eyes on Dorian. Bronx would not distract her. "We've given him nothing. He can't possibly win."

"You've trapped yourselves," Bronx said. "When Cayden gets here, and he will get here, he will have you right where he wants you. You have no escape route, no plan for an evacuation or a retreat. Tunnel vision is your problem. You've served yourself and your comrades on a silver platter."

"You give him too much credit," she said. "Cayden is flawed."

"But acting like he's not is the only way to beat him," Bronx said. "At least for someone in your position. Or Jerry's. If you were to assume he has no weaknesses, then you would drastically even the playing field. Instead, you believe everything you see, like a pathetic child. You allow Cayden to fool you."

Rymera reached her limit. Her patience only stretched so far. She stood, and in one smooth motion pulled the echo sword from the hilt at her side. She brought it within six inches of Bronx's neck and held it there, the violet glow of its echo lighting his face.

"Leave," she said. "Now."

It was unnerving to watch Bronx not so much as flinch as he stared back at her. A smile spread across his broad face, and he laughed in the most mocking way possible. His expression showed no worry. No anxiety. It was as if he knew she would unsheathe her weapon the entire time.

Rymera hated him.

"You are so pathetic," he said, standing up. "So predictable. So . . . disappointing."

"Leave!" Rymera shouted.

Bronx walked away. "Count every breath, Rymera. You don't have many left."

28

THE exit was the trickiest part. And choosing the hardest course was going to make it trickier. But if I was going to stay ahead, I didn't have a choice.

"If I'm reading this right, the path you want to take has an immediate drop," Kalista said.

"Yep," I said. I recognized the strategy of the course builders.

A pinprick of blue light could be seen at the end of the tunnel. It was increasing in size and intensity with each passing second. Our exit.

"Shouldn't you be slowing down?" she asked.

"Afraid not," I said. "I have a plan, though."

"Yes, but it's a *really* steep drop," she said.

It is really steep, Cayden.

I don't need you taking her side.

"You're going to have to start trusting me," I said.

The end of the tunnel was only seconds away. I pointed us upward so that we glided across the ceiling of the tunnel. We would need to exit the course upside-down to accomplish our next trick.

"I do trust you, Cayden," Kalista said, her voice soft.

I let a smile spread across my face. We shot out of the Tube Chute like a missile, and I fired the thrusters with full force as I pointed our nose straight down. The shift in gravity became immediately apparent, as the third course comprised of very little. It caused my stomach to lurch.

The safer pathways split on either side like the two outer prongs of a fork, while my course plunged straight down like a freaking middle finger. To complicate matters, rocky arches lined the path, which would force us into a tight tunnel. Unlike the tunnel of the second course, however, there would be no room for me to maneuver to the side or upside-down. I would have to keep us on the straight and narrow.

The good news was that this path allowed us to drop directly down the cliff face, dumping us onto the main part of the final course much quicker than the safer, less steep paths. Those made a more peaceful climb down the cliff, though much slower.

The third course was given a nickname by the racers. The Nature Walk. Quite simply, the third course was the raw surface of the Racing Moon. There was no more artificial gravity, no more atmosphere resisting the racer's momentum, and creepily enough, no sound.

Creative course placement allowed the designers of the races to move courses one and two around, which meant the final course was never the same. I had yet to see a landscape I ever recognized, despite my many races.

I heard Kalista make an unintelligible sound as we plummeted straight down, narrowly fitting our vehicle through the archways. Without atmosphere, Matilda would be able to reach full speed in a short amount of time.

"Are you doing okay back there?" I asked, my hands white-knuckled on the controls.

"Mmm," was all she replied.

I believe she's focused on not vomiting.

"We're almost through," I said. "The final stretch is actually the easiest part of the race."

I didn't slow down, despite our significant lead. We were at the point of the race when pilots grew desperate. The final course was the safest from a technical standpoint, but more pilots crashed on this course than on the other two combined.

Never underestimate the desperate.

"Here we go," I said, more to myself than to Kalista.

The deadly arches disappeared, and we evened out onto the surface of the moon. I could hear Kalista breathing easier over the headset, and I allowed myself to join her for a moment. As far as obstacles and difficulty of the course went, we were through the worst of it. Now, it was a three-minute race to the finish.

"Is something wrong with his racer?" Kalista asked.

I glanced behind us, and saw an erratic pilot gaining on us fast. He was barely managing to get his vehicle out of the way of the avoidable rock outcroppings on the moon's surface. And he was accelerating at an incredible rate.

That's fast.

That's because he's using illegal boosters.

For shame.

"He's going to pass us," Kalista said.

"He's going to crash," I said.

The problem with the illegal boosters was that they overrode the grav-spheres' ability to keep the vehicle grounded. And with the near zero-g of the third course, the boosters shot the racer around like a runaway rocket.

I banked to the right, giving the desperate racer a wide berth, but its erratic movement kept us within dangerous reach. As I went around a large outcropping, he managed to catch up to me by going around the other side. As we both emerged from the obstacle, he pulled ahead, but was listing lethally to one side.

Kalista gasped in horror as he ran full force into a smaller column of rock. Both the racer and the rock exploded with the unique violence that only raw velocity could deliver. I swerved to the left as the mangled metal of what used to be the cockpit bounced past us, and Matilda's shield resisted the smaller chunks of rock that would have otherwise pelted us.

"Okay," I said. "It's over now."

"Are you sure?" Kalista asked, her voice breathless.

"Do any of the other racers look like they're gaining on us?" I asked.

She took a moment. "No."

"Then we're free and clear," I said. "No one else is going to risk using boosters. Not after that."

"So, we won?" she asked.

"In sixty seconds, yes," I said, swerving out of the way of a large boulder. The finish line was visible now. "Do me a favor?"

"What is it?" Kalista asked.

"Don't get out of the racer when we stop," I said. "Don't even unfasten your safety restraints."

"Why?" she asked. "What's going to happen?"

"I just have a hunch we won't be hanging around for long."

///

Kalista's head was spinning, even as Cayden brought the racer to a full halt beyond the finish line. A large crowd of people were cheering from the stands. She didn't realize until then that they completed a giant loop and were back where they started.

Cayden unbuckled and exited the racer, striding toward a short, fat deeshie announcing them as the winners to the crowd. Kalista stayed in the vehicle, just as Cayden wished. She was learning to go along with what he said. He seemed to know what he was doing quite well, even though she still felt lost.

Certain people were built to play games. Kalista knew that, and she knew Cayden was one of them. Dorian, even; at least to some extent. What her brother lacked in raw strategic skills, he made up for in physical ability and desire for survival. Both of them were built for intensity.

Kalista was not like them. She wanted nothing more than peace. Somewhere, among all of the chartered stars, was a planet with the home she'd dreamed of for so many years. On that planet, there was a petite cottage, weathered by the spray of the beating ocean. Inside was a simple kitchen and small table for four. Old furniture, creaking wooden floors, and the sound of waves crashing onto a pristine beach completed the atmosphere.

Kalista longed for that place. If she were to spend the rest of her days there, she would die with a happiness she couldn't presently imagine. Kalista held no ambitions, no desires for power or money, no need for revenge. Just a wish for a peaceful, uneventful life.

She would wake up in the morning and make breakfast for her husband and two children. They would take long walks on the beach together and fish along the shoreline for lunch. There were smiles. She would smile until her face hurt. Her husband would smile at her, she would smile at him. Their two children would laugh more than they would talk, and Kalista would laugh with them.

Was Cayden that husband? No. He couldn't be. It wasn't who he was, and she knew that. The husband she dreamed of would appear boring to him. He would have a normal job, devote himself to his children and wife, and his personal time would be spent on a non-descript hobby. Kalista's husband would make love to her in a gentle manner, perhaps even with a color-by-numbers approach. But he would satisfy her, and she him.

Cayden couldn't be that. He was a man of passion. Of action. Kalista bore no ill will toward him about this. He was always that way, and whatever part of him that could have been average died long ago in order to survive. Cayden couldn't work a normal job, or raise children, or put down roots in any one location. He lived his life on the edge of a sword, and it was the only way he knew how to live.

Kalista wiped away a tear. There was something odd about her and Cayden. She knew it the moment they finished kissing, and she'd been trying to figure it out ever since. It felt real, but there was something dishonest. She couldn't remember what it was. Every time she thought about it, all she could see was the outline of a wide-shouldered man sitting across from her, his countenance hidden by shadow. He would speak, but it sounded like incoherent babbling, as if he were speaking through a cloth.

Despite this, Kalista carried strong and true feelings for Cayden. She felt something like love toward him, but it could not compare to the passion with which he seemed to have for her. Kalista did find herself smiling at the thought of him making a joke. When he kissed her, she felt butterflies in her stomach. She wanted him, and she knew that he wanted her.

But was that love? They bonded over their shared situation, but did she really love him? Could she ever imagine being with him, escaping death every day by the skin of their teeth? Could a unifying trauma be the foundation for anyone's love?

And why did she feel guilty by the very thought? What was it that held her back? Who was the outlined man in shadow? What was he saying?

Cayden finished his business with the stocky deeshie and was walking back to her, the corners of his mouth tugged upward in a rueful grin. Kalista focused on his gray eyes as they met hers. She blocked the noise of the crowd from her mind, ignoring the movements of everyone else, and forced herself to only look at him. Did she love him? Could she love him?

No. No, she did not, and she could not.

Would it be fair to let him continue risking his life to save someone who couldn't be what he so obviously thought? She was beginning to realize that Cayden's plan was the result of years of dedication. He was risking everything. For her.

Because he was in love with her. Despite his attempts at self-control, she knew he was slipping. He was smiling at her more, and appeared to be upset that he allowed himself to kiss her. It didn't take much effort on Kalista's part to accomplish the kiss. She simply invited it, allowing him to back away at any moment, but he dove forward with the passion of a long-lost lover.

Kalista felt the emotion begging to burst from him, and then felt the abrupt determined halt. He was hell bent on staying focused. Why? Because he knew his plan was built upon years of hard work to accomplish one goal.

She was that goal. Kalista understood now. How could she do that to him? If she truly cared for him, which she did, how could she let him risk everything in an attempt to be with her? How could she let him continue believing she would ever be able to return his love?

Kalista could not. She would not. After they linked back up with Dorian, she would tell Cayden everything she knew and everything she felt. He deserved to know. He deserved a chance to look for happiness elsewhere and with someone who could return the love that she was not capable of giving. And whatever the consequences were, she would face them with a clear conscience.

She allowed the rest of the world's stimuli back in, and was surprised at what she saw. Behind Cayden were two men, clad in sleek gray armor, holding large assault weapons level with Cayden's back. Kalista recognized them instantly as soldiers from the GS. She was about to cry out, but Cayden, still facing her, held up a finger to his lips as a gesture of silence.

The motion caused Kalista to pause long enough for the commander to issue a loud order for Cayden to turn around. Cayden moved with extraordinary speed.

She didn't realize he already retrieved his pistol from its holster before the soldier shouted. He spun, firing two shots, before either of his foes could react.

Cayden's aim was lethal. Both soldiers dropped, sprays of blood and brain matter flying from the back of their heads. The crowd erupted into a panic, and Cayden rushed back to the racer.

From her left, a gun fired in rapid succession from the middle of the clamoring crowd. At least ten more soldiers were trying to fight their way through the panicked throngs of people.

"I think it's time to go," Cayden said, jumping into the pilot's seat. "Don't worry, Matilda's shields won't let their bullets through."

"How did you know they were going to be there?" Kalista asked, as Cayden buckled himself back in.

"I'm a wonderful chess player," he said. "We'll have to play a game sometime. Let's get out of here."

Kalista sighed in frustration. It was always about games. Her whole life was a game. She was tired of games.

29

JERRY'S comm unit crackled to life. Two reasons for this. First, was the captain of his team was calling to inform him the race ended. Or second, he was successfully chasing Cayden into their trap.

Instead, he received panic.

"He's heading straight for you on the racer! I repeat! He's heading for you on the racer!"

The voice was loud, and he could tell they were trying to chase him on foot. Of course, he hadn't thought to give the soldiers an available transport in case something like that happened. Of course, he never factored in the option of his foe using the racer to his advantage. Of course, Cayden outsmarted him and destroyed his plan in one swift motion. Of course, he was going to get away.

Jerry rushed to the docking bay doors, his pistol in hand. Running, one could make it to the docking bay in five minutes from where Cayden and the soldiers were. Flying at hundreds of kilometers per hour on a racer, such a time would have to be reduced to seconds.

He wasn't even able to make it to the doors before Cayden and his love blasted through. Jerry squeezed off a shot, but the bullet ricocheted off the racer's shields as if it were a stone thrown at a well.

"Damn it!" he screamed.

Cayden blew by him in an instant, racing for his ship, and the sleek machine's ramp was already open. He must have owned a remote. Jerry wanted to sabotage the ship, but Cayden installed an advanced security system unit. A strong electric current shocked whatever touched it, even the tracking devices he tried applying.

And just like that, Cayden was gone. In his ship and locked away, safe from harm. Jerry stood still, seething with the familiar rage his foe brought out in him. The chameleon-painted vehicle rose from the docking bay floor, its engines roaring to life. Instead of turning to fly out of the transparent shield that separated the bay from space, he flew around the ship blocking his path.

Jerry's ship.

A plasma mine lobbed from one of the launchers, and as soon as it made contact with the magenta metal of Jerry's mode of transport, it exploded. He ducked, then ran from the fiery debris. He made for the docking bay doors before Cayden could decide to turn towards him and fire.

"Get to the public transports!" Jerry yelled into the comm, moving as fast as his feet would carry him. "I know where he's going. If you get there before me, commandeer one and wait."

"Yes, sir."

///

"Dorian," Kalista said, her voice panicked. "They'll be after Dorian."

"I know," I said, guiding the ship through the watery shield that kept the harsh vacuum of space at bay. "It's going to be all right."

I set our course for Rome, checked the sensors for any pursuing ships, and did my best to calm my beating heart. The turning point of my plan was getting close. Very, very close.

"Are you sure?" Kalista asked.

It wasn't until I looked at her face that I realized how much Kalista cared for Dorian. Her usual soft features were now hard with stress, and her warm hazel eyes were now cold with panic.

"Yes," I said. "I knew they were going to be there. Don't worry. Dorian will be fine. I'm going to take care of it."

After placing the ship on autopilot, I readjusted and gave her my full attention. Kalista, the love of my life, was looking at me like I was a stranger. Her gaze was apprehensive, almost fearful.

"I'd do anything for you," I said. "I've waited all this time. I'm not going to let your brother die."

"Anything?" Kalista asked.

She knelt down in front of me, placing both of her hands on mine. Her touch felt like a drug, and I wanted nothing more than to take her right then and there.

"Do you really mean that?" she asked, her eyes staring into mine, unflinching.

"Yes, Kalista."

"I want you to remember that," she said. "When things get really bad, when you are at your lowest. Remember, you would do anything for me."

"What are you talking about?" I asked. "What do you think is going to happen?"

"Just remember that," she said, her face showing frustration and impatience. "Remember that you would do anything for me. Anything, Cayden."

///

Dorian's fight lasted a solid ten minutes. The large deeshie was marked with a few wounds, but he was still fighting. The yookallan female showed a gash on her right thigh, just above the knee, but it didn't slow her down much. They were tough warriors, but Dorian was responsible for both of their wounds, and was free of any marks himself, save for the claws of the tiger.

Dorian held no desire to kill either of his foes, but they were not the type of warriors who were willing to give up. He would do what he needed to in order to win. His plan to wait wasn't working so far. Nothing changed. The assassins still patiently observed him, and he was only growing more fatigued.

Kalista told him about Rymera, which must have been the one that waved at him with a sick smile on her face. His sister carried mixed memories, but she remembered the competition between the yookallan assassin and him with stark clarity. According to his twin, they were similar in skill, and if that was so, Dorian would need his energy to put up a fight. If he was going to die, he was not going to do so quietly.

The deeshie charged him again, swinging his mace sideways. Dorian made the decision to end the battle and move on to his awaiting doom. He ducked under the weapon and scooted past the larger fighter. The yookallan female met him with a sword-thrust as the deeshie recovered from his powerful swing. The bigger alien stumbled, giving Dorian some time to do battle with the female fighter.

He blocked with his sword and returned her strike with a plethora of his own. Metal crashed against metal with increasing frequency. Dorian was catching them by surprise. His caution during battle was what they were used to, but he abandoned it for a more aggressive attack. He was toying with them, primarily fighting through counters and other defensive methods. The new surprise maneuvers outwitted the yookallan, and his offensive was quicker than she anticipated.

Dorian's sword caught her hand, lopping it off. He then spun and thrust the weapon into her belly. The footsteps of the deeshie were getting close, and he saw the muscle-bound alien heaving his weapon over his head in an attempt to crush them both.

Once again, Dorian proved too quick and too fearless. Most, even a seasoned warrior, would have moved, but he held his ground. Yanking his sword out of the yookallan, he thrust upward at the same moment, stabbing under the chin of his massive opponent and into his brain. The monstrous-sized warrior died immediately, releasing his weapon and falling to the ground with a powerful thud. The yookallan joined him a second later.

It was over that quick. The crowd erupted into maniacal screams, but before the officials could declare him the winner, he saw the assassins descending into the Coliseum all around him. Nine in all, armed and ready to introduce Dorian to Death. There was no chance for him to emerge victorious, not while they surrounded him with their weapons.

The only thing left to do was fight. Though his memories of the people who controlled him were gone, Dorian could understand his personality just fine. He wondered about a good death. Was there a way to die with honor? The question was one that went unanswered, and he knew that it would forever be so. Still, he would use all of his strength to find it.

He located Rymera, walking calmly with some sort of one-edged sword in hand. Dorian stripped himself of armor and tattered shirt, knowing that it would only impede his movement. No armor was going to help against guns or what appeared to be a plasma-echo blade.

Dorian walked to her. To his death, with or without honor.

30

THE soldiers did their job by the time Jerry reached them. There was a small crowd of disgruntled citizens of a variety of races at the public transport station, but Jerry didn't care about their happiness. His soldiers were on board the slow ship, prepping it for take off. Two stood guard, guns pointed at the entrance to keep people back.

Security officers were there already, standing between the crowd of people and the soldiers. Their guns had been taken away, obviously, but they were still attempting to do their jobs. Poor idiots thought they were noble.

As he walked through the crowd and toward the awaiting transport, one of security officers reached out to stop him in a pitiful attempt at protection. Jerry leveled his gun and shot him between the eyes. The crowd screamed, chaos ensued, and the smell of death hung in the air. Jerry's spirits were lifted.

He straightened his expensive black trench coat and continued walking, feeling more like himself. The soldiers parted enough for Jerry to pass through their ranks, and then filed into the transport after him. None of them said a word, not even the captain, as Jerry took the controls and steered them toward their destination at an agonizing, slow speed. They probably didn't want to get shot in the head.

Soldiers were loyalists, not dealers of death. If it were up to Jerry, he would have commandeered the ship, left a string of dead bodies, and commanded the pilot to take him where he wanted to go. Once Jerry was where he wanted to go, he would kill the pilot and move on. But the soldiers weren't like him. They only killed when necessary, and Jerry killed whenever he could.

Common groups of people, such as the soldiers, didn't like having innocent blood on their hands. Someone else took the responsibility. That was their psychology. If a superior told them to kill a child, they would do it. In the aftermath, they would justify their action as being out of their control. Someone else made the decision, not them. At least not fully. They wanted to be the tool, but never wanted to be the carpenter. A tool owned no independence, no choice, and no feeling. It did what it was told.

Jerry loved blood on his hands. If he ever had time, maybe he would bathe in it. Perhaps, in retirement, he would go on a killing spree. Not as a serial killer, though. Killing should have no theme or connective pattern. It was supposed to be random . . . unpredictable.

Maybe he would paint. Kill and then paint with his victim's blood. For as many people as there were in the galaxy, there were that many colors of blood. Painting always attracted him. It was his stress-relieving exercise when he was in training.

Jerry still attacked a canvas every once in awhile. Most probably thought what he painted was horribly grotesque and violent, despite it being abstract in nature, but he saw only the beauty of it. Artistry was perspective.

If Jerry won, he would kill Cayden, and paint the most beautiful image of death with his blood. The thought made him smile, and then the slow speed of the transport wasn't so agonizing.

///

"Hello, Dorian."

The female yookallan assassin held a crazed look in her eyes, and despite her attempt to control her emotions, Dorian could almost feel them emanating from her like heat from a flame. Obsession lied behind her veil of nonchalance. She was trying to savor the moment and not let her passion blind her.

"I see that despite your memory loss, you still fight quite well," she said, indicating the bodies strewn around. "That's good. Very good."

Dorian used every second given to him to take deep breaths in an effort to oxygenate his tired muscles. He was going to need it. Maybe she would talk long enough for him to make the first move, but that was wishful thinking. In fact, it looked like she was out of words already.

"You're not one for long and evil speeches, are you?" he asked.

He should not have responded. The sword lashed out, swinging for his head at a speed that caught him off guard. He ducked, feeling the air above his hair disturbed by both the movement of the sword and the violent plasma-echo that erupted from the weapon. It looked like a purple boomerang in the way it flipped end over end, but it was shaped like the blade of the sword. It traveled a good ten to twelve meters into the arena air before dissipating.

Dorian dodged two consecutive thrusts, each lighting their own echoes, before he walked back several paces. Rymera halted her attack, and satisfied herself by walking around him in a slow circle, like a vulture descending upon a carcass.

For some reason, he was more comfortable fighting her further away rather than being closer. What was interesting about that was when facing a plasma-echo blade, classical strategy taught that it was better to be closer to the opponent, closing as much distance as possible. It made sense. The truly dangerous thing about an echo blade was the disorienting effect.

The echo was released at the apex of the swing or thrust, and so it took a master of the weapon to make it effective. If one didn't know how to use it, the echoes would be released in all sorts of random patterns and do more harm than good. But since Rymera was indeed a master, she could take full advantage of its many uses.

When being located several paces away, she could swing the sword out of range, but the echo could reach where the metal couldn't. And so one waited for the perfect moment to dodge. It didn't sound so bad until one realized the master of the weapon could release any combination of attacks they wished without having to worry about defense. The attack would grow disorienting with speed.

Despite what Dorian knew about the common strategy in defending against an echo blade, he also knew it would not be his game plan. Instinct was his reason, and he had no choice but to trust it. Perhaps the reason was because, in his dodging, he could actually disorient her and gain some sort of advantage.

Rymera held the sword high. Dorian was about to find out if his instinct was correct.

///

"When we get to the streets, find a good hiding spot outside of the Coliseum, and use the screen to shoot the targets," I said as we ran off the ship's ramp and onto the docking bay. I was a bit weighed down by my duffel bag of guns.

"I'd rather shoot from the actual rifle," she said.

"As soon as you open fire, they're going to send at least one to dismantle the weapon," I said, adjusting the bag to my other shoulder. "They will figure out the gun's location by the second time you shoot and will take immediate action. I'll try to intercept whoever they send, but I can't make any promises. That's why it's much safer if you aren't at the gun. We're facing the best killers in the universe, here. Your job is to take out as many as you can as fast as you can. Pick the most available targets and shoot without mercy."

As we turned the corner, a burly man stepped out of the shadows. I dug my heel into the ground to keep from running into him.

Bronx. You need better friends, Cayden.

Outside of you, he's the only person I can trust to help.

We should not be trusting him. We could try to revamp the plan and rely on him less.

We're already stretched to the point of breaking. How many times have we been over this?

"He's . . ." Kalista said, shock written on her face. I'm not exactly sure what she was going to finish the sentence with.

"Relax, Bronx is with me," I told her, patting her on the shoulder. "What's the situation?"

"So far, it's going exactly as planned," Bronx said. "Rymera has eight others with her. Some you'll recognize, and some you won't. Currently, Rymera is fighting Dorian, but I'd give him the odds. She's trying to kill him with a sword. Fool."

"Rymera?" Kalista asked. "Rymera is there?"

I ignored her. "Are all of them armed?"

"Of course," Bronx said, picking something from his teeth. "They are all inside the arena, though. You should be able to eliminate them easily enough."

"Rymera hates Dorian," Kalista said. "She *hates* him."

Bronx turned his cold eyes to her. "I see your memory isn't as damaged as the GS thinks it is. Very good. Tell me, do you remember me?"

"No," Kalista snapped, her response quick and harsh.

She's lying.

It doesn't matter.

Why would she lie?

Bronx smiled, but the expression didn't reach his eyes. "I'll be waiting by the ship. Good luck, Cayden."

He walked past, winking at Kalista, who still seemed to be in shock after seeing him. It was obvious she held some memory of him, and unless my ability to read people severely diminished, there was fear in her eyes.

Ask her about it.

Later.

"Your brother needs our help," I said, grabbing her by the hand. She didn't move.

"I have to tell you something," she said. "It's important."

I pulled her harder until she had no choice but to move. "Tell me after this is over. We're short on time."

31

GETTING there was the easy part. Trying to find a way to mount a surprise attack was the hard part. The stands were still packed full of panicked people. They were evacuating with the organizational skills of a herd of wildebeest.

At first, I tried to avoid them as I marched forward, but their fear was not granting me the same courtesy. I was nearly knocked over several times as I tried to swim upriver, and after one particularly nasty bump, I withdrew my pistol from its holster and held it high.

The effect was instantaneous. The panicked people were paying attention to me now, and actively got out of my way as I marched on toward Rymera's troop of assassins.

It's good that you didn't fire the gun. We still need the element of surprise.

I continued to push past with the bag of laser and plasma-powered weapons across my shoulder. One of the assassins inside the arena decided that the crowd wasn't moving fast enough. He fired his gun into the air, and the whole place burst into an even more frenzied panic. Screaming, running, pushing and people being trampled by other people ensued. I waved my gun with greater fervor than before to ensure my safe passage through the congregation.

I find it remarkable how effective shooting a gun in the air can be for crowd control.

It does tend to turn people into sheeple.

Sheeple?

It's an euphemism for comparing people to sheep.

Why would you do that?

Because sheep are stupid and always do what the other . . . nevermind.

Finally, I found a position, squatting low behind the seats. I was only twelve rows away from the edge of the arena, and so far, invisible to the assassins.

Let's keep it that way.

My guess was that Kalista was going to kill at least two, possibly three before she ran out of targets. The person they would send after my sniper was going to have to run past me. I would eliminate them, and then it would be random. I had enough firepower, Kalista would provide a crossfire, and if I could find a way to get Dorian a gun, the rest would take care of itself.

"I'm going for Rymera," Kalista said over the comm unit.

"Negative," I said.

"She's going to kill him."

"No, she won't," I said. "Dorian's better than her. The odds are with him, even if she's armed and he's not. And if you shoot Rymera, the assassins will open fire on Dorian to achieve their mission. As long as Rymera remains alive, they won't kill Dorian."

"Who do I shoot then?" she asked.

"Go for the deeshie," I said, unzipping the duffel bag. "Aim for the head. After that, you've got ten shots. Take out whoever you want to. The gun has a lock-in targeting system. Once you lock onto a target, it will automatically aim for you. Just fire at the right time."

"What are you going to do when the ten shots are up?" she

asked.

"You think I packed snacks in this bag of mine?"

"Oh."

I began to clip ammo to my waist belt. "Give me sixty seconds, and then open fire."

///

Bronx. It was Bronx. Kalista knew as soon as she saw him. In her memory, the man that hid in shadow, instructing her to form a relationship with Cayden, was Bronx.

Kalista panicked when she saw him, and she was sure that he noticed. Her only fear now was that he would do something to Cayden. But Cayden was working with him.

Kalista knew she needed to tell Cayden everything. Whatever he thought he planned wasn't going to work. Bronx was obsessed with Cayden; that much she remembered. He went to great lengths to shape Cayden's life, and an interest of that intensity did not just disappear.

After they got Dorian out, she would tell Cayden all she knew. They would probably have to go their separate ways, but it would be worth it. Dorian and Kalista would have the money from the gladiator competition, and Cayden would have the money from the race.

"The deeshie," she said, more to herself than to Cayden.

Kalista was huddled in a closet, sitting on an upside down bucket. Cayden insisted she hide during the ordeal, and Kalista did not object. The last thing she wanted was to become a target.

She used the small semi-transparent screen to zoom in on the massive alien. Whatever auto-targeting system Cayden described took over from there. The red flashing icon acquired its target and followed the hulking assassin no matter where he went.

"I'm ready whenever you are," Cayden said.

Kalista took a deep breath and pressed the fire icon on the screen.

///

Rymera went on the attack, swinging her sword in a dizzying pattern, stepping forward with each swing. Dorian matched her movement, but a tick slower, which made the fight feel like a dance with no rhythm.

Though she pressed forward, he was able to stay in congruence with her and avoid the echoes. It was surprising to him how naturally he adapted to the strange form of attack. His confidence grew after matching her movements for a while. Instead of stepping back and copying each movement of hers, he began to anticipate and dodge once to avoid two attacks. The maneuvers threw her off, forcing her to make panicked thrusts and slashes in order to defend against any charge of his.

"You'll make a mistake eventually," Rymera said, panting.

The fight may have caused her to lose her breath, but it was completely exhausting him. Dorian felt like he could barely stand, though he fought hard not to show it to his merciless opponent.

"I don't make mistakes," he said.

Dorian had to make his move in the next attack, or else he would never win. He felt it. The instinct. The indescribable knowledge that came from unknowable senses. Dorian was a natural. Pure potential harnessed for all that it was worth, and when his gut told him to move, he always did. He hadn't regretted it yet.

Rymera swung high. The echo flipped horizontally, end over

end, and Dorian ducked it easily. But instead of stepping back, he charged. His enemy reacted on time. Spinning and swinging her weapon from the ground to over her head, so the echo spun vertically, able to take out his legs from the waist down. It was a perfect move, considering the lowering of his body when he charged. But it was also a downfall to believe that one could achieve a perfect move.

Dorian leapt high into the air before she released the second echo, knowing he would make it by mere centimeters. His left arm cocked behind him, and he saw the fear in Rymera's eyes as the lethal violet light swept underneath him. She made a desperate attempt to swing forward, to catch him before he caught her. Dorian was too fast. His left arm extended, and his hand gripped the wrist of her sword hand like a vice.

As soon as he did this, the head of the deeshie assassin exploded on the other side of the arena. Though it was most definitely an odd thing, Dorian knew it was the work of a sniper rifle even before the sound of the gun erupted into the air. It must have been a good five hundred meters away. He also realized that Cayden, per-haps, did not betray him after all.

Dorian and Rymera tumbled to the ground, each attaining a death grip on the weapon as they rolled. When they stood, it became a power struggle, and that was something he could win. The sword swung for Dorian's head, but he wanted it to. He ducked it, using its obtained momentum to swing it harder at her. She performed the same dodge, and then the sword stood straight once more between them.

The assassins in the surrounding arena were employing basic countermeasures, running past with swift feet and guns aimed in the direction of the shot that killed their colleague. They didn't know exactly where the sniper was, but they did know what direction he hailed from. They would send one to go after him and find appropriate cover.

Rymera kneed his abdomen, but Dorian swung his elbow and caught her jaw hard as an immediate counter. Her grip loosened, and he took the opportunity to rip the weapon from her hands. Though he probably could have killed her then, he instead swung the sword at the nearest assassin, an unsuspecting human female, and sliced her in half with the echo.

By the time Dorian swung back at Rymera, she recovered. A harsh kick intercepted his wrist and sent the weapon clattering away across the arena floor. Two well-placed punches to Dorian's body forced him to take a step back, and then a spinning back kick to the jaw nearly floored him.

He took a defensive stance and was able to block her next two punches. Things were on an even playing field now. Despite his exhaustion, Dorian knew there was a good chance of beating Rymera. He felt comfortable with his hands, even more comfortable than he did with weapons.

A second head was removed by the sniper, and now they knew where Cayden must have been. Still, they lost three members, which reduced their number to five. Four, now that one of them was sent to deal with the sniping nuisance.

The distinct sound of a shotgun sounded not too far from Dorian. Rymera pressed forward, ignoring the losses she was taking. He chose to ignore the outer chaos as well. If he didn't, he would not win.

32

I was ready in half the time I told Kalista, and so waiting was complete torture. My movements with the weapons were automatic, practiced, and far too familiar. I was good with guns, and I hated myself for it. Killing was not something I enjoyed getting used to. But from my youth, I was well-practiced.

Violence is a means to an end.

I could live without it.

Just because you don't want to be violent doesn't mean those around you will help you avoid it.

The sniper fired, and it was go time. The assassins scattered like roaches fleeing the light, and I could see Dorian was now wrestling the sword from Rymera. A second shot made perfect contact just as Dorian used the sword to kill an unsuspecting assassin. Rymera was able to kick the weapon away, and the two of them started fighting hand-to-hand. I knew he must have been tired, but if I was a betting person, I would have still sided with Kalista's brother.

Three assassins were killed in seconds. I ducked behind the seats in front of me and gripped the shotgun like it was going to grow legs and run away. A human male was running down the aisle, no doubt in an attempt to go after the sniper. I waited until I could hear his footsteps.

I turned the corner on my knees, firing the high-powered

weapon at my foe's chest. The impact was impressive, halting his momentum. An explosion of gore landed with a sick, wet sound as he tumbled to the floor, dead.

I stayed bent over as much as possible as I ran past the fallen assassin. The sound of rock shattering indicated Kalista fired again and missed. The rest of the assassins did not spot me, and Kalista's continued shots kept them behind the pillars of the Coliseum. Rymera and Dorian were still doing battle as if nothing else mattered.

Hunkering down, three rows from the edge of the arena, I shoved the shotgun into the bag and withdrew the Gavel 91 sub-machine gun. I modified the barrel to give it greater long-distance range and attached a scope and stock. I set the weapon to fire in three-bullet bursts and took a deep breath.

It's almost over.

No, it isn't.

There were only four assassins left, outside of Rymera. Their full concentration was on hiding from the sniper fire behind the rock pillars that once kept the animals chained. Unfortunately for them, I was in a crossfire position. Rymera planned her attack without regard to basic defensive strategy.

"Keep your aim to the right pillars," I said to Kalista over the comm. "I will take care of the left. They will lose their cover and you should have a clear line of sight."

"Okay," she said, her voice quavering.

Why is she frightened? She's perfectly safe.

Most people are afraid to kill.

Why?

I stood, found my target with the scope, and fired once, dropping the morkallian female before she saw me. Behind her, at the other pillar, her morkallian male partner attempted to put me in his sights, but I was too quick for him. His head snapped back as three bullets traveled through his skull.

On the far side of the arena, the remaining two assassins were sprinting, trying to get within firing range of me. They only had pistols. Kalista hit the one to my right with such force that his leg blew off and collided with his partner, tripping her to the ground. I put six bullets into her torso before she could get back to her feet. Another shot into the head of her one-legged comrade ended it.

"Stay where you are," I told Kalista. "I'll bring Dorian back to you."

I leaped over the railing that protected observers from falling into the arena and landed in a roll. I was very ready to put an end to Rymera with a squeeze of my finger. However, before I made it halfway, Dorian finished the job.

///

Gunfire erupted all around them, but neither cared. Even though Dorian lost all memory of her, Rymera could see that their battle was still personal. Somehow, their competition went deeper than memory.

She fought well, and so did he. It was intense. She landed more punches and kicks, but his were more powerful. They stood apart now, bloodied and bruised from the battle.

This was what she wanted. This was what she came for. Rymera knew her team was already dead. She knew that even if she did kill Dorian, she too would be killed. Bronx was right. Cayden outsmarted them once again. She should have cared. She should have been upset. But all Rymera could do was smile at the prospect of getting the chance to kill Dorian.

He charged her, throwing a flurry of punches. She blocked a right hook, dodged a left jab, and then threw her own. To her surprise she caught him, and was able to clench her hands around the back of his neck. She drove two consecutive knees into his abdomen before he was able to match her grip with his own.

In what she hoped was an unsuspected maneuver, she proceeded with a judo move, by placing her leg on the outside of his leg and throwing him off balance. Again, surprisingly, it worked. He stumbled and she continued with the movement to put him on the ground. Dorian was getting sloppy in his exhaustion.

Or so she thought.

Rymera lost sight of Dorian's hand. Her trip maneuver hadn't worked; it played into Dorian's counter. She felt the intense pressure at the back of her head as his hand secured a death grip on her hair.

It was a perfect grip. A grip that wasn't meant for ripping hair out, but rather for turning the head. And then, as they fell to the ground, she felt the other hand grab her chin. She couldn't stop it or see it because the hand that grabbed her hair already turned her head.

Rymera felt the violent twist, felt the incredible pain, and even felt the snap of the bone. The only thing she never felt, as blackness overtook her, was the impact of the ground.

///

Dorian let his rival fall on top of him, as dead as all her comrades. He took a few deep breaths and rolled Rymera over, sitting up to see what happened. There was sniper fire, but it was also followed by other guns firing.

Cayden was walking towards him, a sub-machine gun in his hands. Whatever Dorian thought of him before, he knew now that

Cayden was serious. The GS lost a lot of assets today, and Cayden was the chief perpetrator of those crimes. Although Dorian could not bring himself to trust the strange man, he was beginning to realize what a powerful ally he might be.

"Can you walk?" Cayden asked, as he offered Dorian a hand. "Are you injured?"

Dorian accepted the help and stood. "I'm fine. Where's Kalista?"

Cayden walked to the exit. "I hid her in a closet at the entrance. She's fine. We have to grab my duffel bag, and then we can blast off from this damn rock."

Dorian jogged to keep up with him. "Did you know they were coming?"

"I had my suspicions," he said. "Setting up a remote-controlled sniper was part of my contingency plan."

"You call that a contingency plan?" Dorian asked.

Cayden ignored him. "My duffel has loads more guns. We're going to have to go in hot to get to the ship. A squadron of soldiers and Jerry are going to be waiting for us."

"Just how do you think we'll get past them?" Dorian asked. "And who the hell is Jerry?"

"A pitiful waste of a human being," Cayden said. "And he's a terrible strategist. Trust me, we'll be fine."

33

THE time for the most complex turn in my plan was soon approaching. Rabid butterflies were fluttering in my stomach, threatening to burst through. I double checked my weapons while Dorian and Kalista had an awkward reunion.

Dorian seemed satisfied by the sight that his sister was unharmed, but she threw her arms around his neck. He didn't return the embrace, instead opting to stand like a statue and pat her on the back. A rock would have emoted more.

There was a part of me that could relate to Dorian. A big part. It wasn't his fault that he couldn't understand emotion. He was modified from birth, genetically and environmentally, to destroy the emotions within. Just as I and Kalista had, but on an even more effective level.

It made sense. Dorian operated on pure logic and instinct. The logic was ingrained, but the instinct was natural. It had to be. The instincts were what kept him alive, and ironically, what kept him human. There were shadows of humanity in him that made him take action. He saved Kalista, kept her safe for three months, and continued to worry about her all because of those shadows.

I could relate. I felt the same thing within me, but one person stepped out of the darkness to give me focus. Kalista. Without her, I could be just like Dorian.

"What now?" Kalista asked, her voice echoing across the empty stadium.

"I don't want to rush you," I said to Dorian. "But the sooner we get there, the less time we give them to think."

"Who?" Kalista said, releasing her brother.

Dorian ignored his twin. "What do you have for me?"

I bent down and unzipped the duffel bag. "Plenty."

Dorian picked up a Gavel 91 identical to the one I was carrying and strapped several ammo packs to his belt. I handed him one of the two Leopard Specials, which I modified for more short range tactics, and he looped the attached strap across his chest, placing the gun behind his back. Standing shirtless, sweaty, muscled, and loaded to the teeth, Dorian looked like a freaking super soldier.

"Who's waiting for us?" Kalista asked again.

I handed her a pistol from the bag. "We're going to have a fight on our hands to get back to the ship."

Kalista recoiled from the gun, but I did not withdraw it. I knew that she did not like weapons, and I couldn't blame her. But it was too important.

"You have to take it," Dorian said. "Just in case."

"I'm no good with them anyway," Kalista said.

"You were good enough with that sniper rifle," I said.

"That was different. I was just pointing and shooting."

"It's the same thing. Just point and shoot."

"We're not leaving until you take it," Dorian said.

Kalista finally grabbed the gun from my hand, and we were on our way. At this point, Rome was a ghost town. Everyone was holed away, waiting for the shooting to stop. The nice part about Rome was, without a police force, no one was coming to get in our way.

It does make things much easier.

Well, it's about to get harder.

This, too, shall pass, Cayden.

///

"Why are you here?" Jerry seethed, watching Bronx stroll into the docking bay like he owned the place.

"I like to watch things, Jerry," Bronx said. "And I especially like to watch how Cayden outwits everyone around him to get what he wants."

Jerry motioned a cluster of soldiers to the left. He was doing his best to create a funnel at the entrance of the docking bay. The soldiers moved a good deal of shipping crates and pallets, stacking them on top of one another to build sufficient cover.

"He's not making it out of this one," Jerry said.

Bronx laughed, his voice full of derision. "You really aren't that bright are you, Jerry? How many times do you have to do this? How many times does Cayden have to beat you?"

Jerry's normally handsome face contorted into a snarl. "I will never stop. Never."

"Such a waste," Bronx sighed. "I had high hopes for you, Jerry. But obsession is a weak man's quality. Weak men die, Jerry. You're going to die."

Jerry's hand found its way to the hilt of his pistol. But no matter how much he wanted to put the gun between Bronx's teeth and pull the trigger, he couldn't. No matter how much he wanted to watch Bronx's brains shower the dock floor, he knew he couldn't do it. The moment he thought of killing Bronx, it was as if he was frozen in place.

"Still trying to kill me?" Bronx asked, looking down at Jerry's hand gripping the butt of the pistol. "Do you feel as if you've gotten any closer?"

"Not yet," Jerry snarled.

Bronx nodded. "Well, Rymera must be dead by now. Either Cayden rescued Dorian or he didn't. If he didn't, Dorian is dead as well as Rymera. If he did, then all of the other assassins are dead and Dorian is alive. What do you think, Jerry?"

Jerry let go of the gun and paced wildly like a caged animal. "Why don't you tell me what you think?"

"You haven't even considered the possibilities, have you?" Bronx asked.

"Like what?" Jerry asked, avoiding Bronx's eyes.

"Cayden could be screwing with your head," Bronx said. "He might have led you on this wild goose chase just to make you look like a fool. He might be coming back here with the bodies of Dorian and Kalista in tow."

"I remember how he was with Kalista. No way in hell he killed her," Jerry said.

"His memory was erased," Bronx said, holding up a finger as if he were teaching a student an important lesson. "He doesn't remember Kalista."

Jerry scoffed. "The memory wiping technique is flawed. It didn't work on Kalista, it probably didn't work on Cayden. Or he recently began to remember."

Bronx clapped his hands. "Very good, Jerry. So, now you have a new problem. Cayden is on his way here with Dorian, and both of them are armed and motivated. What chance do you think you really have?"

"I'll take my chances," Jerry said. "Now, do you mind?"

Bronx smiled, but he finally stopped talking and walked to the side. Jerry double checked the barricades his soldiers set up and ordered them to get into position. Cayden would be there soon.

"No one shoots, Cayden!" Jerry shouted as he ducked behind the center barricade. "He's mine. Take out the siblings and leave Cayden to me."

Jerry didn't need to hear an affirmative from the squadron. He knew they would obey him. That was their purpose. Obey and execute. They would not so much as shoot in Cayden's direction.

But once Jerry heard the first shotgun blast, he realized he made a terrible mistake. Not one that he could fix, because egos held more power than the gun in his hand. Cayden knew that.

And he must have been counting on it.

34

WHATEVER plans Jerry built were shattered by my superior counter move. Life taught me the best way to attack was in response. Never be first, always react.

Jerry followed the strategic rule book on setting up his cover. The soldiers were all in the right position, and their cover was perfect. And if it hadn't been for Jerry's ego, my assault would have been impossible.

Everyone had an ego. It was about control. Does the ego control you, or do you control the ego? In Jerry's case, his ego was always in control. Especially in matters that concerned me.

Such a simpleton.

A dangerous simpleton.

I knew Jerry would want to kill me himself. It was an easy assumption to make, and I confirmed my suspicion back at the races. Jerry wanted me dead, and the soldiers had the golden opportunity to do so at the finish line, but they didn't. They weren't allowed to. Jerry may have wanted me six feet under, but he needed to do the dirty work himself.

Because of my knowledge on this, I knew there was only one person shooting at me. Jerry. And Jerry would be focused solely on me, which allowed Dorian to be solely focused on him. I, meanwhile, would be able to direct my fire at the soldiers without fear of reprisal from them.

With Kalista safe behind us, Dorian and I charged into the docking bay like a pair of lunatics. A soldier to my left was the first victim. He peeked around his cover, and the immediate blast from my shotgun took his head off. Dorian fired at Jerry's position, straight down the middle of the docking bay.

Dorian stayed low and alert, but I walked into the target zones, searching for heads to pop up. I was not disappointed. Anytime Dorian laid down suppressing fire on Jerry, targets appeared in my line of sight. It wasn't difficult to take them out.

Kalista, according to our plan, ran for cover as soon as possible, gripping the pistol like it was her last lifeline. I dropped my shotgun and switched to the Leopard Special. I killed six soldiers so far, and Dorian's fire on Jerry kept my rival cowering behind his cover.

"Fall back to me!" I heard Jerry shout.

Dorian joined me as the soldiers abandoned their hiding spots and ran for the center. He took the ones fleeing on the right, and I aimed for the ones on the left. It was like shooting fish in a barrel. Between the two of us, we took out another eight soldiers before the survivors made it back to Jerry's position.

I motioned Dorian to split to the right as I went left. We both found shelter behind the crates and reloaded our weapons. I turned my head as bullets ripped their way through the crate next to me. It was the first time the soldiers or Jerry managed to return fire.

Dorian looked at me and raised his hand, fingers extended, and raised an eyebrow inquisitively. I shook my head and held up an additional two fingers to add to his count of five. He nodded that he understood and placed the butt of his gun at his shoulder.

After a silent three count, we both turned the corner and unleashed hell on Jerry and his soldiers. I hit at least two, killing one for sure. Dorian took out three. We ducked behind our crates to reload as return fire hit our cover with the effectiveness of a spoon cutting a steak.

Where is Bronx?

He's here.

Yes, but where? We should be seeing him anytime now.

He'll be here.

I turned to Dorian, and he held up three fingers. I nodded. Jerry and his two remaining soldiers weren't going to last much longer.

///

Bronx observed the firefight with the same admiration he had for the theatre. Like an actor on stage, Cayden was putting on an unforgettable performance. Confident, quick, fluid. And like a director, he was guiding events to tell the story he crafted.

It was beautiful.

Bronx was part of Cayden's play. He was waiting for his cue. And then he saw her. Kalista kept low, ducking behind the crates on Dorian's side with Cayden's duffel bag slung over her shoulder. She was armed with a pistol.

Curious. Cayden didn't tell Bronx about the gun. In retrospect, it made complete sense for her to be armed, but Bronx hadn't thought about it. Why didn't Cayden mentioned it? His plan was meticulous, detailed to the finest degree. Why leave out something so glaring?

Did he suspect? Bronx put the thought out of his mind. Cayden was good, but Bronx knew him better than that. He suspected nothing.

The gun would not be a problem, in any case. It was probable Kalista didn't know how to use the weapon, and Bronx was more than confident in his abilities to overpower her.

The smell of hot bullets filled the docking bay atmosphere. Bronx admired the dedication of Cayden. He didn't hesitate to kill the soldiers and did so with little to no protective cover. He knew that without trusting Dorian to keep Jerry at bay, the plan would not work to its full effectiveness. So, just like the greatest of actors, he dove into his role with fearlessness. Dorian, for his part, not only rendered Jerry useless but was also killing any soldier unlucky enough to come within his sight.

The whole assault took less than three minutes. Jerry only had a few soldiers left. Cayden and Dorian trapped them in a devastating crossfire. The cue for Bronx to take his place on the stage was given.

He kept low as he advanced on Kalista. Her focus was on Cayden and Dorian, so she did not see him creeping toward her from the other direction. Bronx pulled out his pistol, and was just about to give his performance, when the unexpected happened.

A bullet blew through the crate just above Bronx's head. The debris flew in his face, temporarily blinding him as a large piece of hard plastic struck his temple. He knelt and wiped away the dust that clouded his eyes. He felt for blood, but there was none. Good. But when Bronx opened his eyes, he found himself staring at the business end of a pistol.

Kalista, a look of determination on her face, held the weapon steady in both hands. Bronx froze. Kalista's eyes told him that he would not be quick enough to disarm her.

"You'll never hurt him again," Kalista said.

Bronx was about to respond, hoping to delay her long enough

for him to expose a weakness, but Kalista didn't allow him to. To his surprise, she pulled the trigger before a word could escape his mouth.

He breathed a deep sigh of relief as the weapon *clicked* uselessly. Bronx should have known. Kalista's determined look morphed into one of panic as she tried to pull the trigger twice more. Bronx slapped the compromised weapon out of her hand and pulled her up by the wrist.

It was all going to be over soon.

///

Dorian caught the movement out of the corner of his eye and stopped firing at once. Cayden, next to him, must have seen the same thing and ceased the assault on Jerry as well. Bronx was walking out, Kalista in front of him with a gun jammed to her temple. He stopped when he was between Jerry's position and theirs.

"Put your weapons down," Bronx said, his voice cool and collected.

Dorian was about to obey the demand, but then saw Jerry emerge from his hiding spot, gun extended with a look of pure glee on his face. Cayden stepped forward, gun pointed firmly at Jerry. Dorian did the same.

"Put it down, Jerry" Bronx said, not bothering to look behind him.

"Like hell," Jerry said.

"Soldiers," Bronx said, his voice booming loud enough to be heard throughout the docking bay. "Relieve Jerry of his weapon. Kill him if he resists."

The two remaining soldiers trained their guns at Jerry's head.

He looked furious. After kicking the crate in front of him several times, Jerry dropped his gun.

"That's better," Bronx said. "Now, we're all going to get on my ship, alive, and take a ride back to the GS."

Dorian thought for a solid two seconds about taking his best shot at Bronx. But he knew it wouldn't succeed. Bronx's finger was on the trigger of his weapon tight enough that the smallest flinch would set the gun off, killing his sister. Dorian opted to drop his weapon.

Cayden slammed his gun onto the floor with such force that it broke into several pieces. "Why?" he shouted.

If Cayden was acting, he was putting on a riveting performance. Tears formed in his eyes, and his face was screwed into an expression of rage. Dorian hoped this was somehow part of Cayden's plan, but his hopes were dashed by his reaction.

"We were so close, Bronx," Cayden said, his voice pleading. "So close. Why are you doing this?"

Bronx looked at him like one might look at an animal trapped in a cage. Admiration, pity, and superiority wrapped in one. Dorian hated that look.

"You can't always win, Cayden," Bronx said. "Let's go."

As the soldiers closed in on them, Bronx put his weapon away and let Kalista go. But then, as if an idea revealed itself to him, he held up his index finger and spoke aloud.

"I need Cayden's bag," he said. "Bring me his bag."

35

OUR ride was quiet but bumpy. Bronx ordered that my ship be impounded on Rome until the GS could figure out what to do with me. Kalista, Dorian, Jerry and I were handcuffed and shackled to the walls of a rental Bronx secured. Jerry was gagged, which gave me a warm, fuzzy feeling deep in my heart.

Sometimes small victories keep up morale.

You're concerned about my morale?

Of course. It directly affects your success. Your morale needs to be high for our next step. It's the most important.

Whatever morale boost I received from Jerry's temporary muzzle was dampened by the rest of my surroundings. The two remaining soldiers were allowed to sit in the dim, ruby-colored cargo hold of the rental ship. The rest of us had been forced to stand, hands held at an uncomfortably high level by the restraints. And the place smelled like an old sock.

Bronx's "betrayal" was the result of years of meticulous planning. The Coyote convinced me to throw Bronx a small curveball by giving Kalista a gun. I sabotaged it, of course, and from what I could see, the whole scene played out in spectacular fashion.

I agree. Kalista thinks that it was a simple, unlucky malfunction. Bronx got the message not to toy with us.

Is that why you did it? I was under the impression that you

thought it would be more convincing if Kalista had a weapon.

That was true. But Bronx needed to know that he can be beaten. He needs put in place, Cayden. The sooner we're done with him, the better.

Soon, Coyote. Soon.

"Your arm is bleeding," Kalista said, breaking the silence of the ride. She was looking at a thin, red line on the back of my wrist.

Observant, isn't she? Do you think she saw what you did?

"It's just a scratch," I said.

I did my best to give her a reassuring smile. I wanted to tell her everything. Tell her that it was going to be alright. Tell her that it was all part of the plan.

But you can't.

No. And I couldn't because I needed Kalista and Dorian to sell their parts to perfection. One hint of deception, and the GS might detect it. I couldn't afford to entrust such an important acting job to the siblings, so I needed them believe it was real.

It's best that way. What they don't know won't hurt them. They can forgive you after we're done.

It's hurting Kalista right now, Coyote. She thinks she's going to die.

Yes, but she's not going to die. Therefore, there will be no actual hurting. So, what pain could she possibly be feeling now?

Forget I said anything.

I never forget.

The Coyote was not capable of understanding human emotion. Only actions mattered, not feelings. He was incapable of comprehending the emotions Kalista was feeling, and the betrayal she would feel after discovering I intentionally kept the truth from her.

"What's the plan now, Cayden?" Dorian asked. There was no

derision in his voice. Only honesty.

"The plan's over, Dorian," I said. "I have no more plan. Bronx tanked it."

"No backup plan?" he asked.

"No," I said. "I put all my eggs in one, insecure basket."

Jerry made a coughing sound that might have been laughter, but it was hard to tell due to the gag in his mouth. If he was smiling, it wasn't reaching his eyes. I don't believe I'd ever seen Jerry's smile reach his eyes. That would signal genuine happiness, and Jerry was not a happy person. He was incapable of it.

"Sorry, Jerry, I couldn't make that out," I said. "Could you maybe repeat that?"

Jerry tried to lunge at me from across the ship, despite being handcuffed to the hull. His face was red, and spittle dripped from his chin as he attempted to either swallow the gag or spit it out. He was far from the picture of his usual chiseled features. The madness of Jerry was now more than evident.

Aren't we all just a little bit mad?

I'd say Jerry takes it to a different level.

"Why do you antagonize him?" Kalista asked. "Why have you always done so?"

Yes, why do you?

Her question took me by surprise. I never gave my hatred of Jerry much thought. It was a defense mechanism I picked up long ago in response to his irrational hatred of me. From what I could remember, Jerry never liked me. I never did anything in particular to warrant his dislike, but the feeling became mutual.

I realized I never liked him. As time progressed, and our trials became more difficult, Jerry's dislike evolved into pure hatred. He would try to kill me, even when we weren't in direct competition. It wasn't hard for me to start hating him back.

"Don't feel sorry for him," I said. "He'd kill you in a heartbeat."

"He can't help himself, Cayden," she said. "No more than any of us. He's been toyed with and turned into what you see now. It's not fair."

I shook my head. "He didn't have to become that."

"What other choice did he have?" she asked. "He adapted in order to survive."

"I would have died," I said, staring into Jerry's maniacal eyes.

"Cayden . . . I need you to understand something," Kalista said.

"Yes?" I asked.

Her mouth opened, but no sound followed. Tears streaked her face, and for a moment, I was worried she couldn't breathe. But she found her voice, though it came out in a halting, insecure tone.

"I . . . care for you a great deal," she said. "I need you to know that."

"We both care for one another, Kalista," I said, confused. "That's why I'm doing this. Well, why I tried to do this."

She closed her eyes, more tears cascading off her chin and onto the floor. "I know. But you and I are a part of something that turns everything upside-down. We could become Jerry. And I want you to know, beyond any doubt, I care for you."

I smiled. "Thanks."

It's nice to feel needed.

///

Kalista couldn't do it. She couldn't tell him. What was stopping her? Shame? Guilt? How could she let such trivial feelings stop her from telling Cayden what he needed to know?

Perhaps it was because there was no point. She would be dead in hours, and Cayden would live on. He would be able to find happiness later in life, and live on believing that she loved him. He would be able to find someone else.

If she told him the truth, what would the consequences be? Would Cayden be okay? Would he be able to recover from her confession? Was her ego so inflated to think such a thing? Wasn't the truth always better than a lie?

The ship lurched violently as it exited the wormhole, and Kalista drew in a long breath as the GS drew closer. Perhaps she would erupt into a panicked state later, but for now she felt quite calm about dying. It was over, at least. No more struggle. No more worrying. Just blackness.

Oblivion.

Dorian appeared to be as calm as Kalista, perhaps even more so. She pitied him. It wasn't his fault that he couldn't relate to human emotions as well as most. Dorian probably felt more relieved than anyone that it was over. He was caught, but there was order in his life once more. He knew where he was going.

Kalista did not fault him for his feelings. Just like she didn't fault Cayden or Jerry. They were all puppets caught in the game, their actions out of their control. Cayden was doing his best to cut those strings, but he still had a few attached. Or did he?

Although Cayden suffered a breakdown when Bronx made his move, he now seemed to be in control of his faculties. And not just in control, but confident. Like he was right where he wanted to be.

Kalista could have been imagining things. With Cayden, it was hard to know what he was thinking, despite her normal knack for being able to glean the truth out of people. With Cayden, she could not detect deception or honesty. He seemed to slip on whatever mask he needed without effort. Had he planned to get caught?

She didn't want to chase the thought. It would give her hope, and hope was not something she wanted to contemplate at the moment. The peace of knowing her end felt natural, and hope would upset that peace.

"Once more unto the breach, dear friends," Cayden said.

Kalista felt like she recognized the words. "Who said that?"

Cayden smiled. "A king."

36

)

MARGARET never imagined that Bronx would make the play. She, in all honesty, dismissed his presence as insignificant. But the more she studied the reports being sent over to her within the last couple of hours, the more impressed she was. He spent years building a con- nection with Cayden so that he could use it as the perfect weapon in the end. It was brilliant.

And intimidating.

Margaret needed to know how Bronx was playing the game. Was he trying to intimidate her? Or was this his way of finally falling into line? Perhaps, it was a way of impressing her.

She put on a polite, subtle smile as he walked down the ship's exit ramp. His expression was neutral, impossible to read, but he kept eye contact with her. Behind him, Cayden, Kalista, Dorian, and Jerry were all led out, by two armed soldiers. All of them restrained by handcuffs, including a gagged Jerry.

"Jerry was disobeying orders," Bronx said, anticipating her question. "He might have killed me to get to Cayden. It's not surpris- ing, but it should be a cause for concern. You may want to have him evaluated."

"I'll take that into consideration," Margaret said with a nod. She extended her hand, and Bronx shook it firmly. "Job well done, Bronx. I'd like you to join me in front of the Council to report on this development."

"Of course. Have you decided what you want to do with these three?" he asked, nodding toward Cayden and the siblings.

"We'll take Cayden with us. The Council wishes to see him," Margaret said.

"Intrigued them, has he?" Bronx asked, a grin tugging at his lips.

"The fact that the memory wipe didn't work on him, and that his plan would have succeeded if not for your interference, has them most intrigued, yes," she said. "I think it might have even scared them."

"Really?" Bronx asked. "I don't believe Cayden was of any real threat."

"Yes, but they pondered the possibilities, now," Margaret said. "Not just of the damage he could of done, but also the resource he could become. You were right, Bronx. Cayden is special."

A cold grin that expressed more madness than happiness, tugged at Bronx's lips. "You have no idea."

"Guards," Margaret said, ignoring the disturbing atmosphere Bronx created, and instead, addressing the four hulking, armored deeshie behind her. "Escort Dorian and Kalista to the holding area. Do not remove their restraints."

The deeshie, each three times as wide as Margaret, moved past her and kept their guns pointed at the twins as they marched them to a secured cell several levels below the docking bay. There were over two hundred and seventy-five levels at the GS base, which was only one of eight other identical bases. They were floating cities in space, shaped somewhat like a chicken egg. She heard that most of the crew used "chick four" as slang for the name of their base, rather than the proper name of GS Base Four.

266

Margaret noticed that Cayden's gaze followed Kalista until she was out of sight. When he turned to face Margaret, he caught her off guard. He winked.

She didn't react to him. Cayden's games relied on manipulating others. He knew he was beaten, and she would not act out in frustration to his cavalier demeanor. He was just trying to establish some kind of control, but those days were over. Cayden's three years of freedom were up. It was time to get back to work.

"Take Jerry back to his quarters," Margaret said, addressing two more deeshie guards. "Remove his restraints and gag when you arrive, but do not let him leave his quarters until you hear from me."

Jerry looked furious. His normally handsome features were red with anger, and he was biting his gag like he wanted to tear it to shreds. He tried to lunge at Cayden before the guards caught him and took him way. Cayden didn't bother to look at Jerry, but held up a brazen middle finger as he was escorted away.

"Bronx," Margaret said. "Let's get this done quickly. Why don't you bring Cayden to my quarters so we can meet with the Council?"

"I'm afraid I need to deposit this in the armory," Bronx said, indicating a duffel bag at his feet. "Cayden has an explosives kit in here that has me concerned. I need to make sure he hasn't armed it as a trap. It should only take me ten minutes or so."

"Trap?" Margaret asked.

"It's nothing to be worried about," Bronx said, waving his hand as if shooing away an annoying insect. "I know how he thinks. I just want to be cautious."

"Cayden," Margaret said, trying to sound pleasant. "How about you save us the trouble and just tell us what you've done?"

"Margaret," Cayden said, imitating her voice with surprising perfection. "How about you go to hell?"

Bronx cocked an eyebrow at her, as if to say "I told you so" with his expression. Margaret gave a frustrated sigh. Why was such a talent so difficult to work with?

"I need to clean up anyway, Margaret," Bronx said. "It's been a long day. I can be at your quarters in fifteen minutes. Would that be acceptable?"

Bronx was close enough for her to smell his body odor. It wasn't offensive enough for her to cover her nose, but if she smelled like that after a busy day, she would want to take a few moments to clean and change clothes.

"Yes, alright," Margaret said. "Fifteen minutes. Don't be late. I won't wait for you."

"Yes, ma'am," Bronx said, picking up the duffel and jogging toward the nearest elevator.

"Guards," Margaret said, pointing at Cayden. Two more deeshie grabbed the young man by his arms and marched after her.

She liked this new version of Bronx. He seemed happy and more cooperative. Why shouldn't he be? He proved his brilliance and now possessed what he wanted all along. The Council, and Margaret along with them, realized that Cayden's value was much greater than previously expected.

"God, you two smell," Cayden said as they boarded the lift. "Margaret, how do you stand it? It's like dirty socks mixed with raw sewage."

The deeshie did have a peculiar odor, but it was something she was accustomed to. Cayden was just trying to rile her up. Get her to react. It wasn't going to work. Margaret knew better. She did not acknowledge him.

"You know, Margaret, you're braver than I thought," Cayden

said. "Those pants with that top? A courage like I've never seen before."

Bronx better hurry.

37

BRONX did not waste time getting Cayden's bag of weaponry to the ninety-third level. There were many armories littered throughout the gigantic base, but all explosives were kept on the ninety-third floor.

This was a mistake, as the volatile plasma engines and jump drive were only ten levels below. Bronx marveled at what ego could do. The GS believed they were untouchable. Cayden was right about them. They were overconfident.

If there was anything they should have learned from Cayden's near success, it was that he was dangerous. Instead, they found him intriguing. They had no sense of foreboding, and that was their weakness.

They would pay for it today, and pay dearly. That was neither here nor there for Bronx. It was a necessary step for his own plans, so Cayden would get what he wanted. At least some of what he wanted. But it wasn't Christmas, and Bronx wasn't Santa.

"Can I help you, sir?" a lithe, dark green morkallian female asked as he entered the armory.

"Why, yes, you can," Bronx said. "I need to have everything in this duffel checked and stored."

"Yes, sir," she said, taking the bag from his hands and depositing it on a tall, gray table.

Bronx took a quick inventory of the room while she carefully removed the guns first. There were plasma bombs, hand grenades, mines, flamethrowers, and several different kinds of explosives kits, much like the Red Sky kit Cayden packed in the bag. All were locked behind transparent, mesh reinforced glass. The room was only about four-by-four meters in size, but it was well organized, allowing for ample room to move around. A table and a single chair were the only pieces of furniture.

The only other thing unknown was a door in the left corner, at the back of the room. Unlike the glass casings holding the weapons, this door was opaque, with a keypad lock, and a retinal scanner.

"It's terribly rude of me not to have asked yet, but what is your name?" Bronx asked, holding out his hand.

"Pheliks, sir" the morkallian answered, shaking his hand.

"I am Bronx."

"I know, sir," she said. "It's an honor to meet you."

"Thanks," he said, his voice light and airy. "Could you tell me what's behind that door?"

"It's our light-sensitive explosives and chemicals," she said.

"Ah, of course," Bronx said. "Well, it must barely be bigger than a closet."

Pheliks shook her bald head. "Oh, no, sir. It's a room that's big enough to walk in."

"Well, that's a bit concerning, Pheliks," Bronx said, his eyebrows furrowing in an exaggerated worried expression.

"Oh? Why's that?" the morkallian asked, mirroring his worry.

"Er . . . well, never mind that for now," he said. "Let's focus on what's important at this very moment. Can you see the explosives kit, Pheliks?"

She peered into the bag carefully. "Yes, sir."

"Does there appear to be any traps set, or is it active in any way?" Bronx asked.

Bronx's worry over Cayden setting a trap with the explosives was genuine. His protege surprised Bronx by arming Kalista, and he wouldn't be caught with his metaphorical trousers down again.

"No, sir," Pheliks said. "It appears to be inert, and I don't see any traps of any kind."

"Excellent," Bronx said.

"Would you like me to remove it, sir?" she asked.

"Not yet," Bronx said. "I'd like to have a look in that room you described."

Pheliks halted for a moment, the concern in her eyes evident. "Forgive me, sir, but may I ask why? The material in the room is quite sensitive."

"I appreciate the delicacy of the situation, but we've recently brought on board a very dangerous individual," Bronx said. "I need to make sure that these sensitive materials are adequately protected from him."

His explanation seemed to calm Pheliks' nerves. She gave him a curt smile and took two long steps toward the door. "Only armorers and the commander have retinal scans that can open the door, and only we know the key code."

"Very good," Bronx said, as he watched Pheliks punch in the code lightning fast and scan her silvery eye.

The first door opened, and there was just enough room for Pheliks and him to fit between it and the inner door. A keypad and retinal scanner were also on this door.

"Apologies, sir," Pheliks said, bending down at an awkward angle to scan her eye. "There will be very little light inside. If you need help reading any of the labels, just ask me, sir. I have excellent vision in the dark."

"Thank you, Pheliks," Bronx said, following her into the over-sized walk-in closet.

"Is there anything in particular you are worried about?" Pheliks asked.

He pretended to see something behind the morkallian, and pointed toward it. "Is that what I think it is?"

Pheliks turned around, and he did not hesitate. She was only a hair taller than him, so it didn't require a great effort to grip her head with both hands. His right covered her mouth in case she managed to scream, and his left found purchase on the back of her skull. Bronx pulled her backward and twisted her head.

The light *pop* of her neck was the only sound made. Bronx caught her limp body before it hit the floor. He laid her down with grace, and checked for a pulse at the base of her clavicle, which was where the main artery ran in morkallians. Nothing.

It was a quicker death than most would experience today. Bronx pushed her body under the bottom shelf to the left. Even if someone else happened to enter the armory, and into the room, they would have trouble seeing the body.

He wiped his hands on his trousers and exited the explosives-filled closet, shutting and engaging each door's locks. He took an extra look at the explosives kit. Everything looked right. He made quick work of repacking the pistols into the bag, placed the remaining guns in a drawer under the table, and swung the duffel over his shoulder.

Bronx swiped his ID badge at the scanner as he exited the armory. Pheliks died so that Bronx could be on record as having taken the explosives to the correct armory, just in case someone was watching.

With that step completed, he was free to take Cayden's explosives kit and arm it on both the plasma engines and the jump drive.

///

The offensive-smelling deeshie guards shackled me to a chair in Margaret's office. Not just my hands this time, but my feet also, as an extra precaution.

Can't be too careful.

Yes, I might just blow up this whole base.

Is that sarcasm or irony?

Irony.

Ah. Thank you.

"Is there anything you would like to discuss, Cayden, before we present you to the Council?" Margaret asked, taking a seat behind her desk and pressing her fingertips together in front of her mouth.

"Like what, Margaret?" I asked.

I was intent on keeping her distracted long enough for Bronx to get back. It was vital that we not make it to the Council meeting. It would only complicate matters for my plan, though it wouldn't derail them entirely.

She smiled in a polite way. "You've certainly made an impression on some very important people. Me. The Council. Do you know what the Council is?"

"No," I said. "But they sound ominous."

"They are the brains behind the GS," Margaret said, ignoring my insubordinate tone. "They are the final stopping point. The true puppet masters."

"I kind of figured," I said. "So it's their fault I exist, then?"

"How did you beat the memory wipe?" she asked, placing her elbows on the desktop.

I shrugged. "With the individual living inside my head and sharing my body, of course."

I love when we get to talk about us.

Me too. It's not often, so savor it.

Just make sure Bronx doesn't overhear you.

He's not here yet.

"I'm being serious, Cayden," Margaret said. "How did you beat the memory wipe?"

"You don't know about him?" I asked, not surprised, but a little disappointed. I hoped that maybe she would know something about the Coyote.

"What are you talking about?" she asked, sounding frustrated.

"He's either some kind of implant or a split personality," I said. "But if you don't know about him, maybe I really am insane."

"You hear voices?" she asked.

I shook my head. "That's ridiculous. I hear a voice, not voices. Singular, not plural."

Margaret's expression of frustration was morphing its way into one of intrigue. She stood from her chair and walked around the desk, leaning against it, only three feet from me.

"You're serious?" she asked. "You actually hear a voice inside your head?"

"Of course," I said. "Isn't that normal?"

"No."

I raised my eyebrows in mock surprise. "Huh. He was right, then. We are unique."

"Who said that?" she asked.

"The Coyote," I said. "Well, that's what I call him. The voice in my head. He's been helping awhile now. That's why I thought he was some kind of artificial intelligence. I thought you would know about it. But maybe he's just a split personality. Wouldn't that be rare, though?"

"What would be rare?" she asked.

"That someone as highly functional as me could operate with a split personality?" I asked. "That's one of the reasons I always thought he was an implant."

Margaret narrowed her eyes in suspicion. "Cayden, if you are trying to trick me, there's no use."

"What good would a trick be now, Margaret?" I asked, doing my best to sound genuine. "You've beaten me. My plan failed. I have no more moves left. I'm trying to finally be honest about what's been happening to me. I thought you knew."

"You call it, the Coyote?" she asked.

"Yes," I said. "I think it fits."

"Is he talking to you now?" she asked.

"No, but would you like to talk to him?" I asked, grinning a little.

Really? Do I have to?

We need to buy more time.

Fine.

"Yes, I would," Margaret said, crossing her arms. She was still skeptical, but she was obviously intrigued as well.

Who wouldn't be?

I closed my eyes, felt the familiar mental tug, and surrendered to it. I was pulled into my own mind, and once again became the observer of actions and words I was no longer in control of. The Coyote was now in control. He was me.

"Is it done?" Margaret asked, looking with curiosity into my eyes.

"Yes," I said. "What can I help you with?"

"You must tell the Council this," Margaret said, apparently ready to believe me with no more than a single sentence. Her skepticism was weak. "There's nothing in your file about this. Nothing."

"And what reason do I have to say anything to the Council?" I asked. "You weren't smart enough to record this conversation. Only you and I know about it now, and I don't see many reasons for me to be cooperative. What's in it for me?"

Margaret paused for a moment, unfolding her arms. She walked back to her chair, laced her fingers together, and propped her elbows on the surface of the desk.

I think your directness is working, Coyote.

Clearly. Only confused people take this long to respond.

"Staying alive isn't motivation enough for you?" Margaret asked, arching an eyebrow.

"This is pathetic," I said. "Do you really believe I don't know how basic employee and employer relations work? Or do you believe that I don't know that you know?"

"Why don't you tell me?" she asked.

"You want to keep me happy," I said. "If I'm happy, you're happy, because I'm doing a good job. I'm more compliant to orders, I find a sense of fulfillment, I cause less trouble, and this all leads to a beautiful symbiosis between myself and the GS."

"Sounds about right," Margaret said, smiling. "If that's still you, Cayden, I'm impressed with the acting."

"I am always Cayden" I said. "You're just hearing a different voice."

Margaret seemed confused for moment, but didn't pursue the subject. "You don't believe the GS can make you happy?"

"You're about to kill his girlfriend," I said.

"Who's girlfriend?"

"Cayden's."

"I thought you were Cayden," Margaret said.

"I am Cayden, but I'm also the Coyote. As the Coyote, I have no physical form and must share Cayden's body and mind, which is Cayden himself. Therefore, I am Cayden, but I do not have sexual attractions. Keep up, Margaret."

"Oh," she said, doing her best to stay in control of the conversation. "Well . . . what if we didn't terminate Kalista?"

I paused for effect, though I anticipated the question. "You would do that?"

Margaret shrugged in a nonchalant manner, but the movement looked unnatural. "It's certainly not off the table. Make your case before the Council. If she's that important to you, they'll be smart enough to know that you'll be most effective if she stays alive."

"And in my care?" I asked.

"Of course."

A buzzer sounded at the door, and I knew it was go time. Bronx had been right on time, and the final chapter was coming to a close.

Make the switch, Coyote.

We traded places inside my head once again, and a shiver worked its way down my spine. It was easier to let go than to grab hold. But I was back in control, and Coyote was back where he was the most effective.

"Come in," Margaret said. "Ah, Bronx. Cayden and I were just having a fascinating . . . what are you doing?"

Before she could make a move to call security, a muffled gunshot sounded throughout the room, not loud enough to draw anyone's attention outside. Blood splattered the walls behind Margaret. She crumpled to the floor, a horrible wound in her stomach.

Why didn't he shoot her in the head?

"Is it done?" I asked.

Bronx stepped over the dying woman and unlocked the restraints holding me to the chair. "You doubt me?"

"I'm careful," I said, rubbing my wrists and standing up.

"Yes, it's done, Cayden," he said stepping back to allow me room. "Your pistol is inside the bag."

"Y . . . you," Margaret said from the floor, rolling onto her back, staring at me. The room was beginning to smell of burned flesh.

"Kill her," I said.

"She deserves to feel it," Bronx said.

I told you to be careful around him. He's a cold-hearted bastard.

"Don't be stupid," I said. "Just finish it."

Bronx shot her in the leg. Margaret tried to scream, but choked on her own blood. Her lungs must have been damaged by the bullet that ripped through her gut.

"What is wrong with you?" I asked, disgusted. "We don't have time for this."

"There's always time to play," Bronx said, and he aimed at her other leg.

Accelerate the schedule.

I clenched my left hand into a fist, and a vibration could be felt throughout the entire base as my Red Sky explosives did their job. "Not anymore."

Bronx glared at me, and I saw for the first time the bastard the Coyote warned me about. Out of instinct, I gripped my gun a little tighter and took a step back. Bronx didn't even look at Margaret as he pointed his gun at her head and pulled the trigger. Blood dirtied the once immaculate office floor.

Do not show weakness.

"We've got twenty minutes," I said, forcing myself to meet his eyes. "Meet me at the escape pods."

I didn't turn around as I walked past him. Instead, I focused on Kalista. I almost had her out. Almost.

38

THE explosion was so powerful and so close that Dorian felt like he'd been punched in the chest. Kalista, standing next to him, dropped to her knees from the impact, but Dorian did not fall. He knew his window of opportunity would be short.

Dorian's hands were still clasped in the heavy restraints, but they were in front of his body, and he was not attached to any wall. Kalista was not restrained, but their cell was sufficient to hold them. At least until the explosion happened. The bolts released, and the door slid open.

"Into the corner," Dorian said, half dragging his dazed sister toward the left corner, near the door. He wanted her in the blindspot.

Dorian walked back to line himself up with the doorway, four paces away. He would be able to cover the distance in a quarter of a second. Still shirtless, and still hampered by the claw marks of the tiger, Dorian kept his ears on high alert and let his fighting instincts take over.

Shouts from the left of the cell block sounded as lights flickered from whatever damage the explosion caused. Boots were hitting the floor. Two pair.

Dorian breathed deep.

Timing was everything, and his was perfect. He rushed the doorway in anticipation and was not disappointed. His outstretched hands found the end of a rifle, which he ripped away as he plowed his shoulder into guard number one, sending him staggering to the floor.

The reaction of the second guard was quick, as his booted foot kicked the gun out of Dorian's grip. Dorian was ready for the move, however. He didn't fight to keep his grip, but instead brought an elbow down across the guard's jaw, and turning his body the other way, brought down his other elbow in the same fashion. The two well-placed strikes were enough to knock the guard unconscious.

The first guard was struggling to his feet, but Dorian already managed to get his hands on a pistol from the unconscious guard's belt, and he did not hesitate to fire three times into his foe's chest. The sound was deafening in the confined space of the cell block hall. Dorian fired another shot into the unconscious guard's head and then ran back to get Kalista.

"Come on," he said. "I need you to help me search them for a key to these restraints."

"Hey, there!"

Dorian's head whipped around to his right to see Cayden's face projected onto their cell wall. He should have known, but Dorian hadn't bothered to take time and think about the source of the explosion or why it occurred.

"Part of your plan, all along?" Kalista asked, getting to her feet.

"Sorry. I couldn't risk telling you," Cayden said. "I had to make sure the GS believed they captured us. It was the only way."

Perhaps Dorian should have felt anger about the secrecy, but he didn't. In fact, he understood. If either he or Kalista gave any hint that Cayden was planning this, the GS would have killed them all. Now, the organization was vulnerable.

"I need you to get to level seventeen," Cayden said. "The command deck. There are life rafts there that we will use. Don't bother trying to get to the other life rafts on other parts of the base. They'll already be taken."

"But the ones on the command deck won't be?" Dorian asked.

"No," Cayden said. "They'll stay and try to save the base, which is hopeless. And without a commander, they'll delay launching their life rafts until the last second."

"And who's going to stop them?" Dorian asked.

"I'm there, now," Cayden said. "Let me worry about that. You just get yourself and Kalista here. Oh, if you see Bronx, don't kill him."

"What?" Kalista and Dorian asked together.

"Who do you think set the explosives?" Cayden asked. "But if you see Jerry, you can kill him. Don't hesitate. He wants Kalista."

///

Jerry was not surprised. Not surprised in the least. It was too clean, and he knew it. He punched the wall in frustration and ran toward the door. If the soldiers there tried to stop him, he would kill them. He was not going to let Cayden get away. He was not going to let him live.

But as he exited his quarters, Jerry encountered no resistance. His protective detail was gone, no doubt called away to deal with the explosions. But Cayden would be nowhere near there. Where would he go?

The command deck.

Of course. If the base was damaged beyond repair, which Jerry had no doubt of, then Cayden wouldn't want to deal with the traffic clamoring for the larger life raft sections. And the command crew would wait last to abandon ship.

Jerry needed a weapon. Lucky for him, a GS security guard was running his way. A male yookallan. He was bleeding from his forehead, his eyes glassy with the signs of a concussion. He wasn't prepared for Jerry's oncoming fist.

The blow knocked the yookallan guard unconscious, and Jerry pulled the pistol from his belt. He gave some thought to shoot-ing the guard, but Jerry knew he would need every available bullet. The small amount of satisfaction he would get by delivering the yookallan into Death's arms was nothing compared to what he would feel by killing Cayden.

Another great shudder reverberated throughout the base, challenging Jerry's balance. Whatever Cayden did, it started a chain reaction. He was planning to use time as his ally.

Jerry knew Cayden, and he knew how he planned. Everything always came down to time. Cayden was a master of it, and he used it as one of his most effective weapons. Cayden's time.

Jerry was going to screw with it.

///

Among the panicked running and shouting, Bronx strode silent and calm to his destination. Level eight. The heart and soul of secrets. The GS had many.

All eight GS bases kept their internal documents on level eight. It was a kind of boring irony they embraced. Outside of a few minor tweaks, the bases were identical in format and function. Bronx knew the bases were vulnerable in specific ways, and Cayden was proving him right.

Three years ago, Cayden asked Bronx to send him the blueprints for Base Eight, his home for the majority of his life. Bronx wondered why. The continuing explosions answered his question.

Cayden didn't tell Bronx his entire plan until the last possible moment. Bronx knew he was going to be planting explosives, but he didn't know where. That was, until Cayden slipped him a small storage chip when Bronx "captured" him on Rome.

He was able to seal off the cockpit of the rental ship to himself and load the chip into a display device. It contained very specific instruction on where to plant each explosive, and how much time there would be to jettison from the base.

The destruction of the plasma engines would take on a life of its own once the fuel began to burn. Destroying the jump drive also added a nice kick. By damaging the drive beyond repair, and destroying the safety shutoff, the drive would try to function. With each renewed attempt to turn on, it would weaken the hull around it. In turn, that would weaken the plasma tanks. Once the plasma tanks released their fuel, the base would go up in one massive explosion.

There was less than fifteen minutes.

Bronx wasted no time inputting his pass code, retinal scan, and DNA marker. Unlike the armory, he had access to this room because he was entrusted to protect its secrets. Margaret was the only other person who was given access to the room. Bronx wished he could have taken more time with her, but Cayden was too squeamish to let it continue.

For all his bravado, cunning, and determination, Cayden still allowed himself an honor code. Such codes were for fools, and he would know it soon enough. Bronx wasn't going to let his protege have the secrets to the GS. Cayden wanted it as collateral protection once he made it off the base, but Bronx had other ideas.

Once the sensor processed the sample of epidermis from his

right thumb, the door to the room slid open with a labored *hiss*. It was a place rarely visited. The air was stale, and the single light fixture flickered on and off from lack of use.

It wasn't a large space, and it was empty for the most part. The only exception was a simple office desk with two drawers on its right side. Bronx wasted no time in opening them.

Most of the items were physical data sheets, but there were storage chips packed securely in holders, and blueprints as well. A go-bag lay beneath them, and Bronx shook it open. He stuffed everything into it, and left the room, not bothering to secure the door.

He was to meet Cayden at the command center, where Dorian and Kalista would join them. The idea was that Bronx would use one life raft, keep half of the GS secrets with him, get rescued by a passing ship, and then he would go back to the GS as the escaped hero who barely survived Cayden's wrath.

Cayden, in his perfect world, would escape with the siblings back to Rome. They would get his ship back and disappear. Bronx was to tell the GS he was unsure of Cayden's survival. He would recommend the GS lick its wounds and learn from the experience with a whole new approach to creating assets. It was supposed to be a win-win for everyone, but Bronx didn't see it that way.

He didn't give a rat's ass about the GS or its goals. He had his own plans, his own passions. And Cayden was a part of it.

39

IT was amazing what a good panic could do to people's observational skills. I passed at least twenty wide-eyed individuals with a pistol in my hand, and so far no one paid me any attention whatsoever.

Perhaps they just wish to survive. Some of them may have noticed you and not cared.

Perhaps.

Or survival makes you blind.

Let's go with that.

I was not looking forward to my next task, but it was necessary. And I would do what was necessary because Kalista was worth it. The command deck was only a few steps away. There were thirty shots in my pistol, which would be more than enough.

You've killed before.

I've never liked it, Coyote.

You're good at it. Perhaps it would be healthier for you to enjoy the things you're good at.

That would turn me into Jerry.

Ah. That's what that looks like.

I was only ten paces away when the frosted doors slid open and a young man stepped through, panicked. He looked right past me, and I was ready to let him pass, but then he froze. A look of recognition dawned, and I did not hesitate to raise my gun and pull the trigger. His body crumpled to the floor in a heap, like a marionette that had its strings cut.

He was only a puppet, anyway.

Pistol raised, I walked into the command room firing with lethal accuracy. It was not hard to end the twelve additional lives. No weapons allowed on the command deck, so there was no resistance. Security guards were nowhere to be found.

No one managed to escape because I picked off those nearest the doorways first. The others ran over each other in an attempt to try and get away. I placed my shots as mercifully as I could, aiming for heads when possible and the heart when a head shot wasn't clear. A few times, I had to shoot twice.

It was the screams that got to me. The begging. The pleading. The fates of those on the command deck were determined a long time ago. I was here to fulfill that fate, but I did not enjoy it. I could not.

After eighteen bullets, the room fell still and silent. It was a slaughter. The multicolored blood of humans, morkallians, deeshie, and yookallans mixed on the floor in swirls. Empty eyes and faces frozen with expressions of terror gazed into nothingness.

It's done.

Not yet.

"Hello, Cayden."

I turned. Standing like a fashion model in the light of the doorway, was a black-clothed Jerry. A pistol was pointed at my head, and at a distance of only five meters, he would not miss.

"Hello, dickhead," I said, tightening my grip on the gun. I just needed a small window of opportunity.

"Drop the gun," Jerry said.

"Screw you. I'm not dying without a fight."

"You're not fast enough," he said, baring his perfect white

teeth.

"You're not smart enough," I said.

Two seconds.

Until?

My question was answered by the biggest explosion yet. Either one of the smaller plasma tanks erupted or part of the level beneath us ruptured into space. Whatever it was, it sent me tumbling to the floor, and I hit my head hard on the cranium of a dead morkallian. I saw stars, and then realized I lost my gun.

Jerry lost his balance as well, and perhaps because he attempted to charge me, flipped over a console and landed only three feet from my position. He failed to keep his balance on the landing, and crashed over the bloated body of a deeshie.

Get his gun.

I didn't delay. I made for my opponent's weapon. Jerry was trying to get to it as well, and I managed to secure a grip on his pistol just as he did. A hard knee collided with my chest, but I didn't let go. Jerry couldn't win.

I would not let him.

That's the spirit.

///

Dorian was carrying dead weight, and he needed to get rid of her. A team of guards was on their heels, and Kalista was slowing him down. They made it to the command deck level, but just barely. It was hard to keep someone alive, and it was even harder to not allow his instincts to take their course and face the seven attackers head on in battle.

"How far?" Dorian asked, pushing Kalista around a corner to

avoid gunfire.

"Not far," she said. "It's straight ahead."

Before he could make a decision, a violent quake leveled them. It was the strongest one yet, and Dorian knew they must be running out of time.

"We can't risk fighting these guys all the way there," Dorian shouted over the alarms that were blaring through the halls. Apparently the ship's emergency system was just now doing its job.

"I'm not going to leave you," Kalista said.

"I'm better off if you do," he countered. "I can take care of this, you just get to the command deck. I won't be long."

Dorian was happy to see that Kalista only hesitated a moment. She nodded and then took off running. A gunshot struck the wall just behind her head, and Dorian turned the corner, fired three shots, and killed two guards.

Unfortunately, he didn't see that one guard advancing along the far wall. The morkallian male chopped down on Dorian's arm, and the weapon clattered to the floor. The remaining four guards charged.

Now, it was a real fight.

40

FIGHTING Jerry was not my idea of fun, and I hoped to avoid it. But my rival always had a knack for getting in my way at the most inopportune times. His singular focus and unpredictable actions made him difficult to plan for. I knew his nature, which I could always take advantage of. But when pressed into a corner, Jerry did not behave in a manner similar to anyone else.

During our childhood, if that's what it could be called, we faced off against one another more than any of our peers. Jerry was physically skilled, but lacked brains and discipline, which were the two attributes I had in spades.

I'm betting on you.

Thanks.

It was perhaps the most awkward fight in history. I gave up on securing Jerry's weapon, instead, opting to slam his hand into a console hard enough to break bone. The gun released from his hand and clattered onto the floor, among the bodies. Jerry made me pay for it. A sharp elbow split my lip, and a textbook trip put me flat on my back.

Pull him with you.

I learned long ago to trust the Coyote's recommendations. He had a way of seeing the big picture that let me stay a step ahead of my opponents. It was a valuable advantage.

I found a grip on Jerry's shirt and pulled him on top of me as I fell. Old defensive techniques surfaced to the forefront of my mind, and I deployed every single one that I could.

Using my legs like a spider monkey, I pinned Jerry's right arm to his body, and used both of my hands to secure his other wrist. I swung my hips as hard as I could, and it was enough to flip Jerry to the side, pulling myself on top of him, reversing our positions.

Strike.

I did not hesitate to use my elbows to pummel into Jerry's head. He covered up, but some of my shots got through, and blood became visible on his pretty, blond head. In an instant, his hand shot up and hooked around my neck, pulling me down. I felt him push off and begin to flip me, but I jumped to my feet to counter the move. We both stood across from each other once again.

"You know that I'm going to kill you," Jerry said, his eyes glancing to one of the pistols that lay between us.

"How many times have you said that?" I asked, ready to fight him for the weapon.

Then, the plan changed.

I was careful not to alter my gaze, but out of the corner of my eye, I saw Kalista enter the room. Jerry's back was to her, and she froze on the spot.

I'm not so sure about this plan.

It's perfect. And poetic.

If she goes through with it.

She will. She loves me.

You would know that better than I would.

"I'm going to kill that bitch you're trying to save, too," Jerry said, baring his teeth. It must have been his attempt at a smile.

"Way to keep that positive attitude," I said, laying the sarcasm on thick. Jerry hated it when I got sarcastic. "You keep thinking like that, and you'll go far in life."

"Your jokes aren't going to save you or your girlfriend," Jerry sneered. "I'm going to eat your heart, Cayden. And her liver. I'll paint with your blood. It's going to be beautiful."

The butt of the gun between us was sticking up, and Kalista was directly in my line of sight. I would have to be quick and accurate, but I would also have to beat Jerry. Not an easy task. But when he got like this, he was easy to distract.

Idiot.

"Just how big will that portrait be, Jerry?" I asked.

My rival's large, white, predatory teeth were more visible than ever as he spread his arms wide to indicate the size of his fantasy painting. It was a fatal mistake. I darted forward, and Jerry, because of his momentary distraction, attempted a dive to beat me there. Assuming that I was going to try and grab the gun, he abandoned any form of defensive posture and instead laid out completely in an attempt to reach the weapon.

Instead of grabbing, however, I kicked. It was a solid shot with my left foot, and the gun sailed over Jerry's arms. I had only a tenth of a second to make my next play. The weapon flew through the air, and Kalista caught it out of instinct. I didn't know for sure if she would do what I needed her to, but if I was going to trust anyone, it had to be her. We were destined to have a long relationship together, and if this wasn't a healthy trust exercise, I didn't know what was.

Jerry's momentum sent him crashing into my lower legs, which he tried to restrict with his arms. I wouldn't allow it. In what looked like an awkward dance, I jumped out of his grip and kicked at his body. Jerry rolled away from me in a crouched position. He still didn't realize Kalista was in the room, much less armed. His focus was his weakness.

Kalista saw no clear shot at Jerry yet, and if she attempted one and missed, he might be able to get to the other gun. I needed him in the open.

"Come and get me, dickhead," I said, standing tall and making myself an easy target.

I might as well have waved a red cape in front of a raging bull. Jerry charged like a madman, screaming at the top of his lungs.

Such emotion. Such weakness.

Jerry's hands reached forward, shaped like claws, ready to strangle me. He devolved to reacting with pure savagery, and I took full advantage. Ducking under his arms, I plowed my knee into his midsection.

Spin and uppercut.

My blow gave Jerry pause, but he reached for me again. I spun my body completely around, fighting off his grasping hands, and planted my feet. It was the perfect punch, and I put as much power as I could into it. Jerry's head ducked at just the right moment to get in the path of my rising fist, and I hit his forehead hard. Pain sung through my knuckles, but I didn't care.

I hoped I landed a knockout blow, but there was no such luck. Jerry stumbled backwards, stunned. He regained his composure quick enough, but stayed where I wanted him. Now, it was a waiting game.

"It's going to take more than that to stop me," Jerry said, wiping blood from his nose.

"You mean like a bullet?" I asked, hoping it would cue Kalista.

She pointed the gun at Jerry, holding it with both hands. Perhaps she was going to say something to stop him. Perhaps she was just taking an extra long time to aim.

Perhaps this wasn't a good plan.

"You have no bullets," Jerry said.

He still hadn't noticed Kalista, despite her being in his periphery. But that was what tunnel vision did. It disoriented people. Made them sloppy. Even trained killers.

"You should just let me have you," Jerry said, stepping forward. He was only six paces away.

Give yourself up.

It took me only a moment to understand the Coyote's thought, and I embraced it. A pang of guilt struck me that I was going to force Kalista's hand, but I saw no other way.

"Sure, Jerry," I said, raising my hands high above my head. "I'm all yours."

It worked. Jerry was about to charge me, but before he could take a step, two deafening gunshots shattered the silence. The first struck his left shoulder, and the impact jerked his body around toward Kalista. Only half a second passed before the gun fired a second time, and Kalista's aim was more lethal.

The bullet pierced Jerry's torso, just below the heart, and my rival from childhood fell backward to the floor, gasping for precious air. Kalista dropped the gun, a look of horror on her face.

I ran to her. I needed to comfort her. We were almost there. Almost.

41

BRONX slipped on a pair of dark, over-sized, protective lenses. He would need them soon. After hacking into the video feed of the command deck, he watched from a safe room down the hall.

Bronx opened the door, but didn't leave the confines of his haven. The sounds of Dorian killing several guards with his bare hands reverberated from his right. The sound of Kalista killing Jerry came from his left. Bronx had to wait for the right moment. He tossed the small viewing tablet to the floor and dug into his pocket for the single flash grenade he took from the armory.

It was non-lethal, but powerful enough to take a group of people out of commission for several minutes. It sounded like Dorian was finished. He was only thirty paces away, around the corner. If Bronx stepped into the hall, the view of the command deck would be clear. He checked that his pistol was fully loaded, and placed it back in its holster. He didn't need it yet.

Soon.

Bronx twirled the grenade in his left hand and placed plugs into his ears with the other hand. He pulled the pin on the oval-shaped device, tossed it aside, and kept his thumb firmly on the "hold" button. Turning the dial on the side, he set it to a one second delay.

By his count, there was only six minutes until the base was

destroyed. He needed Dorian to hurry. Adjusting his protective eye shields one more time, he waited for his moment.

Just as he predicted, Dorian made quick work of the last remaining guard. Bronx heard his running footsteps, and he exited his room. Dorian paused at seeing him, but did not raise the assault rifle in his hands.

"Here you go," Bronx said, tossing Dorian the grenade.

Before the assassin could realize what it was, it went off with a spectacular *BANG*. The explosive decompression punched into Dorian with enough force to throw him to the floor. The gun clattered away harmlessly. The light was so intense that it hurt Bronx's eyes, even behind the protective lenses. His ears rang from the sound, despite the earplugs.

Bronx didn't waste time. Tossing his eye protection aside, ignoring the writhing Dorian, he withdrew his pistol, switched off the safety, and pulled the hammer back.

Ready. Aim.

42

KALISTA was quite distraught. I didn't blame her. There was no feeling like killing, and I made her do it on two separate occasions today. It wasn't fair, but the reward would have to be worth it. I hoped it was.

"It's okay," I said, pulling her into a hug. She was shaking. "It's over, now. We're getting out of here."

"Dorian?" she asked.

"Wouldn't dream of leaving without him," I said, caressing her back. "We're all getting out of here, and then we're free. Forever."

Kalista nodded, and she wiped away the tears staining her cheeks. She was gorgeous. And in minutes, I would have her free of this hellhole. I would have her to myself. And she would have me.

"Cay . . . Cayden," a gravely, choking voice said. "Cayden."

Wow. He's still alive.

He's a determined son of a bitch.

It was Jerry. Despite the growing pool of blood over his body, mixing with the blood and bodies of everyone else, he was still taking labored breaths. It was no use. He wouldn't escape death today.

"Don't," Kalista said, holding my arm in an attempt to stop me.

I scooped the pistol from the floor, and walked to my fallen enemy. I shook Kalista's grip, but did so with as much gentleness as I could muster. "This won't take long. I'm going to finish it."

Dying men hold no secrets back.

What is that supposed to mean?

"How?" Jerry said as I approached. "So . . . weak."

"How what, Jerry?" I said, coming to stand beside him.

My once intimidating rival was broken. He spit blood as he choked out more words. "You were . . . so weak. How did . . . how did . . ."

"How did I always beat you? How did I always win? How did I thrive? How did I do all of this?" I asked, waving my arms at our surroundings.

He nodded, all manner of spite gone. It was almost like looking into a child's eyes, and I couldn't remember a moment when Jerry appeared as innocent as he did now. I almost felt sorry for him. Almost.

"I had help," I said, quiet enough that only he could hear me. I wasn't afraid of Kalista knowing, but I wanted to explain on different terms.

"Who?" Jerry said, gasping, trying to pull in enough oxygen with each breath, but failing.

I put a finger to my temple. "He's up here. They did something to me. Something they didn't do to anyone else. It helped me beat you. Helped me pull off what I did today. Why do you think I called myself, Cayden the Coyote?"

Jerry's eyes grew wider as the meaning of what I was saying dawned on him. There was a panic to his expression. Almost as if what I was telling him was more important than the fact that he would be dead shortly.

"You . . . you heard it, too?" he asked. "I thought . . . it was just me."

What?

Oh my God.

"Jerry, what are you talking about?" I asked, bending down to get closer to his face.

"I haven't heard it in years," he said, his eyes beginning to glaze. "That damn . . . voice in my head. Couldn't sleep. Had to . . . kill it."

"Jerry," I said, grabbing him by the fabric of his shirt. "What did you hear? You heard a voice?"

"Drove me . . . crazy," he said, what little color that remained in his face disappearing at an increasing rate. Blood was trickling from his mouth. "Wouldn't shut up. Always . . . had to kill it. Couldn't . . ."

Death adhered to no schedule. And Jerry was taken by it. He heard one, too. A voice.

Coyote?

Don't ask me. Maybe we're not so special.

But he's right. I nearly died before you began talking to me. I was the weakest candidate in the Betas. Until you.

Cayden, it's okay. That's why we have Bronx retrieving the documents. We're going to find answers.

A *bang* sounded in the hallway, and I spun around, releasing my grip on Jerry. Kalista turned around as well, searching for the source.

"Dorian?" I asked her.

Kalista's face filled with fear. "Cayden . . . I'm sorry."

Then, my world was ripped apart in the span of a second.

43

IF I had a voice, my ears did not hear it. A single bullet ripped through Kalista's chest and out her back. She fell backward with the grace of a fallen angel. I know I was screaming, but the only thing I could hear was a shrill ringing. I couldn't even hear the Coyote.

After tripping over at least three bodies, I made it to her. She was still breathing, though only in labored gasps. I cupped her face in my hands. My voice came back to my ears.

"I've got you," I said, though I had no idea what those words meant or what good they would do. "I've got you. I love you."

"No," she said, but her voice was coming out in a painful groan. "Don't look . . . don't love . . ."

She managed to push one of my hands away from her face and turned away from me. I didn't know what to do. She gave one shuddering breath, and then she didn't breathe anymore.

"No," I said, turning her face back to me. But her eyes were empty, her expression blank.

Cayden, we have to go.

I'm not going anywhere.

Cayden.

I'm not going anywhere!

"Let me talk to him," a deep voice said.

I looked up to see a large blur enter the room. I wiped away the tears gathering in my eyes, and my vision cleared to see Bronx walking forward. There was a gun in his hand.

"Let me talk to him, Cayden," Bronx said, pulling me to my feet. "I need to speak with him."

Don't, Cayden.

"You," I said, my voice weak. My knees felt like they were made of jelly. "Did you kill her?"

Bronx smiled, his expression cold. "Of course I did. But I don't have time to discuss that. Now, let me converse with that lovely voice in your head."

"What are you talking about?" I asked.

Bronx's backhand was so hard that it sent me tumbling over a console and into a group of bodies at the floor. But it woke me up. I was going to kill him. I had to kill him.

Yes.

"Don't play dumb with me, Cayden," Bronx said. "I've known for a long time. I knew before you knew."

I wasn't interested in talking. Instead, I charged my large opponent. My punches and kicks were wild and random, but they were connecting. It didn't matter. Something hard rammed into my abdomen and knocked the breath from my lungs.

"I don't have time for this," Bronx said.

He wrapped one massive hand around my throat, lifted me into the air, and slammed me down onto a console. I struggled against his grip, but he kept me pinned to the surface and leaned over me.

"Want to see something fun?" he asked, handing me his pistol. "I want you to shoot me, Cayden. Go ahead."

Don't think. Just do it.

I didn't think. If Bronx was trying to play some kind of game, I wasn't going to let his one mistake remain unexploited. I took the gun and aimed it at his head, despite his hand still pinning me down by the throat.

Nothing happened.

Pull the trigger.

I'm trying to pull the damn trigger!

It was as if my hand became paralyzed. My fingers were frozen. Bronx smiled, his expression monstrous.

"Do you want to know why you can't kill me, Cayden?" he asked. He tapped his free finger against my temple. "Because I created it. I gave you that voice, and I put safeguards in place to protect myself. You'll never be able to kill me. That thing in your head won't let you."

Coyote?

I'm not . . . It's not true.

"I'm the stronger one," I said, struggling to talk through Bronx's vice-like grip. "I control it."

Bronx laughed, his voice sick and harsh. "Is that what you think? Fine. You don't want to let it talk to me, then just listen. I created you for one reason, and one reason only. A challenge. Someone to face me that's worthy."

"You're sick," I gasped.

"No. Just bored," he said.

"I'm going to kill you," I said. "I'll find a way."

Bronx smiled again. "That's what I'm counting on."

A spray of bullets whizzed by us, and Bronx released his grip. Dorian. Bronx ran, but not before a bullet ripped the bag he was carrying. Half of the contents spilled to the floor, and when Bronx tried to pick them up, another bullet struck him in the shoulder.

"Kill him, Dorian!" I shouted.

Yet another explosion ripped through the ship, and the floor shook with a renewed violence beneath our feet. Bronx managed to propel himself toward one of the life raft hatches.

"No," I said. "Dorian, shoot him!"

Kalista's brother got back to his feet and aimed his rifle, but it was too late. Bronx made it through the hatch, and before I could protest, he launched the life raft.

There's still one more. Get to it.

I told you. I'm not going anywhere.

Cayden, snap out of it.

Dorian was staring at Kalista's corpse, his expression blank. Perhaps there was frown there, but it was hard to tell with Dorian. Emotional expression wasn't exactly his forte. But there was no mistaking his cold gaze as he leveled the weapon at my head.

Cayden. Don't do this.

You want to live, Coyote. I don't. Everything I was living for is lying there at his feet.

Live for revenge.

Why?

"Why are you hesitating?" I asked Dorian, a renewed batch of tears spilling down my cheeks. "Kill me. Get Kalista out of here."

Dorian didn't move. The gun remained very much pointed between my eyes, but I saw no muscles working in his arm to pull the trigger. In fact, his finger wasn't even on it.

"Fine," I said, collapsing next to Kalista. "But if you're not going to kill me, then leave her with me. I don't want to be alone. You don't have much time."

Cayden, please.

I'm not going anywhere, Coyote. It's over.

Don't do this.

Something sharp struck the back of my head, and blackness

reached out, pulling me into its cold embrace. He did it.

He killed me.

44

DORIAN didn't kill me, as it turned out. Something I was not too thrilled about when I regained consciousness aboard the life raft. There was a nasty shouting match between us, but he put me in my place.

I owed him. I owed Kalista. The GS deserved to be destroyed, and I was the only one capable of doing it. It took a while, as we floated in space, but I calmed down and rethought the prospect.

Yes, I'm much more fond of Dorian, now.

Kalista's brother knocked me unconscious, collected the documents and storage chips that spilled from Bronx's pack and dragged Kalista's body into the life raft. Then, he came back for me. We jettisoned with only a few seconds to spare. And, according to Dorian, the explosion of Base Eight was quite the sight.

We floated in space for a long time before a transport picked up our emergency beacon. I didn't mind the time. Dorian was gracious enough to let me lay by Kalista and cry my eyes out. I wasn't ashamed of it. He said nothing, and when I was finished, he even gave me an awkward pat on the shoulder.

We held a bond that had been lacking before. I couldn't quite explain it, but there was a trust between us, and we were in full agreement on what to do next.

Destroy the GS.

Kill Bronx.

That, too.

I could not speak on how Dorian felt about Kalista. It was more complicated than my own feelings, but his focus was just as singular as mine. He took care of me the past couple of days, and even arranged a small funeral for Kalista. We cremated her, with only the two of us as witnesses of her passing.

She deserved more.

"Do you have any kind of documentation to give them?" Dorian asked, walking alongside me down the streets of Rome.

"No," I said. "We may have to get creative."

"Should we have brought a gun?" Dorian asked.

"Probably," I said, shifting the urn from one arm to the other.

We stopped at the entrance of the impound lot. Somewhere, behind the dilapidated shack before us, was my ship. And we were going to get her back.

The documents that Dorian obtained were most helpful. Many secrets of the GS were now known, and I was going to use those secrets to destroy them. But I needed my ship to do it.

"I don't want to kill if I don't have to," Dorian said.

"Only do what is necessary," I said. "But we need her."

I came up with a name for my ship. *Most Beautiful.* Not only would it sound fun in a sentence, but it was also special. It's what Kalista's name meant.

It was what she meant to me.

ACKNOWLEDGEMENTS

No one can do this alone, and I'm no exception. I'd like to thank all of my family and friends who have encouraged me through the years, but there are a few I want to single out.

S.P. Outside of myself, no one has spent as much time and given as much energy to this project. Your determination and drive made me realize this was possible. Thank you.

Linda. Thanks for your ceaseless encouragement, and all that time you spent reading what I wrote.

Daniel. Growing up, thanks for never telling me to shut up when I droned on and on about the stories in my head.

Crystal. Thanks for your sage advice.

www.ingramcontent.com/pod-product-compliance
Lightning Source LLC
Chambersburg PA
CBHW032151190626
46814CB00005BA/1937